BOOKS BY KRISTIN CAST

THE KEY SERIES
The Key to Fear
The Key to Fury

WITH P. C. CAST:

THE HOUSE OF NIGHT: OTHER WORLD SERIES
Loved
Lost
Forgotten
Found

THE HOUSE OF NIGHT SERIES
Marked
Betrayed
Chosen
Untamed
Hunted
Tempted
Burned
Awakened
Dragon's Oath
Destined
Lenobia's Vow
Hidden
Neferet's Curse
Revealed
Kalona's Fall
Redeemed

THE SISTERS OF SALEM SERIES
Spells Trouble

THE KEY TO FURY

KRISTIN CAST

BLACK STONE
PUBLISHING

Copyright © 2022 by Kristin Cast
Published in 2022 by Blackstone Publishing
Cover design by Kathryn Galloway English
Book design by Amy Craig

Printed in the United States of America

First edition: 2022
ISBN 978-1-9825-4804-9
Young Adult Fiction / Dystopian

Version 1

CIP data for this book is available
from the Library of Congress

Blackstone Publishing
31 Mistletoe Rd.
Ashland, OR 97520

www.BlackstonePublishing.com

To my mother, who was only a little offended (but extremely whiny) when I didn't dedicate the first book to her.

INCOMING PRIORITY ONE ALERT FROM THE KEY CORPORATION

TO HEALTH. TO LIFE. TO THE FUTURE.
WE ARE THE KEY.

The Key's slogan and red logo unfurled in front of the eyes of every citizen in Westfall. The corporation had coded the livestream as Priority One, and all Priority One messages from the Key Corporation overrode any videos, calls, or chats. Even people in virtual reality meetups or educational simulations had their program paused and taken over by the corporation responsible for saving humankind. According to the Key, some messages were too important to hear secondhand.

As the logo faded, Holly walked in front of the camera. She stood in the center of a nondescript white room. No, *walked* and *stood* weren't the right words because no matter how convincing, Holly wasn't a person and therefore couldn't *walk* or *stand* anywhere.

Holly, aptly nicknamed by the citizens of Westfall after the latest upgrade took her from a voice to a fully realized holographic projection, simply *existed* in every home, building, and citizen implant.

"Good morning, Westfall." She clasped her tawny hands in front of her hips and rested them against her knee-length pencil skirt that shone an even brighter shade of white than the room around her. "It pains me to announce that our number one rule, the rule that has kept us safe for nearly fifty years, has been broken."

It was curious that the word *pain* was programmed into the speech. As Holly could not truly walk or stand, she most certainly could not feel pain. Nevertheless, the word had made it into her announcement. What did it say about the Key that they so wanted their people to identify with, trust, and depend on a hologram? And what did it say about the citizens of Westfall that they were so eager to abide?

"Please do not be alarmed." She continued without needing to specify which rule had been fractured. Touching had been outlawed for five decades. For most citizens, the thought of placing hands on another human had never occurred. After all, most citizens had been born into this new world of social distancing and hands-off protocols. But there were some, born into it or not, who were never quite fond of the rules.

"To protect every member of Westfall who was at the Rose Festival that day, the Key immediately shut down the commemoration and beamed the Violet Shield throughout each Zone."

Holly paused as if awaiting applause. No doubt some were whooping and hollering their support for the swift actions of the Key.

"Out of safety concerns for the culprits' family and friends, the Key will not be releasing either of the guilty party's names at this time. Rest assured that those who may have been exposed to any pathogens have been taken to the MediCenter and placed under a mandatory fourteen-day quarantine."

Holly brushed her hair from her shoulders. It was curlier today and framed her fuller, rounder cheeks in a familiar way. The minds at the Key were always tweaking the hologram. Whatever features polled higher with the citizens of Westfall inevitably made their way into Holly's code and then projected as real life.

"For many years, the Rose Festival has served as a way for the people of Westfall to come together and celebrate the Key's unparalleled generosity. Their life-saving medical advancements not only rescued us from the deadly virus Cerberus but also provided the means for havens around the globe where civilization has once again flourished."

Us. Another purposeful choice. As if a hologram could understand what it meant to be denied access to saying a final goodbye to the dead or see bodies stacked in refrigerated trucks like slabs of meat. There was no *us.* With technology, there could never be. But that didn't explain what was happening with Holly. What the citizens of Westfall *sought out* in the hologram. It seemed that no matter how far removed from them she was, it was always better to be together than to face the world alone.

"With the Key's hands-off protocols and social distancing guidelines, we, and the rest of the world, have been virus-free for fifty long years. With continued effort, we can ensure that Westfall stays the greatest city in New America." She smiled around the words, her voice nearly identical to Blair Scott's.

It was rumored that Blair had encoded her vocal pathways into the hologram as a sort of signature after hours of hard work on the program. Others whispered that she had done it because she knew that the former MediCenter director (rest his soul) was not far from being put down and the act would force the Key Council to add her to the short list of replacements. However, most also knew that Blair would have to beat her adoptive mother, Dr. Cath Scott, for the position. No matter how talented and dedicated the younger Scott was, besting Cath was a challenge she could never win.

Holly tugged on the sleeve of her Key Corp—red blouse and smoothed the silky fabric between her thumb and forefinger as she spoke. "But Eos continues to threaten us. That is why now, more than ever, the Key needs your help. Just as the corporation saved humanity, they need you to save our way of life and ensure our city isn't overtaken by these domestic terrorists."

Her expression hardened as she placed a slender hand to her hip. Her hips had also undergone an update and were more curved and fuller than before.

"Stay vigilant and alert, and immediately report suspicious behavior or activity. Together, we can protect our family, our neighbors, and our community."

Again, she clasped her hands and smiled, her lips a bit plumper than they'd been the last time she'd appeared. "The Key is always protecting you. Take pride in this land and its people, and remember—no touching today for a healthy tomorrow. For your safety, and for everyone."

Holly and the white room dimmed to gray before disappearing completely as the livestream ended. Programs, videos, and chats resumed as the citizens of Westfall continued on with their day, most reinvigorated by the Priority One announcement. But though the livestream was over, the hologram was not at rest. Holly was watching, sorting through gathered information with the delicate swiftness of a spider spinning its web. Projected and scripted by the Key Corporation, the holographic woman had bridged a gap between corporation and citizen. She'd given one power, and the other purpose.

But, as everyone knew, or would have known if books, history, and facts hadn't gone up in smoke, *power tends to corrupt, and absolute power corrupts absolutely.*

I

Smoke filled Zone Seven. It choked out the blue sky and trapped the sun in a thick orange haze that settled over every inch of the charred forest. But Elodie and Aiden had made it—they had been through hell, and this was the last bit, the outer rim, the final test before absolute freedom.

Elodie's lungs burned and her eyes teared, but she forced herself to stay facing the grays and blacks of the forest and not turn around to gaze at the box truck that had dropped Aiden and her off in the middle of this wasteland. There was no use in looking in a direction she could no longer travel.

The truck's low grumble turned into a distant purr before fading from existence on its trek back to civilization. Silence bored into Elodie's ears as she balled her hands into fists and made herself move forward, one foot in front of the other, until the muffled *thud thud* of each step was as soothing as a metronome.

Next to her, Aiden was her shadow at high noon. Goose-bumps crested against her skin as his arm grazed hers while they silently trekked deeper into Zone Seven. Having him there and knowing that they'd been through everything together was a comfort. It was true that misery loved company, but more than that, misery loved being held close and told everything was going to be okay.

"How are you?" Aiden finally broke the silence.

"Fine." The word came out a croaky whisper, and Elodie swallowed past the dryness in her throat. "I'm fine."

"You can't die in VR, El. It's not real." Astrid's voice pounded against Elodie's ears.

Turns out, that wasn't true. Once again, her misery reared its ugly head, and Elodie blinked back the image of her best friend's glossy black ponytail swimming in a sea of fresh blood.

"Getting out here was easier than I thought it'd be." Her stomach twisted. Fleeing the city had been less complicated than expected, but there was nothing *easy* about what she and Aiden had been through.

The memory of blood spraying from Cath's body temporarily stained her vision red. "I'm sorry," she whispered.

She wanted to be everything he needed, everything *they* needed, and move forward without dragging the weight of the past with them. She wanted to forget the last day and banish the memories that haunted them like the ghosts of her best friend and Aiden's adoptive mother. But there was no escaping what had happened.

Tears burned Elodie's eyes. This time, it wasn't the smoke. She stared up at the dingy orange sky to keep from crying. The mask she'd made from a red bandanna she'd found in her pack pressed against her parted lips as she inhaled. It had stopped raining, but ash still fell from above like snow.

"You don't need to apologize." Aiden draped his arm over her shoulder and squeezed her against his side. "I get it."

His arm left her back, and she shivered in its absence, surprised that it felt so good to be touched. Elodie shook away the heat that built in her cheeks and met his gaze. He blinked, his eyes shining with unshed tears.

The empty arms of the jumpsuit he'd changed into before arriving in Zone Seven hung loosely around his hips. With the top half of his suit unzipped, its arms tied around his waist, and those heavy brown boots he was never without, he looked almost the same as the first time they'd met. But a part of this Aiden was missing. It had died in his sister Blair's office along with his adoptive mother Cath Scott, and Elodie didn't know what would come to fill its place.

She wiped the chalky flakes of ash from her lashes and squinted ahead at the wasteland of Zone Seven. There was no end in sight—the Key had burned the forests outside Westfall to the ground. They had said it was to keep its citizens safe from Cerberus and eliminate the risk of other zoonotic diseases. Elodie assumed that was also why there were hardly any birds or squirrels or bugs in the city. There was no real reason for them not to exist, no biological or evolutionary explanation for their absence. They existed in virtual versions of the past along with cats and dogs and other pets that the people of Portland, the name of the city pre-Cerberus, used to cart around attached to leashes, in buggies, and in cars. Decades ago, studies showed that there was a small chance that Cerberus could infect dogs, so the Key had exterminated all pets. It wasn't long before all critters ceased to exist within the Zones. Burning, exterminating, all done in the name of safety. But, up close, this didn't look like protection. Or perhaps it only appeared differently now that she knew the Key was lying.

The corporation that had saved mankind from the brink of extinction had been telling the same story for so long that no one had stopped to ask whether or not it was still true, still needed. No one except Aiden and Eos.

She glanced back up at Aiden as he swiped his fingers under his eyes. She averted her gaze. Men didn't like to be seen crying.

"I read this banned book," Elodie blurted, needing to fill the anguished silence and the vast, unending nothingness of Zone Seven.

Aiden blinked down at her as if she was holding a copy of *Death by Violet* in her hands.

"I mean, I *used* to read it. Back at home." The brittle, black remains of a tree branch crunched under her feet as she stopped. The realization that Westfall was no longer her home sunk to the bottom of her stomach like a stone.

He paused alongside her. "You never told me that." Shielded by his makeshift mask, Aiden's expression was as indecipherable as his tone.

She rolled the pointed end of her bandanna between her fingers. "Well, you don't know everything about me." She'd meant it to sound cute, coy even, but the words came out as flat as Aiden's.

He grabbed the canteen dangling from the strap of his backpack and unscrewed the lid. "What made you think about that?" The top of the canteen disappeared under his bandanna as he took a long drink, his eyes never leaving hers.

Elodie's cheeks heated and her lashes dusted the top of her makeshift mask as her attention fell to the ash-covered earth.

"The series is about Violet, this woman, this *assassin*. She breaks all the rules, but it never seems wrong, you know?" She looked back up at him, his green eyes and red bandanna the brightest things in the desolate Zone. "Vi does all the wrong things for all the right reasons."

"Like us." Aiden dropped the canteen. It swayed back and forth, thumping against his side in time with the accelerated beat of her heart.

"Like us." Elodie yearned to reach out and twine her fingers around his, but she wasn't used to making the first move, and she was even less familiar with making this one.

"So, how does Violet's story end?"

"She falls in love with this guy who seems all wrong for her but ends up being totally right because he understands her in a way no one else ever could." Elodie choked back an embarrassed giggle as her cheeks cooled and her heartbeat steadied. Vi would never feel embarrassed for speaking her mind or saying how she felt. That's part of what made her relationship with Zane Cole, fellow assassin and all-around bad boy, work so well—she was honest with him, and he was honest with her.

Aiden cocked one ash-dusted brow. "So, it's a love story . . . but with murder?"

"Yes," Elodie said and slid her hand into his.

Aiden stared down at their joined hands, both chalky and dry with the steadily falling ash. He nodded to himself and squeezed her hand.

His hand warmed hers, melting her like a flame to wax. "Vi and Zane both have hard lives, but they're able to make it through because they've chosen to face everything together."

She bit her lip. With each step forward, she got further and further away from *Death by Violet* and closer to her reality with Aiden. She was writing her own romance novel.

Aiden released her hand and stuffed his into the pockets of his jumpsuit as they started moving again. "Sounds like quite the story."

Elodie stilled. The distance between them increased as Aiden marched on without her. She didn't know how to navigate this space between their new lives and their old. There was so much in their way. Plus, Elodie hadn't told the truth, not entirely. She hadn't finished Violet Jasmin Royale's books, and from what she *had* read, she knew the ending wouldn't be a simple happily ever after. Violet's story was about pain and rebirth, and heartache was written only a few pages ahead.

11

Holly's transparent image pixelated and faded from Blair's vision as the Key's Priority One transmission ended. Her pulse thundered inside her veins, threatening to shake her to pieces while she waited for the doors of the Council Hall to open and her trial to commence.

Preston Darby had done it again.

Rage sloshed in Blair's gut, so hot her throat burned. It didn't matter that he was the Council Leader. She would find a way to sink him. She had to, and fast, or one day she would wake up to discover that she'd been replaced by a hologram.

Major Rhett Owens cleared his throat, alerting Blair to his presence as he made his way to the two rows of chairs that lined each side of the corridor outside of Council Hall. Since he and Blair had both been caught red-handed (literally *and* figuratively) after Cath's death, they would be reprimanded for any wrongdoing together. The thought that Blair would lose her job never once crossed her mind, and not only because she had more pressing things to think about. The Key couldn't afford to lose Dr. Cath Scott and Blair Scott at the same time—no matter the reasoning, the citizens would take the death of one and the firing of another to mean that trouble was brewing within the corporation. The Key hadn't maintained power all these years by sowing unrest and fear. Well, at least not the fear that the corporation was unstable and therefore couldn't keep its citizens safe.

"Blair." Rhett forced her name between clenched teeth as he dropped into the chair opposite her.

She didn't respond. If she wasn't careful, she would open her mouth and drown this corridor with the wrath that bubbled up her throat. Not even Major Rhett Owens deserved that.

Rhett crossed his thick arms over his barrel chest, the jacket of his Key Corp–red dress uniform stretching and creasing with the motion. "I, uh, well, I just wanted to say that—"

"Don't," Blair whispered.

Rhett blinked. There was still a purplish bruise around his eye, but it was healing nicely. "I only meant that—"

"Don't," she repeated, her gaze skewering his. It wasn't a request, but a warning.

She wanted to blame him for Cath and her brother and for putting her in the position she was in; sitting in this hallway waiting on people who thought they were better than her. Blair wanted to blame someone that was still alive for everything that had happened in her office the night before and for everything that had happened every moment since. But the only person Blair could blame was no longer available for punishment. Cath had removed herself from the equation.

"If I want to hear from you," she growled. "I will address you directly."

Rhett's white-blond temples pulsed, and he fixed his glare to the ceiling.

Satisfied, Blair tugged on the sleeve of her Key Corp–red blouse, rubbing the silk between her thumb and forefinger in a gesture identical to the one Holly had made in the transmission. Heat licked her skin as she shook out her hands and forced them flat against her bespoke pencil skirt.

There *was* one person she could hold responsible. One person who deserved far more than her wrath. Council Leader Preston Darby could be blamed for the tragedy of Cath, and the loss of her brother. She could blame the Council Leader for many, many things.

Blair brushed her wild curls away from her round cheeks.

Darby had issued Aiden's death warrant. Without it, she could have saved her brother, saved her whole family. But Darby had pushed her to act too soon.

And then there was the continuing matter of Holly . . .

Maxine's kitten heels clicked against the tile as she hurried down the hall toward Blair. "I was so worried the meeting had already begun." She gracefully lowered herself into the chair a mandated six feet away from Blair. Maxine had been calling the trial a *meeting* since Blair had received the message demanding her presence at Council Hall. The Council didn't have *meetings*. The Key Corp Council held trials and heard complaints.

Rhett grunted something unintelligible, or perhaps Blair simply wasn't paying attention, before clearly snapping, "Couldn't start without you, now could they, *Ms. Wyndham*?"

For every strong woman, there was a man who despised her for no reason.

Maxine's skin smoothed over her sharp, angled features. Blair's assistant wouldn't give the major the satisfaction of getting a rise out of her.

Good little monster.

Maxine pursed her lips and continued as if Rhett Owens had never been born. "Everything in your office has been sorted. The bots just finished cleaning and—"

Blair held up her hand. She didn't want to hear about bots cleaning the blood from every surface of the space she'd once thought of as her fortress. She wanted to distance herself from the hurt that came with thinking about her office and her adoptive mother and live inside the rage instead. She was comfortable there.

The Council Hall doors hissed open and a steady stream of violet light illuminated the entrance to the great open space. As she stood, Blair smoothed down her skirt and mindlessly straightened the collar of her blouse. She plunged into the Violet Shield, a practiced grin plumping her cheeks.

Without looking at him, she felt Darby's eyes pressed against her, studying her. What piece of her would he cut away next to paste onto Holly?

Heat washed up Blair's throat and sharpened her tongue. She was ready for battle.

III

Blair Scott would be the next MediCenter director if it killed her. And it might. Being forced to stand in front of Preston Darby was enough to make her feel as if the end was nigh. Not to mention the fact that the past twenty-four hours had been . . . *taxing*, but she had proven her worth.

The gunshot memory rang between her ears, making her eyes water and her chin tremble. She balled her gloved hands into fists. The familiar ache of her raw cuticles and gnarled nail beds was muted by the second skin gloves given to her by her dutiful assistant, but Blair wanted to rip them off and reveal the truth under the perfect facade. More than that, Blair wanted the pain.

She'd lost two people: first her birth mother, then Cath. Each time there had been blood. So much blood. It was amazing how much pulsed inside a body. Buckets and buckets. The ringing ceased, and Blair's breath caught. She blinked away the images of both her crimson-spattered office and that night so many years ago when her parents' blood flowed in rivers down the stairs.

Her life had been filled with death and trauma. Others would have broken, but Blair remained steadfast and loyal to the Key. They certainly wouldn't find that strength in any of the cube workers or titleholders who flitted around the MediCenter like mindless drones. Even her brother wasn't made of the same stuff. Their birth mother's death had left within Aiden an open, seeping wound that Eos sniffed out and infected. But not Blair. Instead, she had found purpose in the mission of the Key. She had found life in her MediCenter office and in keeping Westfall in order. She had found her own kind of joy in squishing men beneath her stilettos as she climbed the ladder of success.

All of that had happened in the *after*. After the death of her parents. She only remembered bits and pieces of her life before. Her memory had dammed away that night and everything before it in an attempt to keep her safe from what had happened. That was, until last night. Now there was a *before* Cath, too . . . And *this* was the *after*. Flooded with new horrors, it was too much for the dam to hold. It was cracking, small fissures leaking red.

Blair unclenched her hands and flattened them against the long metal table where she and Major Rhett Owens sat six feet apart in the middle of Council Hall—a chamber with walls so curved and white it was like drowning in a glass of milk.

"I noticed, *Council Leader*, that more updates were made to Holly's appearance," Blair said, doing her best to iron the hostility out of her voice.

Darby stared at her from the elevated platform where each of the five council members sat behind individual tables. "The hologram is always undergoing updates." A grin shuddered against his lips. "Did you like what you saw?"

Blair's throat tightened as she struggled to keep her voice even and calm. "I only wish I was consulted before the update went live."

"Now, Ms. Scott." Robin Wilson leaned forward, her long, slender arms like twigs in her brown blouse. "You must know that, even though you assisted with the original program, the Council Leader is under no obligation to run changes by you."

Blair tugged on the sleeve of her blouse and looked up at the elevated bench where the five council members awaiting her reply. She had known the members for most of her life. She'd gone to school with Darby and had met Yasmine Green, Dr. Teresa Palazzo, Robin Wilson, and Dr. Osian Normandy while running up and down the hall outside the vaccine lab her mother shared with Dr. Normandy. The days of playing doctor in the corridors of the MediCenter weren't too far behind her, but now they felt like a different time, someone else's life.

"Of course, Councilwoman Wilson," Blair said. "What I meant by that was—"

Dr. Normandy cleared his throat, a roaring crackle that echoed around the hall like thunder. "It seems Ms. Scott is unhappy with the payment she received for her work on the hologram." He pushed his glasses farther up the bridge of his thin nose. "Was having the program's vocal pathways based on yours not enough thanks?"

The piercing ring returned, flaying her nerves and setting her teeth on edge. She swallowed the saliva flooding her mouth and kept her attention fixed on Dr. Normandy even as she felt Darby's eyes graze her skin. "That was not my choice."

"No," Darby's breath seemed to quake from between his lips. "It was a gift."

Blair pressed her back against the cool, metal chair as wave after wave of dizziness overtook her. If only the ringing would stop, and Darby's dark eyes would cease boring into her.

"I asked you a question, *Ms. Scott.*" Preston Darby's thin nose wrinkled with a sneer.

Before an automatic answer, an automatic *no* slipped off her tongue, Blair took a breath and pressed the soles of her feet firmly against her shoes, grounding herself. She had underestimated Council Leader Preston Darby before, and he'd turned her into a computer program and nearly murdered her brother.

"Would you repeat the question, please, Council Leader?" she asked, the ringing between her ears fading into a haunting echo.

Darby tented his fingers and leaned forward, the fluorescent lights glinting off his shiny black hair. "This council was convened to determine whether or not you and Major Owens deserve punishment or a parade, but before we proceed, do you have any more to say about the great honor that I bestowed upon you in syncing Holly's voice to yours?"

Each council member stared down at her. They didn't understand what was happening. They couldn't see how Preston Darby collected pieces of her and filled in Holly's gaps with bits of code until they were whole again, and the hologram resembled her even more.

"Have you found my brother?" she blurted.

Darby leaned back in his chair and ran his fingers along his tie. Before he could settle on an answer that best tortured Blair, Robin interjected.

"We are in the process of locating Aiden and . . ." She glanced down at her holopad. "Elodie Benvidez."

Rhett straightened and his squared jaw pulsed with a clench of his teeth. *"Ben-AH-videz,* Councilwoman."

"Either way," Darby leaned forward again. His flat stomach pressed against the lip of his white lacquer desk. "We will find them. And when we do, they *will* pay."

Spots flashed across Blair's vision as she released a trembling exhale. "Your death sentence still stands?"

"Do you think a virus like Cerberus, one that spreads through touch, cares that Aiden Scott is your brother? An example needs to be made." Darby crossed his arms over his chest, and Blair swore she saw the corners of his lips twitch with a smile. "If he wasn't being put down for breaking our society's most important law, a law that has helped protect us for the past fifty years, he'd be put down for treason. For being a member of Eos, a known terrorist organization." The Council Leader cocked his head and narrowed his dark eyes. "Do you disagree with this council's ruling?"

This was a test, a trap. Tell the truth and Darby would sign her death warrant as fast as he'd signed Aiden's. Blair parted her lips and sucked in shallow gulps of air. Darby would take everything from her, whittle her away until she was nothing more than raw pulp. "I would never disagree with the Council."

Black.

She felt nothing for the lie as she packed it up and tucked it away with the others. Black lies were to be used and then discarded just as quickly.

"Then we'll proceed." Darby's attention slid to Dr. Normandy, who nodded stiffly, before it returned to Blair. "Yes, we'll move forward."

She glanced over her shoulder at her assistant. Maxine stopped typing on her holopad, and her mouth sharpened with a smirk. She'd seen it, too.

Blair knew Darby was too inexperienced to sit at the head of such an important entity. After all, his title had been gifted to him, wrapped up in the Darby bloodline and secured with the macabre ribbon of his father's untimely death. And anyone who knew anything about the inner workings of the Key knew the late Council Leader and Dr. Normandy were the best of friends. Add the late Director Holbrook, and the three were thick as thieves. For all intents and purposes, the Council was a monarchy. But kings were rarely seen looking to their court for permission.

Blair's spine tingled. She could use this information. She *would* use it. The only question was, *how?*

Darby tapped his finger on his desk, his gaze never leaving Blair. Rhett might as well go home. Darby's torch only burned for her, and the Council Leader had been carrying it a long, long time.

"Holly," Darby cleared his throat and looked up as if the holographic assistant was a god and not a program. "Play the recording from Blair Scott's office last night."

Blair stiffened as Maxine squeaked behind her. Without looking, Blair could see her assistant's pink lips tighten into the O she reserved for only the best Westfall gossip. But this was Blair's life. Blair's mother.

The Key's red logo unfurled in the empty space in the middle of the Council Hall. "To health. To life. To the future. We are *the Key.*" The hairs on the back of Blair's neck rose as Holly repeated the Key Corporation's slogan. The citizens found comfort in

Holly, the hologram that was everywhere and nowhere. She was in every Key building and, with the latest implant update, in every Westfall citizen. A best friend, assistant, therapist, Holly was anything and everything. That is why the council believed that Blair should be grateful for the *gift* its leader had given her. But how could she be grateful for her image that he'd stolen, repackaged, and beamed in front of the whole world to see? To the Key, she was the villain for not appreciating the violation, and he was the hero for perpetrating it.

The Key's logo faded, and the center of the white room transformed into a perfectly rendered version of Blair's Medi-Center office. Her onyx desk sat in the corner like a fresh grave. The gun Maxine had fetched for her stuck out against the smooth black surface like a shark's fin. Blair didn't focus on Elodie or Aiden, both pressed against the rendered wall, or Rhett, or even herself. She could only see Cath. Holly had perfectly captured her adoptive mother's halo of golden curls and gently clasped hands.

"Cath . . ." The whisper dusted Blair's lips and she gnashed her teeth to keep her jaw from trembling. She eyed Rhett. He hadn't moved since he'd corrected Robin. His large hands were flat against the table and he stared, unblinking, at a point across the room. The panel seemed to think he was paying attention, and, if Blair hadn't spent hours with the major and the ego and opinions he carted around like an ass with a wagon, she would have assumed the same. But Rhett Owens was miles away, most likely retracing the steps that had led him to this very moment.

"Holly, please record the events in the room."

Blair's heartbeat quickened and her eyes darted back to the

center of the Council Hall as the past version of herself spoke. Her holographic image stood in the office with her arms crossed over her chest just steps away from Aiden. What Blair wouldn't give to be just feet away from her brother once more. Last night, she hadn't saved him. She'd been too emotional, too human. She wouldn't make the same mistake again.

"If you want to save your son, it's now or never, Mother."

Cath Scott glided forward and stood between Blair and Major Owens. She took a breath and nodded slightly. At the time, Blair hadn't seen her adoptive mother's quick nod, the subtle acceptance of her fate.

No, this wasn't her fate. Cath had made a decision. She had prioritized terrorists over her children. *Adopted* children. That was the difference. Blair had always known Cath hadn't loved her. Now she knew Cath hadn't loved Aiden, either.

Blair bit the sides of her tongue. She needed the stab of pain, the sudden distraction from what was coming.

"My name is Cath Scott, although, to many, I am Echo." She lifted her chin and drew her shoulders down and back. Her soft curls glinted like twinkling stars in the harsh overhead lighting. *"I've been a member of Eos since their inception,"* she continued, her tone slow and even. *"I regret nothing. I only wish I could have done more."*

Maybe Cath *had* loved them. Maybe this wasn't her fault. Blair's nostrils flared. This was Eos. Those terrorists made this happen. They stole Cath and then they stole Blair's little brother.

"I love you both deeply."

Blair closed her eyes. There was comfort in the darkness. Just the gentle lilt of Cath's voice and the steady hum of the Hall's fluorescent bulbs.

"You were the best decision I have ever made."

Blair bit the tip of her tongue and copper coated her teeth.

She wanted to remember these words forever but knew she wouldn't. That wasn't how memory worked. It didn't keep the nice things, the warm things, the things that, in the moment, felt like they'd be everlasting. No, the memories that survived being dammed up and hidden away were hauntings. Ghosts of the *should haves* and *could haves*, the traumas and the horrors. Blair would remember Cath like she remembered her birth mother—bits of flesh in an unending ocean of red.

From the hologram, there was a strained grunt and a sickening *thwack* as Cath tackled Rhett, sending his head into the corner of Blair's stone table.

Next to her, Major Rhett Owens stifled a groan. Blair's eyelids fluttered open and she cut her gaze to the soldier. His bruised eye twitched and sweat beaded against his hairline.

Blair shook her head and glanced at the three female council members as they watched the holographic scene unfold. Each wore the same shocked, wide-eyed expression that deepened the wrinkles along their foreheads. Dr. Normandy ignored the scene completely, focusing instead on wiping his glasses. And Darby did what he always did when in a room with Blair—he watched her.

She swallowed and affixed her gaze to the hologram and the unconscious, slack-jawed mound that was Major Rhett Owens. Cath's shadow darted across Rhett's red uniform and a sob tore through the center of the Hall. It was Blair's hologram crying as her adoptive mother picked the gun up off the desk.

Blair's fingers twitched and she forced her palms to stay firmly against the table. She wouldn't cover her ears and muffle the sob. *Her* sob. She hadn't known it then, but within that cry were the *I love you*s Blair had never said and the *thank you*s she hadn't bothered to offer. That sob had been her goodbye.

"After the storm comes the dawn!"

Blair didn't flinch when the gun fired, and she pressed her bloody tongue against the back of her teeth as Cath's body hit the ground.

IV

The gunshot reverberated through Council Hall. Once again, the ringing returned loud and sharp between Blair's ears. She looked through watery eyes at Councilwoman Robin Wilson who clutched her chest and inhaled so deeply Blair felt the current pull her forward. Or maybe that was guilt, regret, the part of her she'd buried so deep that it had nearly rotted away? Blair hadn't experienced the emotion in so long that she couldn't know for sure.

"Holly, end transmission." Yasmine Green tugged at the collar of her lilac blouse as the scene in Blair's office pixelated and then vanished. "Council Leader, we could have done with a transcript of the events. To put Ms. Scott through the whole ordeal again is callous." She smoothed down her collar. "A very difficult thing to endure."

Dr. Normandy shook his head from side to side. "I am quite sure it was distressing." He paused. The fluorescent lights reflected white rectangles in the lenses of his glasses. "For those who hadn't already seen what had transpired, that is."

The air thickened as the realization dawned that Robin, Yasmine, and Teresa were the only people in the Hall who hadn't already watched Cath meet her end. The three women shared a glance. They were on the outside. The Key's governing hand no longer had five fingers. Darby adjusted his tie and nodded at Dr. Normandy. It had two.

Between Blair's ears, the ringing muted and a headache took its place as the Council Leader cleared his throat. "Dr. Normandy and I discussed the matter and decided that showing the recording was necessary. We need all the facts if we are to rule fairly."

Blair almost snorted. When it came to her, nothing Preston Darby did was *fair.* He'd been trying and failing to knock her down since grade school when Blair had sent a glitch to his cuff and turned his Violet Shield puke green. When she'd seen him a few days ago and embarrassed him in front of an entire floor of cube workers, Cath had warned her it wouldn't end well. Darby had even said it was the last time Blair would make a fool of him, but she had never paid much attention to *Derpy's* whining. Then he'd become Council Leader and had sentenced her brother to death and leered at her while she watched her adoptive mother commit suicide. If she could go back and replace the bullying with kindness, or even no attention at all, would that change how he felt about her?

She smoothed her silk sleeve between her fingers. It wouldn't matter. Nothing she had done then or now warranted Preston Darby's particular brand of twisted obsession.

The Council Leader glanced down at his holopad. "You don't seem to have much luck with them, do you Ms. Scott?" He met Blair's gaze and cocked his head. "Mothers, that is. Seeing as both of yours are dead."

Those decaying feelings inside of her continued to claw out of their grave. "Cath Scott was not my mother."

Red.

The lie cut through the Hall and the wound on the tip of Blair's tongue started to bleed again.

Darby's full lips curled, and he let out a dry chuckle. "Then this process should be easy for you." His smile faded and his dark temples pulsed with each clench of his jaw. "I know everything else has been."

Text from Maxine Wyndham.

With a thought, Blair accepted the message and a transparent gray box formed over one side of her vision before the message thread she shared with her assistant appeared.

> We will destroy him. We will make
> it through this, and then we will
> destroy him.

Blair didn't respond. She stared through Maxine's text, through Preston Darby, through the curved white walls of the Council Hall. She was past Zone One and in the suburbs of Zone Two. She walked, no, she *ran* down the sidewalk, shedding years with each step. Her childhood home was a burst of yellow sunlight amidst the neighbors' grays and blues. She was barefoot in the grass. Dewy blades squished between her toes as she squealed and chased her brother. Her Denny. *But where was he now? How had everything ended so badly?*

Heat flooded her eyes. Blair swallowed the blood pooling against her tongue and blinked back the tears. She told herself it was the pain of the cut and the headache, not the grief or regret or guilt she couldn't keep from breaking out of their sepulcher.

You are strong.

Maxine's text appeared in bold letters. Blair blinked and she was back in the oval room.

Remember that you are Blair Iris Scott. Remember why you are here.

Blair smoothed down her shirt, and with it, her emotions. "Oh, little monster . . ." She whispered and cleared the text box from her vision. For a moment, Blair *had* forgotten. She'd lost herself, she'd retreated. But she remembered now. Blair Iris Scott was power. She was determination. She would burn Preston Darby alive if it meant finding her brother and getting what was hers.

Darby's eyes pressed against her. He could look, but he wouldn't find a chink. Blair was a fortress, a stronghold.

"Exactly what process are you referring to?" She brushed her hair from her shoulders. She'd had to wash it last night. *Really* wash it. With water and liquid soap. She'd even done it twice. But it hadn't been enough—she still felt pieces of Cath stuck in her curls. "Because this—" She gestured to the empty space where the hologram had been. "This is not a process. It's a show."

Darby sat back, blinked, and glanced at Dr. Normandy. "This is a tribunal." He leaned forward, his slick black hair gleaming under the lights. "You are on trial. I could sentence you to Rehabilitation."

Rehabilitation. Oh, she could never go there. She would survive, but there was no guarantee she wouldn't break.

Councilwoman Green inhaled a cluck of surprise. It was no wonder she had been left out of the real decision-making. Weakness fell off her like unspooled thread.

Blair clenched and unclenched her fists. "I am good at my job. Better at it than anyone else. That's not arrogance. It's fact. Yet, I am here." She pressed her fingertips against the metal table. "Not being questioned, as anyone would be during a trial, but wasting my time and this esteemed panel's." She stood and clamped her hands onto her hips. "You want me to do my job? Great. You want me to succeed at another? Sign me up. You want to end my time with the Key? *End it.*"

Blair's throat tightened with a coppery swallow.

"But showing me my dead *adoptive* mother, a traitor to this corporation and to me, and dissecting my response will not keep the world spinning."

Each word burned as her tongue struck her teeth. Each word was a reminder that nothing motivated quite like pain.

Dr. Normandy's chair creaked as he leaned back and once again slid his round glasses down the bridge of his thin nose. "It is true that this council had chosen Dr. Scott as former Director Holbrook's successor and are now faced with the difficult task of choosing another." He rolled the arm of his glasses between his thumb and forefinger. The lenses swept back and forth like a fan blade. "You were our very next choice." He paused, his mouth opening and closing with an unspoken thought. "Tell me, Ms. Scott, why should we appoint you? Your judgment seems . . . *questionable.* Don't the citizens of Westfall deserve better?"

Blair resisted the urge to cross her arms over her chest. That's not what Cath would have done, and she had fooled everyone. "I assume the questionable period you're referring to is my work with Major Owens. You all know Major Rhett Owens?" Blair asked as she gestured to the soldier whose Key Corp–red uniform burned against the white tile like the setting sun. "I asked him to apprehend my brother and Elodie Benavidez and bring them to me. I set a trap. A trap that snared Echo." Blair glanced at the foggy outlines that surrounded Rhett's sweating hands on the metal table before returning her attention to the Council.

"You see, Doctor Normandy." She beamed a practiced smile at the aging scientist. "Like my career, my judgment is impeccable."

Behind her, Maxine sucked in another breath. They both knew that this was the fun part. This was the kill. And it felt like flying.

Blair ignored Rhett's penetrating stare and clasped her hands in front of her as she'd watched Cath do so many times before. "I intended to bring Echo here, to you. *Alive*. I did not, however, count on Major Owens's failure."

Rhett's breaths were deep growls that thrummed against Blair's ears.

"Relying on Major Owens to complete this operation was not a lack in judgment. The Key would not have given him his current title if he was not capable." Fighting through her headache, Blair tented her fingers in front of her chest and pursed her lips. "I'm afraid Rhett was distraught over learning that his fiancée was a traitor who had so easily manipulated him. To put it simply, Major Owens's emotions got in the way of his being an effective soldier."

Rhett surged from his chair, fists clenched at his sides. "You only knew Echo existed because of me!"

Yasmine cocked her head and frowned, "Yes, Ms. Scott, I do see what you mean."

Rhett's uniform seemed to bleed into his neck and paint his cheeks red. "The mission was flawless. My men and I uncovered the Eos warehouse and brought the civilians to Ms. Scott's office where—"

Teresa held up her hand. "Why did you not bring them to us?"

Rhett shifted and sweat glistened against his white-blond temples. "Ms. Scott requested that I escort the civilians to her."

Penelope rested her pointed chin on her fist. "Ms. Scott's plan was not without vision, but, Major, you are exceedingly familiar with the chain of command. I am inclined to agree with Ms. Scott's assessment. Your emotions did indeed inhibit your ability to be an effective soldier."

The ruddiness spread from Rhett's cheeks to his forehead and scorched the tips of his ears.

Blair cleared her throat and reclasped her hands in front of her hips. If she could keep Rhett from sinking himself, she would bring him back from this. And then she'd do the same for her brother.

"Following my direction rather than the proper chain of command may have awarded us a unique opportunity." She took a measured inhale, letting her brilliance bloom before the panel like a rose. "Echo is gone. Westfall's citizens will believe what they should, that the Key has beheaded the beast that is Eos. And their heroes? None other than the woman whose voice represents the future of our great corporation and the man whose efforts in securing Westfall's perimeter have been beamed to every billboard from here to Zone Six."

Blair lifted her chin and drank in the cool air above the heat and tension that radiated off the major. "The Council has more than enough information to make its decision."

Her head pulsed as she smoothed her hands down the front of her pencil skirt and stepped around her chair to the side of the table. "Now, if you'll excuse me, I'll be getting back to work until the panel has made its decision."

Blair held her breath as she motioned for Maxine to collect her things. She wanted to bottle this moment, drink it in whenever she doubted her greatness. She was a magician. A storyteller.

If the Key was smart, it would destroy her like it had all the other fairy tales.

Since first grade, Blair Iris Scott had been challenging Preston. Although, back then, she wasn't a *Scott*. The trauma of her parents' deaths hadn't been the thing to kick off her bold and aggressive behavior. Blair had been born a challenger.

Preston had expected a reaction from her after Holly's Priority One Alert. What he hadn't anticipated was her desire to play games. She would never thank him outright for creating an immortal monument to her, but it was there. He only had to look hard enough, study her expressions long enough, to find it.

Preston chewed the inside of his cheek as his gaze swept the round walls of Council Hall only to land back on Blair. No matter how much he tried, he couldn't keep his eyes from her.

His stare slid down the full hips and toned hamstrings that strained against her perfectly tailored skirt to the gentle slope of her calf and the delicate sigh of the meat giving way to her ankle.

Challenge accepted.

He smoothed his fingers along his tie, down and up and

back again. If he focused, tuned out the rest of the world, he could feel the pressure straight through his body to his spine. Like he was reaching through himself, a real human hand stroking his own back.

What would it be like to reach *into* a person, feel what they were truly made of?

No one did that anymore. Not doctors, not scientists, men, women, *humans.* Everyone was a body with parts open to the world but closed to each other. That's what he loved about coding Holly—his own chance to reach inside.

On his left, Osian drummed his fingers against his desk and nodded down at Blair and her petite assistant as they prepared to leave.

"Blair!" Preston's voice quivered slightly.

She was always keeping him on his toes.

He cleared his throat and began again. "Ms. Scott." He smoothed his fingers down the blade of his tie a final time. "After Dr. Scott, you were next in line for the directorial position. It's only right that we close up this matter as open wounds do tend to fester."

Her eyes were on him, but they no longer held a demand. She blinked, and her gaze glistened against the bright lights. She was pleading to him. Yes, he could see it clearly now. Blair was asking him for a favor, begging him for help. And he couldn't say no to her.

"You have the position now, but leave your brother and the Benavidez girl to us. As you said, you have enough work to keep the world spinning."

Blair's swallow rippled down her throat as she smoothed the fabric of her shirt between her thumb and forefinger. "It would be my honor to serve the Key as director of the MediCenter." Her round cheeks swelled with a grin. "I will not let you down, Council Leader."

Preston's heart clicked against his ribs as he once again dragged his fingers along his tie. It would be difficult for Blair to ever let him down. And, if she did, he'd have a backup waiting. It was just one of the many plans he had for himself and for Westfall, and one of the many tests he was conducting. After all, what was a scientist without his experiments?

VI

Elodie hadn't been happy before. Not truly. How could she have been? In Westfall, she'd existed in a small box with high walls and even higher expectations. The high expectations hadn't troubled her—she was used to reaching every goal. She was always at the top of her nursing studies classes. She participated in virtual reality meetups for the precise amount of time the Key Corporation recommended for optimal health. She ate the prepackaged meals the Key's bots delivered to her home every week. She'd even agreed to marry Rhett Owens even though, when her mother had rushed into her room that fateful evening, Elodie wasn't completely sure she was ready to make such a commitment. Not that that mattered. With no other suitors, denying Rhett would have made her look defective, and no one wanted a defective match.

Aiden's racking cough pulled Elodie back to her original thought: she hadn't been happy with her life in Westfall. *But was she happy now?*

Elodie watched Aiden as he adjusted the shoulder straps of his backpack and continued to trudge through the ash that had accumulated on the charred, black earth, like paper-thin frosting that burst into clouds of smoke with each step.

There was no way to ever be truly happy in Westfall. The Key had made sure of that. It also wasn't possible to be happy here, tripping along the ancient freeway—a decrepit spine, battered and crumbling under years of neglect and the flame of the Key—that led Elodie and Aiden farther and farther away from the only home either of them had ever known. Her life as she knew it was over. But whatever awaited them at New Dawn had to be better than the past.

She stared down at her once bright-white tennis shoes. The dirt that marred the rounded toes was now buried under layers of soot and ash. The blood was buried, too.

Elodie widened her eyes to keep from blinking. She couldn't allow the moment of darkness, not now. Not since she'd thought about the crimson droplets, bits of Dr. Cath Scott, that had stained the tips of her shoes. Her eyes watered, and her body abandoned her, forcing her lids closed. Red flashed across her vision. Not the red of closed eyes against the muted sun, but the vibrant scarlet of fresh blood. Elodie's stomach roiled. She could taste the metallic liquid that had seeped between her lips in Blair's office, and she could feel its sticky warmth against her skin. It coated her hands and—

She sucked in a breath. Her eyelids flew open, and she held her trembling hands out in front of her. No blood, not Astrid's or Cath's. She was clean and free from the death and destruction that the Key inflicted with one hand while the other lulled society to sleep.

New Dawn will be better.

Everything in the distance held the promise of happiness. It was shiny and new and not yet realized. A few weeks ago, that's what Aiden had been, too.

Elodie studied the back of the guy she'd literally followed to the ends of her earth. His curly mohawk and deep brown skin were chalky with ash, as were the clunky boots that seemed to be welded to his feet. He was the greatest adventure, the only adventure, of Elodie's life. He'd gleamed with the possibility of change and true happiness. Elodie thought both had already been realized in Wonderland and at the Rose Festival.

That kiss . . .

Her cheeks warmed with the thought, and her heart fluttered against her ribs. She'd foolishly believed, at each point, that she'd reached the peak of happiness; that she could never possibly experience one more ounce of joy. She'd been wrong. True bliss awaited just ahead, just out of reach. She'd follow Aiden all the way to New Dawn to find it.

New Dawn wasn't the mythical place the Key made it out to be. It existed. It was a safe haven for everyone like her—everyone who desired a life of choice. A life outside the box. After all, the corporation had convinced most citizens that no one could survive past Zone Six and that Zone Seven and beyond were monster-filled wastelands. She couldn't much argue with the *wasteland* aspect, but there weren't any monsters, and she was surviving just fine.

She hooked her thumbs around the straps of her pack and swallowed past the lump in her throat as a charred stick cracked and crumbled beneath her foot. But what if *this* went on forever? *No!*

She wouldn't think that way. Besides, that wasn't how the world worked. She couldn't give up *everything* in the search for freedom and happiness and not be rewarded in the end.

New Dawn is out there. New Dawn is out there. New Dawn is out there.

She repeated it over and over, until, once more, she believed.

"I know we'll find it," Elodie said aloud, more to herself than to Aiden.

"New Dawn?" He quickly shook his head. An immediate acknowledgment that his question was superfluous. "I mean . . ." He paused. His makeshift mask fluttered against his mouth as he exhaled long and slow. "Yeah, we'll find it."

Elodie wrinkled her nose, glad it was covered by her own red bandanna. Aiden didn't believe. Luckily, Elodie had enough faith for both of them.

VII

"Yeah, we'll find it." The lie came without effort. Simple as an exhale and just as quick.

Maybe lying was coded into Aiden's genes. Maybe, when his parents were ready to choose and design each of their two children from their harvested genetic material, they had asked the Key's Gestation Unit to make sure their kids could twist the truth and make anyone believe. After all, that was his sister's gift. Blair couldn't take a step without leaving behind a lie. And this wasn't Aiden's first time spilling an untruth. From the moment his parents died, his life had been anything but honest. To the people who knew him as Cath Scott's adopted son, he was an entitled brat who felt like the rules didn't apply. To those who knew him as Echo's son . . . well, they didn't feel any differently.

He watched Elodie as she stared up at the trees with childish wonder. No matter what anyone thought of him, he'd do anything to reset the past few weeks and undo what had gotten him here. He should have stayed in the morgue with pink-haired

Tavi and pumpkin-orange hazmat suits. Then, he'd have Cath but not Elodie. Then, he would have only ruined one life—his own. But Aiden wasn't a stranger to unhappiness. The morgue, the sameness of every day, the small bites of joy Wonderland provided, that could have been enough. Instead, he'd gone after life, tried to suck the marrow from its bones. They'd splintered in his throat, slashed his insides, and he'd filled with blood until everything around him was red.

If he could do it all over again, he would choose his family, not his freedom.

Elodie removed her bandanna and swiped it against her forehead. She met his gaze and smiled, gray ash streaking her smooth skin. She was always smiling at him, looking at him with those curious dark eyes that deserved to be shown the realities of life and the hope that rested on the other side of truth. But he'd taken advantage of her desire to live a different life. He'd wanted so badly to have his own recruit and prove to Eos that he could be a leader, like Blair, like Cath, that he hadn't given Elodie a choice, not really. He'd made himself her mentor.

Within the Eos organization, every new member stayed with their mentor for months, sometimes years. They were partners, soldiers, comrades. Good that happened to one, happened to both. Same with the bad. Aiden hadn't been given permission to be a mentor, but Aiden hadn't been given permission to do a lot of things. He chose to do them anyway.

"I know you don't really think we'll make it to New Dawn," Elodie said as she retied the bandanna over her nose and under her dusty ponytail. "But there's no way we could have made it this far just to wander around a burned-up forest for the rest of our lives."

She was so optimistic. A beacon shining in a sea of darkness, unknowingly surrounded by sharks.

She settled her eyes on his and waited, like he held all the answers, like he could give her what she was missing. Back in Westfall, Aiden had thought he could. But all he'd managed to do was take her from her safe and planned life and thrust her into chaos, the desolation of Zone Seven, and an unknown promise called New Dawn.

He'd been the shark and the darkness.

Perhaps that was who he was meant to be all along. Someone had to be. Not everyone went through life *good*. Evil was part of the world for a reason. Without the weight of darkness pressing on the other side of the scale, what was hope, kindness, joy, love? Evil must have been coded into his genes along with his penchant for telling untruths. It wasn't simply floating around in the air ready to be breathed in by just anyone. Darkness was born and, like anything else, grew slowly, silently, like a mold, suffocating goodness as easily as falling asleep.

Aiden stopped in his tracks and swallowed, his mouth suddenly dry.

That's what had happened to him. After he'd been recruited to Eos, after finally succeeding at something, he thought he'd been leading a life of virtue and glory, when in fact, he'd been applying a slick layer of darkness over everything he touched. It was only a matter of time before the light around him was snuffed out. And that's what he'd done to Elodie—snuffed out her light.

"I need some space," he blurted. "To figure stuff out."

Ash leapt from his shoulders as he charged forward and continued walking away from Westfall, from Elodie, and from the one person he couldn't let himself think about. He'd filed Cath's death away with his mother's and his father's. If it was up to Aiden, he'd never see the color red again.

He stared down at his ash-covered boots and forced his thoughts far from his sister's office. The muted blacks, dirty whites, and hazy oranges of Zone Seven were a comfort. He deserved to be here. Maybe he'd be here forever.

Behind him, Elodie sucked in a breath. He lifted his gaze. Just ahead, there was pure, living green.

VIII

Preston was the first person headed toward Council Hall's wide exit. He didn't much care for getting snagged by the chattering group of councilwomen all clustered together like a bunch of grapes while discussing things that could be handled just as well, and a lot more quickly, in an email. The solution to making the perfect hasty escape, he'd learned, was not to keep your attention fixed on the floor. He'd made the mistake of employing that method for years. It only resulted in people concocting stories about him and assuming he lacked confidence. No, the correct and most effective way to dodge the sticky-booger folk who wanted to glom onto him and prioritize gossip over action was to appear extraordinarily busy.

He furrowed his brow and picked a point ahead of him, nodding to himself as if engaged in an important message exchange. His attention faltered as he passed Blair, caught up in conversation with her assistant. He inhaled deeply, breathing the warm scents of vanilla and lilac that rolled off her in hypnotizing waves. A shudder vibrated beneath his flesh as his gaze lingered on her velvety skin and soft curves.

A flash of red snagged the corner of his vision. Major Rhett Owens circled Blair like a ravenous beast. She had made him look like a fool controlled only by his emotions. If the major knew Blair as Preston knew her, he would take it as a compliment.

"*Preston.*" The way Normandy hissed his name always brought goosebumps to the back of Preston's neck.

Preston turned, half expecting to see the doctor maniacally stroking his chin in a shadowed section of Council Hall. But shadowed spaces were for areas other than the sterile rooms and corridors of the MediCenter, lit brightly enough to cause a flash burn.

Preston sighed and threw one more cutting glance in the oblivious soldier's direction before fixing his gaze securely on Normandy.

"I must commend you . . ." The doctor paused and pressed the delicate frames of his glasses up the bridge of his nose. "You're finally deserving of my congratulations."

Preston's jaw turned to steel as he walked with Normandy through the Violet Shield and into the open hallway. He had done many things deserving of praise, but when it came to Normandy, every one of Preston's accomplishments may as well not exist until vetted by the good doctor.

"Holly looks superb," Normandy continued. "More and more like her every day."

Preston's chest tightened, and his stomach warmed. "Yes, she's coming along quite nicely."

Normandy motioned to a gap between the evenly spaced chairs that lined the corridor. "And the others?" he asked, peering at the Council Leader over his round lenses.

Preston crossed his arms over his chest and leaned his shoulder against the wall. "As planned," he said, silently congratulating himself on the aloofness of his tone and the casualness of his posture. Normandy was always sticking his thin nose where it didn't belong. "Ironically, I finished updating the program last night."

"And, luckily for you, you were able to capture and install the vocabulary and vocal pathways?"

Preston clenched his toes within the narrow tips of his custom-designed boots.

You shouldn't be nosing into things you don't fully understand.

He swallowed the response. "As I said, the program is finished."

Councilwomen Green and Palazzo emerged from the open doorway, their conversation falling to a hush as they passed the men.

Preston's head bobbed acknowledgment of each of the women, who were no doubt discussing how they'd been left out of the proceedings; how *if his father had been there* things would have gone differently; how he let his emotions, instead of his mind, appoint their new director.

Preston's teeth creaked as he clenched his jaw. He'd made the correct choice. After all, promoting Blair had really been the only choice, and not because they shared something special, *indefinable*, but because she had been correct—losing both Cath and Blair would make the corporation appear unstable.

"Don't worry yourself with them," Normandy said, returning their polite nods with one of his own. "They're hens. They'll always follow the biggest cock."

"I'm not worried." Preston winced as his voice cracked and the words flew from his lips.

"Oh?" Normandy's gaze locked onto his.

The doctor's blue eyes stared at him, unblinking. A scream

tore through Preston's skull—the old part of him he'd long ago locked away from the outside world.

One day, he'll be gone.

For Preston's whole life, Normandy had always been nearby. Same with the former Director Holbrook. They'd both been close friends of his father. Growing up had been like watching three prized flowers wilt. Now, two were dead and there was only one left to go. No matter how much the old doctor tried, he wouldn't live forever.

He'll be dead, and I'll still be here. No father, no Holbrook, no Normandy—finally free.

Preston cocked his chin, returning the same cold, perceptive stare. "What's the status of the girl? Patient Ninety-Two, wasn't it? Last I heard, she'd expired." A smile trembled against his lips as the doctor blinked, his gaze slipping back to the open door to Council Hall.

"Science is not linear." Normandy removed his glasses and wiped his frames on the fabric of his lab coat. "It's a complex cycle—"

"Yes, Doctor. Thank you." Preston didn't keep the condescending tone from sharpening his voice. "I also studied science and am aware of its more free-form nature."

"Oh, young man, they have fooled you into believing you know too much." Normandy rested his glasses back on his nose. "Virtual lectures and cadaver simulations, conducting experiments through a bot . . ." The wrinkles around his eyes deepened as his gaze hardened and he shook his head. "Perhaps *you* are the fool for equating high test scores with true intelligence."

Preston's heartbeat roared between his ears as another silenced scream rattled his chest. He couldn't catch his breath, couldn't force his mouth around a quick reply that conveyed his *true intelligence*.

"How is our newest project advancing?" Normandy asked, taking the opportunity to seize control of the conversation.

Preston cleared his throat. "*Our* project?"

It wasn't *their* project. It was *his*. His ideas, his program, his rules, but somehow Normandy had taken it over simply by drawing breath.

"Surely you're aware of its status."

That flash of red was back, drawing Preston's attention from Normandy and his rage to the doorway of Council Hall and the major who stood taller than anyone yet seemed like the smallest in the corridor. Preston understood that feeling all too well. Not the sense of being tall—Preston Darby was always the shortest man in the room—but the feeling of worthlessness. It was a vulnerable place, a malleable place, a room filled with mirrors that reflected each imperfection, and Preston prided himself on being able to create the most wonderful visions from each blemish.

Preston unclenched his fingers, stiff from the fantasy of wrapping them around the doctor's neck.

"Major Owens!" Preston waved the soldier over.

"Is this the decision you want to make?" Normandy asked, knowing Preston's plans before he'd had the chance to speak them aloud.

Preston didn't answer. Instead, he grazed his teeth along his lower lip and reminded himself that one day the old man would no longer be in this city, on this earth, in his space. And that day couldn't come soon enough.

"Council Leader. Doctor Normandy." Rhett nodded stiffly to each man as he approached.

"Major Owens," Normandy began, filling the gap in the time it took Preston to inhale. "You have shown extreme promise. I believe I have a place for you on my team. How would you like to truly make a difference in Westfall?"

Preston's fingers clenched back into fists. He should have known better. Osian Normandy was a bottomless pit of a man, just waiting for the right idea to fall into the darkness.

Rhett's chest inflated. "It's my duty to serve Westfall. A duty I take very seriously."

Unspoken words stuttered against Preston's tongue as he bottled his anger and stored it away with the others.

Maxine's high-pitched laugh sent Preston's gaze flying to the doorway. She was never far away from her boss.

Blair's dark curls bounced against her broad shoulders as she led her chattering assistant and Councilwoman Wilson from the Hall. Her hazel eyes found his, and in that moment, they were the only two creatures on earth. Her lips remained still, turned up in the corners in the mischievous smirk she must have been born with, but her eyes were ablaze with an emotion he knew all too well—passion. She didn't have to speak for him to understand how she felt. That was the strength of their bond, their intense hunger for each other.

Soon. He thought as he breathed in the last traces of her heady scents. *Soon, and then*, forever.

"Preston?"

Another hiss of his name and goosebumps lifted the hairs on the back of his neck.

"You'll have to forgive the Council Leader. He is prone to daydreaming," Normandy said as he peered through the glasses resting on the tip of his upturned nose. "I suppose that's the life of a creative. Being a man of science myself, there's no way I could know for sure."

Preston's projects were their own brand of science just as Normandy's lab was filled with its own kind of art. They were both creators, both architects of their unique visions of man. Normandy got lost in his beakers and test results whereas Preston was overtaken by the letters and numbers that could be computed to create a person.

"I am working on a project that is very important to the Key. I'm sure, Major, that you'll find it interesting on a personal level as well." Darby emphasized with a lift of his brow. "It must be looked after more often than I am able, and you fit the job perfectly."

Rhett's chest puffed a bit more. "I am honored, Council Leader."

"Two offers in one day." Normandy removed his glasses and wiped them on his lab coat. "Your work is very important to the corporation, Major Owens. And so is your discretion. We wouldn't want others to think we're playing favorites, now would we?"

Rhett's attention lingered a little too long on Blair.

Preston's teeth were sandpaper as he clenched his jaw. "That'll be all, Major."

As Rhett walked away, Normandy tilted his head, his blue eyes resting on Blair, but not in the way Rhett's had. No, that had been something else entirely. "Do you think we'll glean any information about our new director from the young major?"

Fire scorched the back of Preston's throat as Rhett's gaze remained on Blair as he walked past. "We'll learn something, that's for sure."

"Do you think we can trust her?"

"Absolutely," Preston said automatically. No matter how many games Preston and Blair played, how at odds they seemed to outsiders, they were linked. A link *no one* could break.

Preston stared at the major's broad back as he continued down the hall. On paper, Major Rhett Owens would easily best him and win Blair's affections, but power couldn't be categorized or put into words the same way physical features could.

Blair glanced over her shoulder, no doubt feeling his gaze roam her body.

There was also no way to categorize history, the shared space and feelings and moments had with another. In that, Preston's chips were stacked higher than Rhett's could ever be.

His insides quivered as she looked at him before turning on the pointed heels of her stilettos and marching toward the elevator, flanked by her petite assistant.

Preston could win her, *would* win her. And that wasn't even the best part. He pressed his fingers against the blade of his tie. A chill ran up his spine as he dragged his fingers toward his neck and down again. The best part was that she would choose him, open to him, bloom for only him, her softness pouring out until it enveloped him, warm and sweet. They were made for each other. She just had to quit playing these games.

IX

Elodie had stopped looking at the world around her. After spending hours in the forest, she'd come to realize that the forest was the forest was the forest. It was all trees and ferns and ivy, pinecones and bark, birdsong and wind. It was beautiful, but it was all the same beautiful over and over again.

Instead, she focused on the cords of tension that tightened and flexed along the sides of Aiden's neck. They sloped down into his shoulders, hiked close to his ears like he was bracing himself against the cold and rainy winds of a Westfall winter.

As if her thoughts had come to fruition, rushing water sounded in the distance. It was calming, better than the crunch of pinecones and leaves beneath her feet or the occasional grunts from Aiden as he brushed past a prickly pine branch. He'd said he needed his space. It had stung, but she could understand. She also knew that he would be better soon. Elodie would help him get better. All they had to do was make it to New Dawn.

She sighed, long and slow. Her vision blurred around the

edges and her legs switched to autopilot as her mind traveled to the wonders that lay ahead at New Dawn. There it was. Perfect. Fields of blooming flowers, fruit trees, and vegetables. Like the crops and buds in Wonderland, but expansive and even lusher. So many yummy growing things that the fields had no choice but to stretch into the horizon, stained orange and pink by the rising sun.

And the people . . . An exhale slipped past her lips as she pined for the place she hadn't yet discovered but already knew. The people talked freely without shame or consequence, and they hugged. Her cheeks plumped with a grin. They hugged and held hands and stood close to one another, unafraid. And they kissed, deeply and passionately, losing themselves in one another. She pressed her fingers against her warm lips as her stomach filled with fluttering wings.

Back in Westfall, she'd told Aiden that she would never be with him. She was engaged to Rhett, *matched* to Rhett, and she would honor that contract. She didn't have a choice. But now . . . she could do what she wanted. *Be* who she wanted. Choose who she spent life with. She pictured Aiden in the fields of New Dawn, beckoning for her to follow as he disappeared behind a wall of vining flowers. The distant hum of water morphed into the steady buzz of bees as she, lost in a daydream, chased after him. Laughter bloomed around her as bright and yellow as sunflower petals. They were happy and everything was perfect.

"I miss you, El."

The words fell over her daydream as an imagined Aiden slipped behind a row of cornstalks.

"Rhett?" she whispered. She could hear his voice as

golden-orange light bathed the field. The light warmed her back as she parted the cornstalks and dipped into their shadows.

"I don't think I said enough stuff like that."

His words wrapped around her the same way the words in Vi's books had—clunky at first until she was fully submerged in the story and each word played like a movie behind her eyes.

"Maybe if I had . . ." Rhett's voice was soft and smooth like a memory, a journal entry that her mind uncovered in a time of stillness when the terror and anguish and excitement of the past day had drained away everything but this.

"We were perfect, weren't we, El? At least, I thought we were. I thought you were happy. I was."

No longer was Elodie in the fantasy of New Dawn. She was back in the forest, trailing the real Aiden as he ducked beneath low-hanging branches and shriveled leaves crunched beneath his boots. And Rhett—at least his voice—was there, too.

"I had no idea you were involved with Eos." Rhett continued as if her subconscious were one of the Christian confessionals Cerberus took down along with mankind. *"You were good, El. Good at hiding your feelings. I'm trained to detect and take down threats, Eos being at the top of the list, and I never once suspected. How could I have missed it? How could I not have known you were a member?"*

Perhaps this was Elodie's guilty conscience? It would make sense that it would speak to her as Rhett. She'd betrayed him the most of all. Her heart knocked against her ribs as the memory of fresh blood, slick and red, warmed her fingers. *No*, she had betrayed her best friend far more than she had Rhett. And Astrid had paid with her life.

"I don't think I ever really knew you."

Elodie glanced down at her trembling hands before stuffing them into her pockets. There was no way Rhett could have really known her when she didn't even know herself.

"I've been going over it again and again. Why didn't you come to me? Were you scared? I wouldn't have reported you."

Elodie stared at Aiden's pack strapped to his back like a shell. It wasn't hard to believe that even her subconscious would lie. She'd grown up with lies, been swaddled in half-truths and false facts from the moment she was cut out of the gestation bot and handed to the caregiver. What had held her, changed her, cradled her when she cried had been nothing more than metal and wires wrapped up in lab-grown skin. It was normal, but was it right?

"That's not true," Rhett sighed. *"I would have taken you in myself. I shouldn't lie. Not anymore. Not to you. Is that what got us here? All the lies?"*

"Yes," she whispered to herself. The lies were exactly why she was tromping through the forest outside of Zone Seven on the search for true happiness.

"I remember the first time I saw you. At that virtual event. You remember?" His laughter mirrored her own as she thought back to that night. *"You had on that puffy dress and were so nervous about dancing in public that you sat on that bench next to that giant plant the whole night. The bench's legs were glitchy and wouldn't sit on the floor quite right and those leaves kept flashing over your dress."*

Elodie had gotten the very best, most exciting version of Rhett that night. Actually, when Gwendolyn had burst into her room two days later breathless and atwitter about receiving a Match request from the Key, Elodie had been nervous, but she'd remembered Rhett. He'd seemed alluring and refreshing, and she couldn't wait to find out what excitement lay ahead. The memory flooded back.

"I'm not going out there, Astrid." *Elodie settled on the wooden bench next to a potted fern and pressed her back firmly against the wall. She couldn't feel the bench under her legs or the wall against her back, but she knew they were there the same way she knew that, in the real, she was curled up in her desk chair in sweatpants and bunny slippers. Spending hours in VR had acquainted her with virtual spaces, although she had to admit that she was looking forward to the next update that was rumored to make VR feel like real life, wooden benches and all.*

Even in the safety of her own room, Elodie's palms became clammy with the thought of being forced onto the virtual dance floor. "You know I don't dance in public."

"Elodie," Astrid whined, pulling the name from her mouth like rubber cement. "What's the point in coming to these events if you're not going to get out on the dance floor?"

Not even the force of a Fujimoto's pleading could wrench Elodie from this spot. She flattened her hands on her legs in an attempt to squash the layers of pink tulle that bloomed like petals against her thighs.

"I don't even want to be here. You mentioned this ridiculous function in front of my mom on purpose because you knew she would force me to come."

Astrid stroked her pointed chin conspiratorially. "Ol' Gwennie is good for some things after all. I'll bet she's dying right now. Not being invited and everything."

Unfortunately, Gwendolyn Benavidez was not dying. Although, as soon as Elodie logged off VR and rejoined the real, she knew her mother would make every effort to convince her daughter that she was, indeed, on the precipice of the great, unending sleep.

Astrid shook her head. No doubt brushing away the mental image of Elodie's mom sobbing about not receiving an invite to the very exclusive celebration for the Key Corp's newly appointed military officers with a sharp swish of her jet-black ponytail. "But you're here now, and all the fun is happening out on the dance floor." She pointed over her shoulder to the black-and-white tile and the gaggle of people gyrating at its center.

Elodie shook her head and released her petal pink layers, blossoming into full wallflower status. "Sophie is out there. Go dance with her."

Astrid twirled the end of her ponytail and tapped the toe of her checkered shoe on the tile. "I can't just go straight up to her. I have to chum the waters a little bit. You know, make her want to take a bite." She drew slow circles with her narrow hips. "I never make the first move."

Sophie hadn't taken her eyes off Astrid all night, and she'd flipped her blond, waist-length hair enough times to make Elodie's neck hurt.

"Any more bait and there'll be a feeding frenzy."

Astrid's perfectly shaped brows arched, and her lips softened into a smirk. A feeding frenzy was the stuff of Astrid Fujimoto's dreams.

Elodie rolled her eyes. Astrid was gorgeous and outgoing and fun. There was no need for bait. Just being herself, Astrid had more suitors than she could handle.

"Go out there and live your life."

Astrid's tongue glossed her lips as she glanced over her shoulder at Sophie. "Fine," she said, all pleading erased from her tone. "But don't log off without telling me."

Elodie's gaze hung on Astrid as she danced her way over to Sophie. She couldn't wait to hear what grand VR adventures the two of them had before the spark wore off and Astrid was onto her next conquest.

Beside her, the fern glitched, covering her chest in green fronds before adjusting and settling back into its pot.

That's what happens when people don't take the time to code the rooms in advance. Last-minute changes are never stable, *Elodie thought as her gaze left the dance floor and floated to the opposite end of the ballroom. Against each wall sat benches and potted plants just as glitchy as these, and the benches were all empty.*

The crowd shifted as the DJ changed from a slow, winding tune to one fast and sharp. Elodie tapped her feet in time with the music as her attention returned to the bench across the room. It was no longer vacant. A man sat on the bench a few feet from the glitching vegetation. His Key Corp–red officer uniform seemed brighter than the others as he ran his hand through his closely cropped white-blond hair and smiled. Elodie stiffened. He couldn't be smiling at her. *Her feet ceased tapping as she glanced at the empty space next to her.* But he was. *Her cheeks warmed, and she smiled back.*

He leaned against the wall and stared at her, a question poised along the small crease between his eyes.

Elodie swallowed as he dragged his thumb back and forth across his bottom lip. She was hot and cold all at once and had never felt more exposed.

She forced her spine straight and clasped her hands to keep her fingers from tangling in her hair like a giddy schoolgirl. He was mysterious and wonderful. All dark shadows and rough edges which peaked and ebbed under his custom-coded suit.

He hadn't said a word, hadn't slid into her texts or stalked across the dance floor. He was speechless, yet his gaze sang to her like a siren's.

That's who she wanted to be. Not a wallflower, but a storm—a powerful force that bent others to its will. Elodie tilted her chin and brushed her hair behind her ear before licking her lips in the same slow, mesmerizing way Astrid had to Sophie. He bit his bottom lip and lowered his eyes in response, sending shivers through her. Maybe she *would message* him.

"*Everything around you glitched, but you . . .*" Rhett's voice invaded the memory. "*You were perfect.*"

Elodie took a deep breath of pine-scented air. There was no use remembering things that didn't matter. Rhett had turned out to be as dry and rigid as the intro of her Nursing Studies 101 textbook. Her subconscious should know better.

"*I should have been there for you. I tried to make you feel safe, make the world safe for you, but it didn't—*"

Elodie's eyes burned as emotion strangled Rhett's words.

"*It doesn't matter.*"

She stared up at the swaying tops of the pines and kept the tears from falling.

"*Look at me about to cry over this. Over a woman. Over you,*" he growled. "*I've spent too much time around too many women.*"

Rhett was gone then. His voice vanished just as quickly as she had the night of the officer event, logging off when the blond-haired mystery man had finally gotten up from the bench and walked toward her.

Still wrapped up inside herself, Elodie crashed into Aiden as he abruptly stopped in front of her.

"Sorry," she said automatically. "I wasn't paying attention."

He stared down at his feet and shook his head. "Like I said

before, you don't need to apologize." He opened his mouth to say more but paused and shook his head again.

Elodie remained silent, her lips pressed tightly together as she waited for him to speak.

"I was wrong to shut you out. I don't—" He took a deep breath and brought his green eyes to hers. "You didn't do anything. It's me, but I'll sort it out. I promise."

Elodie smiled. Aiden was coming back to himself, back to her. Soon, everything would return to normal. They would be in New Dawn where she would finally be happy and stay that way.

She cleared the dryness from her throat and reached for her canteen. Empty. She lifted Aiden's and shook it. "We need water."

Aiden turned toward the direction of the subtle whooshing that had created the perfect backdrop for Elodie's daydreams and remembrances.

"Have you ever seen a waterfall?"

Elodie squeezed the straps of her backpack to keep from squealing. There were so many good things waiting just ahead.

Aiden followed the rushing sounds of water. He hadn't much thought about refilling his canteen or eating since he and Elodie had been dropped off in Zone Seven. Despair had numbed those parts of him, but they would need clean drinking water if they had any hope of making it to New Dawn. If New Dawn was even out there.

He rounded a tree trunk nearly the size of a Pearl transport and paused. In the distance, water slipped down a wall of rocks like silver strands of hair.

Westfall had been named for its western location and the waterfalls that dotted the landscape around the city formerly known as Portland, but Aiden had only ever seen one. A pitiful stream that dribbled over algae-covered rocks, it had looked more like tears than the thunderous water crashing over rocks he'd read about in books.

Next to him, Elodie inhaled and squeaked with glee. She grabbed his hand and pulled him toward the water. They reached it, breathless. Elodie grinned from ear to ear as she stared down at her reflection in the shallow lagoon so clear and clean that he didn't have to squint to spot the small gray-striped fish that darted from the frothy white bubbles to the rocks.

Elodie's hand slipped from his as she knelt by the water's edge and plunged her cupped hands beneath the rippling surface. She laughed as she splashed water onto her face and neck, cleaning soot from her cheeks before refilling her hands and taking a long, slow drink. He'd been like that, wide-eyed and amazed by the world, when he'd met her. That's how he'd gotten her, poisoned her, infected her. His darkness had camouflaged itself in curiosity and joy and excitement.

"We should jump in." She smiled up at him. Water droplets clung to her skin and glinted in the sunlight, bathing her in stardust.

"I don't have anything to wear."

"From what I've seen in VR, underwear will cover way more than a bathing suit," she said as she slipped out of her pack and began to untie her ash-covered shoes.

Aiden tightened his grip on his shoulder straps. "It's cold. The water's from the mountain, snow melt, and—"

"I know you're not okay. I know you probably never will be. I get it." Her swallow was audible as she shook her head and blinked back unshed tears. "But we have to try. If not, what was all of it for?"

Guilt washed up his throat and stung the back of his tongue. He averted her gaze and stared out at the rushing water. He couldn't trust himself, but he could trust her.

Aiden shrugged off his pack, and it landed on the rocky shore with a *thump*. "You ever been swimming before?"

Her fingers seemed frozen around the jumpsuit's zipper she'd pulled up to her neck. "No one swims in the real."

"No one kisses at the fair or searches for New Dawn," he said, hopping on one foot as he tugged his boot off the other.

"I've taken a water shower."

He smiled his first real smile since Westfall. "That doesn't count."

Ash plumed around him as he unzipped his jumpsuit and shrugged out of it. He'd left his blood-spattered shirt and pants in the back of the box truck that dropped them in Zone Seven and now stood in front of her in only his underwear. Elodie's cheeks reddened as she stared at him, a smile pinned to the corners of her lips. For a moment, he thought about asking her what she saw and felt when she looked at him, but he didn't want to give the evil parts of him the advantage. He didn't want his darkness to know how she truly felt. It would use it to get closer to her, coil around her like a snake and squeeze.

"I'll get in first. Test the water," he said, breaking the silence.

He charged into the lagoon. It was as cold as he'd imagined. Aiden welcomed the icy chill that gnawed on his bones and sucked the air from his lungs. He inhaled fully and dropped beneath the surface. Completely submerged, the water wasn't as cold. Maybe this was a lesson, a note to give in to his demons. That they weren't so bad, if only he would take the plunge.

His lungs burned, and he rocketed to the surface. His long legs steadily kicked, keeping him afloat, while he shook water from his ears and wiped his eyes. A gray ring of ash and soot yawned away from him—the remnants of Zone Seven. His gaze scanned the shore, his breath hitching when it settled on Elodie and her bare stomach and legs and the thin triangles of fabric that hid the rest.

The Key had outlawed touch nearly fifty years ago. With that change came many others. The textbooks he'd skimmed during the entry-level courses of his various MediCenter careers had taught him about the hands-on hospital procedures of the past and the dangers that accompanied them. They also educated him on the science of sexual intercourse and sterile Release Pods, an "advancement" the Key had made in the name of "safety." Nothing had taught Aiden about lust or desire. He'd figured those out for himself. Maybe they were a part of his darkness, too.

Aiden tipped onto his stomach and swam closer to shore. Water rained from his cupped hands with each effortless stroke. Cath had taught him how to swim at the same place he'd seen the sad waterfall. The water had only gone up to Cath's hips and was muddy brown with Aiden's failed attempts at getting his arms and legs to work together, but that hadn't mattered. He would have taken lessons in a dirty puddle if it meant being with his second mom. He blinked away the memory along with the water that had dripped into his eyes.

Don't think about her. He scolded himself as he strode toward the shore. He offered his hand to Elodie. It shook slightly as he shivered against the gentle breeze.

She reached out but stopped before she took his hand.

"I'll keep you safe," he murmured.

Her dark eyes gleamed with the reflection of the sparkling water. *"I'll keep *you* safe."*

She grabbed his hand and he pulled her into the lagoon. She hiccuped back a breath, her eyes widening with the cold.

"It takes a minute to get used to." Aiden wrapped his arm around her waist and pulled her away from the shore.

She clamped her hands onto his broad shoulders and straightened her legs into arrows.

He brought his hand to her chin and tipped her face to meet his. "Breathe." He instructed and demonstrated with a deep inhale and exhale.

Elodie sucked in a breath and released it slowly. She relaxed her grip on Aiden's shoulders and deepened her breathing, her chest pushing him away and drawing him back in with each deep breath.

"I'm sorry," he blurted. He couldn't stop the apology.

Elodie tilted her chin, her forehead wrinkling. "For what?"

"I'm the reason you're out here. I'm the reason you can't go home. I'm the reason for Astrid." *And Cath.* He choked back a noiseless sob. "If I would have known that any of this would have happened, I would never have—"

Elodie pulled him down to her and pressed her mouth to his. Her tongue slipped between his parted lips and explored the unspoken apologies.

He couldn't be all bad. Elodie wanted him. Because of her goodness, she wouldn't have been with him when she was still matched, but this was a new day. The rules of the Key no longer applied. She was free to do what she wanted, and what she wanted was him.

His fingers tangled in her hair as he pulled her closer. They fit against each other perfectly, shaped from the same bit of stardust.

Her kiss deepened with a whimper, a growl, a need for more.

"Elodie . . ." He loved the way her name tasted in his mouth.

Elodie wrapped her legs around his hips and flattened her hands against his back. It was his turn to moan, hot and low against her lips as he smoothed his palms down the slope of her waist. He cupped her ass and slid his hands to her thighs. Elodie locked her legs around him as his fingertips pressed into her skin.

Maybe she could uncover the goodness still within him. The pieces of him that had yet to be snuffed out by the dark.

Aiden buried his head against her neck and his tongue drew slow circles down the slope of her shoulder.

She guided his mouth back to hers and ran her fingers along his stubbled cheeks.

Maybe she could breathe new life into him, inject him with her light until he beamed from the inside out.

But what would be left of her?

Aiden's eyelids flew open and he pulled away. Cold water snaked between them, no longer heated by their coiled bodies and flaming desire.

That had been his evil talking, wanting to take from her, drain away her goodness until she was nothing but the husk of the woman he'd met in Westfall. This evil he carried was insipid, insidious. *He* was insidious.

"Aiden?" she asked, her brows lifting.

Twigs snapped and bushes rustled.

Aiden stiffened as his gaze swung to the shore.

"Monster," he breathed. Silt buried his feet as he clenched his toes.

The creature stood on the shore, its face blurred by the quaking shadows of swaying tree limbs. Key Corp–red smoke encircled its torso like wings, and its paper-white legs dug into the sand like two sharpened twigs.

"Where?" Elodie's whisper was the frantic beat of a bird's wings.

"Stay behind me," he murmured.

"Aiden, I don't see anything."

The monster's throat undulated with a clicking growl, and thick strings of foamy drool hung from its shadowed chin.

Aiden held his arms near his side. His muscles were rigid and at the ready, guarding Elodie against the creature. His heartbeat roared between his ears and drowned out the splashing waterfall and the words Elodie spoke against the breeze. Small rocks bit the soles of his feet and the gentle wind felt like ice against his goosebump-covered flesh as he led them, inch by inch, out of the water.

The creature's nostrils flared as it sniffed the air. The strand of drool dangling from its chin broke and plopped into the trembling lagoon waters. Its neck flexed with another round of clicks, and its bony fingers stabbed the air as it searched for a line to reel them in.

"Put your shoes on. When I say run, don't hesitate," he said, stuffing his feet into his boots.

"But, Aiden, I—"

"Run!" Aiden shouted.

Elodie paused behind him, and he grabbed her arm and catapulted her forward. Aiden didn't look back. He'd learned from his sister Blair that looking back only slowed you down. His pulse beat against his ears. How far would they have to run to be safe?

Suddenly, heat seared Aiden's calf and a silent scream wrung the air from his lungs. There had been no hammering footsteps behind him, no warning, only the tear of his skin and the warmth of his blood seeping into his shoe.

Aiden fell onto the ground. He dug out fistfuls of earth as he crawled forward, dragging his injured leg behind him. Elodie was ahead of him, jaw slack and eyes wide. Aiden couldn't force the word *run* from his lips. But it was no matter. He would die protecting her like he should have for Cath and for his mother.

His vision blurred, and his head pounded as he jerked his attention over his shoulder.

The monster was on all fours, paces behind him. Its thick hips twitched and the bands of muscle shaping its legs tensed. It sprang forward and released a gurgling screech as it shot through the air.

Aiden dropped to his forearms. Cracked pinecones and splintered sticks dug into his flesh as he fought to gain ground. Fiery pain exploded through his leg as the creature landed and sank its claws into him.

Aiden's arms shot out from under him as the monster dragged him backward and flipped him over. The back of his head bounced against the ground with a *thwack* and the scene before him burst into stars.

Weight pinned Aiden's legs to the earth. He blinked the flashes of light from his eyes. The monster was on top of him, a blur of white and red. A scream scorched the back of his throat as the creature's talons pierced his shoulders. It snarled, baring teeth as jagged as mountaintops.

Aiden opened his mouth to shout for Elodie to run away and never look back, but pain had sucked the moisture from his mouth and glued his tongue to his teeth.

His fingertips were cold, but the blood pouring from his leg and shoulders was a warm bath on a winter's day.

"Aiden!"

The world around him spun as a familiar voice pierced the monster's snarls and growls.

"Aiden!"

Reds and whites swirled in front of him like the birth of a sun. Maybe this was death—witnessing the creation of the cosmos and being called home. He should have expected it. Evil was always vanquished in the end.

"Aiden, can you hear me?"

His vision darkened around the edges and the shouts of his name turned to birdsong as he fell into blackness.

EOS NETWORK SECURE COMMUNIQUE

SPARKMAN: Council meeting adjourned.
No eyes or ears inside. Heard
anything?

TFUJIMOTO: No. Try Wonder Boy. He's always in
the thick.

SPARKMAN: Lost track of Aiden after we
got his recruit out of VR and
Key soldiers took Wonderland.
I barely made it into the tunnels.

TFUJIMOTO: Elodie?

You saved her?

SPARKMAN: Aiden was with Violet Royale.

TFUJIMOTO: Her name's Elodie Benavidez. Just
intro'd her as Violet Royale. Thought
I was protecting her. Joke's on me.

SPARKMAN: She's working for the Key?

TFUJIMOTO: No.

My father found Astrid dead in her
VR chair.

Key Corp soldiers hacked her VR
program looking for Elodie.

She got my sister killed.

SPARKMAN: They killed her in VR? The update?

TFUJIMOTO: The update and Elodie.

My father feels like it's his fault.
He gave the Key access to Astrid's
program.

SPARKMAN: He couldn't have known what they
would be ordered to do. Or what
they are capable of.

TFUJIMOTO: I hope she wasn't scared or in pain. I
hope it was fast.

Why did they want Elodie so badly that
they killed my sister to find her? I need
to talk to Elodie and find out what she
knows. I have to get answers.

SPARKMAN: We need Echo.

Echo will get you answers, but first,
we need intel on what happened in
Council Hall.

TFUJIMOTO: Has Echo scheduled a virtual meet?

SPARKMAN: I haven't received a response to any of my urgent messages.

TFUJIMOTO: Wonder Boy. I'm tellin' you. He has a line in with Echo. Find him, and you'll be able to reach command.

I'll make some calls, too. See what I can shake loose about the meeting and about Elodie. I need the distraction.

SPARKMAN: Understood.

TFUJIMOTO LOGGED OFF

-:-:-

Sparkman logged off the secure Eos network and tucked the custom holopad back into the hidden pocket in the lining of her Key Corp–red military jumpsuit she wore under the lab coat Normandy insisted she don whenever working with him. The stiff, white fabric constricted her arms, and the seams groaned and popped each time she moved. Without it, she could complete her duties much more efficiently. However, as she was continuing to learn, others' perceptions of the doctor— and therefore of her—trumped both ease and speed in his mind. Until Eos no longer needed her eyes and ears in his lab,

Sparkman would continue to be uncomfortable in more ways than one.

Her strawberry-blond braid brushed the wall as she adjusted her tight-fitting lab coat and wiped the sweat from her brow. Eos's techs had fully mapped the MediCenter and Zones One through Six for spaces safe from the Key's ever-watching eye. Throughout the whole of Westfall, there were only a handful of places in which Holly and the corporation's CCTV didn't cover—Dead Zones. This bot charging station around the corner from the bank of MediCenter basement elevators was one of them.

Sparkman ran the toe of her boot over an uneven section of tile. Years ago, there had been a collection of ornately detailed wrought iron posts that sprang from stamped and polished concrete like ocean spray. They'd held a potted plant—faux, of course. Dirt had always been too much for the Key. But real or not, Sparkman had always felt a sense of calm when she hid in this corner next to the crinkled plastic fern. Then one day, the fern was gone and a door installed, four charging stations placed inside on top of the concrete that had been covered by the same bleach-white tiles that blanketed the rest of the Medi-Center's hallways. But the bots hadn't been able to take away the memory. A lump remained in the floor in place of art, and a lump was better than nothing.

Sparkman's braid slid over her shoulder as she manually slid the door open and peered out the narrow crack. When she reappeared from the Dead Zone and back on CCTV, no matter what bot was watching or who it reported its information to, Sparkman would look like she'd been doing her job. Normandy didn't trust bots to fill his lab's medicine vials and had delegated that task as part of her duties. He didn't trust Sparkman, either.

Had he, she wouldn't be crouched in a corner discussing a way to best extract information from a closed meeting. She would have been in Council Hall with him. His trusted apprentice. That was her job, after all. Her *real* job. The job Eos had tasked her with. But every step forward with Dr. Normandy was ultimately followed by two steps back.

The elevator chimed and its metal doors slid open. The door to the charging station remained open as Sparkman sank into the closet's shadowed, warm interior. Her muscular legs tensed, and her toes dug into the soles of her boots as she watched and waited.

Major Rhett Owens strode from the elevator, his shiny dress shoes clicking against the white tile. While it was true that anyone could visit the MediCenter's basement level, it was also true that not anyone could enter the rooms, labs, and offices tucked along its wide corridors. Only certain people had the correct permissions coded into their Key-issued cuffs, and there was no reason for Owens to have access to such permissions.

Sparkman's movements were liquid, silent and fluid, as she slid the door open and poured herself down the hall after him. She paused as he turned the corner and waited two breaths before she stole a glance. Owens stood outside a closed steel door, the word MAINTENANCE in small block letters against its glossy front. He passed his cuff beneath the scanner. It lit up green, and the distinct *click* of a disengaging lock bounced around the sterile hallway. The door hissed open, and purple light drenched the doorway as he disappeared inside.

Major Rhett Owens was featured on billboards and commercials that reinforced the rules of the corporation and how indebted society was to their great leadership. Maintenance was far from his purview. But, thanks to Dr. Normandy, it wasn't far from Sparkman's.

She tugged on the lapels of her starched lab coat and marched to the maintenance-room door. She passed her wrist beneath the cuff reader. It flashed red. Again, she passed her cuff beneath the scanner. Again, it denied her entry.

Sparkman pressed her ear to the metal. Owens's voice droned, tinny and low against the steady beeps and hisses she knew all too well. Her stomach tightened, and her hands balled into fists. There was no maintenance station behind this door. No, behind this door, was a lab.

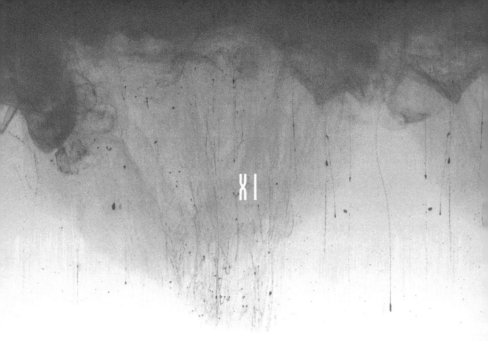

XI

The Darby Zone One estate was the farthest a person could get from the downtown MediCenter without entering Zone Two. Actually, if any citizen bothered to study a map of Westfall closely it would show a small bulge in the otherwise perfect circle that encompassed a portion of the winding, forested roads of Southwest Hills. Why hadn't the original Zone cartographers maintained the integrity of the circle and merely made it wider?

Simple. There was nothing exclusive about letting everyone in.

Preston tapped his foot against the black rubber floor mat of his custom-designed Pearl as it motored down the twisting drive that led to the family home he'd only lived in since his father died. Before that sunny day when Clifton Darby slipped at the top of his mansion's marble staircase and hit every blunt edge on the way to the floor, his head cracking against the ninety-degree corners like a ripe melon, Preston had resided at the Darby's country estate. He'd grown up taking long car rides into town to attend in-person school days and was never invited to play dates that took place in the real because of how far away he lived from the other children. At least, that's what he would shout while tearing apart the country house's rooms in wild angry bouts, and the staff never contradicted him.

Now that his father was dead—rest his soul, (if the bastard had one)—Preston was the man of the house and held all the power. Not only in the mansion tucked into the wooded hills of Zone One, but as Council Leader for the most influential body in the entire New American West Coast.

The Pearl stopped in the middle of the crescent-shaped drive, the interior flashing that annoying purple shade as the door noiselessly opened. The chunky heels of his boots tapped the pavement as he marched to the front door. There was an almost imperceptible *click* as the high-tech sensor logged the information from his cuff and automatically opened the house's grand, wooden doors. No one was there to greet him as he entered the still house. No dutiful wife or cherublike toddler, rosy cheeked and breathless from running through the house to excitedly meet his father. He could have had that; been matched to someone he loved who loved him in return. But his father had stopped the matching process before it could get started. Preston needed to *be more of a man* before he could be a husband. The love of his life, a.k.a. the only woman who had managed to chase Blair from his thoughts, had been matched to another man, had given her genetic material to create another man's fat, angelic baby, another man's happily-ever-after.

Preston snorted as he dragged his fingers up and down his tie and stared at the floor at the bottom of the double staircase. It was a shame his father would never see the man his son had become. Although, if Clifton were alive, he wouldn't have noticed anyway.

These thoughts of his father stoked the anger in his stomach. Heat bubbled in his core and a faraway scream echoed between his ears.

Before he could attend to the part of himself that he'd locked away years ago and had only recently begun to stir from its long slumber, Preston's attention was drawn to a yellow puddle of sick crusted against the shiny white marble. He only had to walk a few feet to find another. And another. And another. It was amazing that his mother vomited at all. She never ate. At least, he never saw her eat, and the caretaker bot he'd reprogrammed to look after her never reported success at mealtimes. Hate was the only thing that kept his mother alive. Perhaps it was all that was left of her and each foamy, bile-yellow puddle was a piece of her humanity that the rage and spite had evicted.

"Holly." Preston forced the hologram's name between clenched teeth. "Where are the bots in charge of cleaning this mess?"

Holly materialized before him with her delicate hands clasped in front of her newly voluptuous figure. She glanced down at the crusted puddle on the floor before motioning upstairs.

Preston cocked his head. "She locked them in again."

It wasn't a question, but Holly answered anyway. "I was going to alert you, but I knew—"

"Not while I'm with the Council," he interjected.

Holly nodded. Her short brown hair dusted her pointed chin and her Key Corp–red gem earrings shuddered with the motion.

"How long has she been up there?"

A swallow rippled down Holly's lean neck, and Preston couldn't suppress the goosebumps that crested across his arms. He'd programmed that swallow—the gentle push of saliva into the contracting esophagus. For hours, he'd watched Blair's neck before he had programmed Holly. The slight motion that was missed by so many of the living was absolutely perfect in this hologram. Before releasing the update that transformed Holly from a voice to an image, Preston had dictated a paper on the importance of adding details like this perfect swallow to the hologram that helped not only the citizens of Westfall, but the planet's entire population. Then his father died, and the only things the Key's publicity department wanted from the Darby household were images and papers written by the Darby that had been taken from the world too soon. Even in death, Preston's father outdid him.

Another silenced scream roared to life from deep within him.

Holly moved her attention to the grand staircase that glittered under the warm glow of the foyer's decadent crystal chandelier. "She called in the bots and locked the door right after you left."

Blair was correct when she'd said that basing Holly's vocal pathways on hers hadn't been her choice. It had been his, and he allowed her to take credit for the achievement. He didn't even expect her to say thank you. That's not how it worked between them. Blair Scott showed her thanks in other ways.

Preston clenched his jaw. This time, he'd gotten ahold of himself and suppressed the shudder that purred against his spine.

Holly blinked. The reflection of the chandelier sparkled perfectly against her dark eyes. "Because of what happened last time, I chose not to override your mother's code and unlock the doors myself."

"You *chose* not to?" He'd said it as if her ability to choose was a discovery. In truth, he already understood the inner workings of the hologram. He understood how she learned and evolved. How she only needed a body to be fully realized.

"Would you like me to go in with you?" Holly asked as he walked past her and headed toward the stairs.

He stopped, his foot hovering over the first step. He didn't have time for this, not anymore. He was the head of the most important and influential entity of the entire New American West Coast. He wasn't a bot, and he was no longer a child. For all he cared, his mother could rot up there.

Preston tugged his tie free from around his neck and draped it over his shoulder as he backed away from the stairs and cut through the library to the guest quarters that occupied their own wing of the Darby's Zone One estate. His fingers shook as he unclasped his belt and untucked his starched button-down from his pressed pants. His clothes showed no signs of the overnight session he'd held with Osian Normandy before meeting with the three other council members inside Council Hall, but Preston felt the sweat and dead skin that had flaked off throughout the long hours sticking to his body like dew. He had to change before he went back and held court once again. He undid the delicate oyster-shell buttons of his button-down and let the rush of filtered air sweep over him as he marched to his haven inside the house that had never been his home.

"Open," he commanded. The glossy white door obeyed and noiselessly retracted into the wall. He dropped his tie on the shiny black tiles that showed dirt and grime better than white ever could before stripping out of his shirt and dropping that, too. If his mother could leave piles of mess around the house, so could he.

A ripple of anxiety rushed through his chest, and he paused in front of the open bathroom that sat across the wide hall from his bedroom. Trying to ignore it, he pulled his belt free from its loops and savored the gentle swipe of pressure across his low back. He took a deep breath and stared up at the smooth white ceiling as he let the belt dangle from his fingertips, the tapered end grazing the black tiles. His stomach hardened into a rock, and he turned his attention to the hall behind him, empty except for the discarded shirt and tie. He fisted his hand around the metal belt buckle and went back to retrieve his dirty clothes.

He wasn't like his mother—a filthy animal. He was in control of all parts of himself, those at the surface and those he'd imprisoned.

He tucked his clothes under his arm and stood a little taller. Preston Darby was powerful. Preston Darby was king.

XII

Blair wasn't a stranger to stares, whispers, or cutting glances that lit the air with the neon green of envy, but the looks she now received from the MediCenter cube workers were not filled with jealousy or curiosity. A hush spread out around her like she had detonated and sent out a paralyzing shock wave. Sets of eyes followed her, as wide as saucers, while she walked from her last meeting through the publicity and marketing department's open workspace. Next to her, she felt Maxine swell, her petite frame seeming to grow until she filled the space, choked out all the air. Blair narrowed her eyes. She'd have to make sure her assistant didn't suffocate them both.

An office door opened, and a cube worker shuffled through the Violet Shield that rimmed the entrance. Gaze glued to her holopad, she nearly walked into Blair.

Maxine sucked in a breath. "Watch where you're going," forcing the words between clenched teeth.

Blair affixed a smile to her face and clasped her hands in

front of her. She was mercy and softness with an attack dog by her side.

"Director Scott, I didn't see you. I should have—what I mean is that I—" The worker tripped over her words as her knees buckled in a graceless attempt at a curtsy.

The news that named the new director had spread like fire through Zone One and the MediCenter gossip mill and was no doubt torching Westfall's remaining habitable zones. Although, Blair hoped that would be the first and last curtsy she'd have to endure.

"Condolences on your loss. Dr. Scott was a great person." The young woman's thin lips nearly disappeared as she pressed them together and took a deep breath through flaring nostrils. "And congratulations on your achievement." She looked up as she said the last bit, staring directly at Blair. *Challenging* her.

Blair's throat went dry. For the first time in a long time, she didn't know what to say. No lies sprang from parted lips or seeped through her expression like poison.

She thinks I killed Cath.

The ringing was back—a siren wailing in the distance, growing louder and louder with each passing second. The buttons of Blair's blouse strained against her chest as she struggled to fill her lungs. Her gaze darted around the workspace. The cube workers' eyes were no longer saucers but heavy-lidded looks of agreement.

They all think I killed her.

Maxine tapped a pointed nail on the screen of her holopad and her lips moved in clipped precision, but Blair didn't hear a word over the ringing in her own ears.

Whatever she'd said had done the trick. The young woman

blanched and scurried toward the open cubes. Blair watched her go and watched the judgmental gazes grow back into saucers.

She and Maxine approached the elevator and Maxine scanned her cuff. Her lips had relaxed now, moving in the rushed way they did when she told Blair things she knew neither of them found important but needed to know nonetheless.

Blair entered the elevator first and didn't turn around until she felt the rush of moving up. The wailing sounding between her ears subsided as she leaned against the cool metal.

Maxine's fingers flew across her holopad. "The news hasn't even been officially released yet, and it's already tracking so well," she said without looking at Blair. "They love you, *Director* Scott."

If Maxine had sensed the young woman's accusation, she didn't make it known.

They think I killed her.

The idea wriggled between Blair's ears.

"As publicity said, the Council will do what you suggested and tell the citizens that you, their new director, along with *Major Rhett Owens*"—Maxine's top lip curled as she peered down her nose at a digital memo—"captured the leader of Eos."

They all think I killed her.

"Then you'll no longer have to hear about what a *great person* that terrorist was. Everyone will know the truth."

But that *was* the truth. Dr. Cath Scott was a great person. She was also a terrorist. Blair couldn't make the two fit together. Did one automatically exclude a person from the other? If so, why had Cath taken Blair and her brother in after they'd been through so much and had no one to turn to? Then again, Cath had never loved her. Maybe she wasn't such a great person after all.

"I wouldn't be surprised if there was a parade in your honor,"

Maxine continued. "You're only the second director this Medi-Center has ever had. That's monumental." Her lips tightened into that delightful little O. "A *monument?!* Holly, contact Lani in PR and set up another time to talk." Her fingers resumed their speedy taps. "Scratch that, Holly. I'll go back down there myself." Maxine's cheeks flushed, and her brown eyes brightened. She looked so alive, lit up from the inside out by the job she most likely lorded over others.

Blair had been like that once.

"Lani and the rest of the marketing heads would *love* to do the new director a favor. They'd sooner die than say no to me face-to-face."

Blair almost wished for the ringing to return to drown out Maxine's spark. Being around it was nauseating. Like being sober while everyone else was drunk.

"What do you think about replacing that eyesore of a fountain near the river with a larger-than-life-sized statue? Marble, of course." She paused and tapped her pointed chin. "No, *onyx*."

The elevator slowed and the doors slid open.

Blair dragged herself to the exit and paused, the metal doors shuddering as she blocked them from closing. "Maxine, what exactly are they saying happened to Cath?"

The petite assistant hiked her thin shoulders. "They didn't. They're waiting to see what the public wants—Rehabilitation, her head on a spike . . ." The corners of her mouth ticked with a sly grin. "Whatever it is, you'll have a hand in giving it to them."

The elevator doors grunted and stuttered in another attempt to close.

"Does the public think I killed her?"

The reflection of Maxine's paper-white holopad glowed in

her brown eyes. "Do you want them to?" The holopad flashed against her pupils and stole her attention. "I'll work on a few whisper-campaign ideas and send them over."

The pealing between Blair's ears started again as she stepped back, and the doors quickly swept closed in front of her. Her stomach lurched, and she pressed her hand against her mouth and ran to the closest restroom.

She couldn't breathe. Everything was too tight. She tugged at the rigid waistband of her pencil skirt and scratched at her silk blouse and the pearl buttons made rigid with each of her labored breaths. This wasn't right. Cath was supposed to be here. *Aiden* was supposed to be here. But she'd lost them both, and they were never coming back.

The door to the restroom hissed open, and Blair charged into the single-stalled room. Her legs trembled and she flattened her palms against the wall to keep from melting. She blinked through the tears swirling her vision. Red. Everything was red. The color slipped down the walls in rivulets and pooled onto the floor. She could still smell the copper tang and feel the puddles squish warm and sticky between her toes.

Momma! a small voice inside her screamed.

She clapped her hand over her mouth and pushed open the stall door. She bent over the porcelain and heaved. A stringy glob of yellow bile coated the inside of the toilet. She sagged against the metal wall and blinked through teary eyes. There was no blood on the walls, no death. Only the blazing violet light that automatically switched on when the restroom door opened.

She wrapped toilet paper around her trembling fingers and dabbed her lips before throwing the wad into the basin. Water spun inside the bowl as she smoothed down her skirt and headed to the light station in front of the mirror. Her hands still shook as she passed them under the stream of color changing light, but the ringing had ceased and her stomach had settled. She hadn't eaten anything since last night. A fact made obvious by the lack of food to purge. That was the problem. She'd feel much better once she ate.

Blair wiped a stray hair from her blouse and stood a little taller as she glanced at herself on the way out. As the door to the bathroom hissed open, the room once again lit up in violet.

She cleared her throat and stared down the well-lit corridor that led to her office. On either side, the glass-walled meeting rooms were empty. Blair was alone. Except for her brother, she had always been alone.

"Denny . . ." His nickname slipped from her lips like a prayer.

She hadn't lost Aiden. He'd been taken. First by Cath, and again by that girl, *Elodie*. Blair tugged on the sleeves of her blouse and marched down the hall. She had once vowed to burn West-fall to the ground to save her brother. Now she was director, ruler of the New American West Coast, and she would make good on her promise.

She rounded the corner to her office and nearly smacked into a red-clad soldier.

The man spun on his heels. "Director Scott." Rhett straightened and removed his cap. He'd chosen wisely during the trial at Council Hall and kept his mouth shut. She could thank him, but what would she gain from doing so?

He took a step back to make room for her in the narrow hallway that led to her office. Still, there was barely enough space for her to slide between the sturdy major and the white wall and keep from touching either. The tight entryway was one of the things she liked about her office. There would never be a gaggle of people waiting outside her door, unlike Cath's. The door to Blair's adoptive mother's office was out in the open. Anyone on the ninth floor could stop by, chat with the elderly secretary, chat with Cath—

Bile burned the back of Blair's throat. None of that was real anymore. Cath was *dead*. And by now, Cath's office had been reset to the drab MediCenter standard, and her septuagenarian assistant had been forced into retirement.

"Is everything okay?" Rhett leaned forward. His breath tickled her eyelashes.

She frowned and slid her Key-issued cuff beneath the door's sensor. A purple waterfall of light spilled against her as she strode through the Violet Shield and into her office. "Maxine didn't inform me we had an appointment, Major."

"I didn't schedule one."

She tried to be normal, but Blair couldn't turn to face him. She could only stand in the middle of her office and stare down at her shoes. She hadn't been back since it had been thoroughly cleaned and running into Rhett had ensured that her thoughts were far from what would be waiting for her on the other side of the door.

It had been less than a day since Cath had entered Blair's office. Blair inhaled. She could still smell Cath's earthy scents, still see her halo of blond curls, still hear her voice ablaze with motherly intensity.

"I love you both deeply. You were the best decision I have ever made."

Blair hiccuped back a sob and kicked off her shoes. The fuzzy white puff of a rug had been scrubbed clean. She spread her toes and let them sink into the fibers as her eyes roamed the ceiling and slid down the wall of windows. All at once, copper and the acrid scent of burnt skin and hair hit her senses. Cath had been everywhere. Now she was gone, and Westfall would praise Blair for her demise. The Key had made everything perfect.

"Blair?" The concern in Rhett's voice brushed against her like a cold breeze. "I wanted to see how you're settling into your new position and offer my services if and when you need them."

She shivered and forced herself free from her memories.

He cleared his throat, and his boots squeaked against the pristine tile. "I never knew Elodie. I see that now."

Blair balled her hands into fists. "Oh, yes, I'd almost forgotten. I promised you a new match." Ice splintered in her veins as she slid her feet back into her stilettos. People were always so ready to *take*, and it would be worse now that she had more power to deliver.

Rhett stood in the doorway. The Violet Shield rained against his white-blond hair, tinting it lavender as he stared down at the cap in his hands. "You haven't been matched. Maybe I shouldn't be, either."

Blair walked to her desk and ran her fingers along the edge of the stone. She stopped when she reached the corner that had nearly taken the good major out of the game. "We are very different people."

His attention rested on the onyx slab. His bruised eye twitched. "We're not as different as you'd like to believe." His gaze found hers. "I have power. You have power—"

"But a match will never take your power. A *woman* could never take your power." She bit the raw bump on the tip of her tongue as she opened her desk drawer. The same woman had hurt them both, but anguish didn't make for strong allies.

"A woman like you could." His growl was barely audible—a thought meant to stay tucked within.

Blair unwrapped a cinnamon mint and popped it into her mouth.

Rhett stood still, his jaw flexing as he tightened his grip on his cap.

This wasn't anguish. This was hate. And hate . . . Blair's stomach warmed, and her heartbeat quickened. Hatred was as strong as iron shackles.

She rounded her desk, leaned against the edge, and crossed one leg over the other. She was comfortable here, she was *powerful* here, when a man gave into the heady bliss of testosterone. Most of them thought this was *feeling*. She bit her lower lip to suppress a chuckle. It was weakness.

"I have yet to hear an apology, Major."

"An apology?" Heat peeked out over his collar as he crumpled his cap in his hand. "You have a lot of nerve." He charged into the room and the door slid closed behind him. "You practically begged me to help you with your brother, and then you went in front of the Council and lied. *To get a promotion.*"

Blair's curls slipped from her shoulder as she cocked her head. His energy had changed. It no longer filled the air, gritty and humid with pride and ego. Now it felt electric and prickly and sparking with change.

"That doesn't sound like an apology."

"It isn't." He stalked closer. In this light, she could see the streaks of cleaning solution on the squared toes of his dress shoes.

"Oh?" This time, she didn't hide her laugh. Rhett was used to intimidating, used to getting his way. If it wasn't so amusing, she would stop him. She flexed and unflexed her foot before uncrossing her legs. His ferocity stirred something within her. Something dormant. Something . . . *interesting.*

He inched closer, wringing the space from between them as he spoke. "The only thing I'm sorry about is that I thought you were a slightly less cruel and poisonous woman than you actually are."

The redness in his cheeks subsided as he planted his hands against the desk on either side of her. Heat spilled off him and caressed her shoulders. He was close, too close, but she wouldn't let him win.

She tipped her chin toward him. The scent of cinnamon stained the air between them. "You came to offer your services, but it seems as though you don't like working for me, Major."

"Working *for* you?" he growled. "That's not the only thing I dislike. You're cold and twisted and wicked. I like nothing about you."

"Oh, come on." Blair leaned forward, their lips almost touching. "There must be something you like."

His jaw flexed and his amber eyes narrowed.

"You see, I think you do like me." She snaked her tongue across her lips.

His muscles tensed and a low, gentle groan thrummed behind his closed lips.

Blair's nerves quaked beneath her skin, and she gripped the edge of her desk to keep from dissolving. "Don't you, Major?"

Another restrained moan.

She dug the tips of her gloved fingers into the stone. "Say it."

"I like you." He grunted, rough and husky.

"Then prove it." Heat flooded her stomach. This game had gotten away from her. She no longer knew what she needed to prove or who was in control. She could only feel his warmth and smell cinnamon, his sweat, and see his amber eyes burning into hers like the sun.

Then Rhett backed away, and Blair inhaled fully for the first time since she'd run into the major.

He cleared his throat and shook out the cap that he'd balled in his fist. "As a military member of the Key corporation, I serve at the director's disposal."

In his absence, Blair's skin cooled. "I expect nothing less."

Rhett nodded and averted her gaze, staring blankly at the windows behind her.

The ringing was back, clanging between her ears. Blair crossed her arms over her chest. She needed him gone. Not forever, but definitely for now. He'd found a chink in her armor. Or perhaps *he* was the chink. She pushed away from her desk and strode to the high-backed chair she'd had fashioned after a throne.

"Aiden and Elodie. My brother and your fiancée—"

"*Ex* fiancée." His golden gaze washed over her.

"Find out where they are. Bring Aiden to me along with the girl's location."

Rhett's throat bobbed with a swallow.

"Is there a problem, Major?" Her eyes teared as she focused through the ringing and ran her hand along the metal accents pressed into the chair's soft velvet.

"I can't give you that information," he said, his attention firmly fixed on a point behind her. "Not after what happened with Echo."

Blair gripped the metal bobbles. "You *can't give me that information?*"

He shook his head. "Not after last time."

A headache sprouted, a flame thrower torching the back of her eyes. "I am the MediCenter Director."

"Yes, ma'am," Rhett cleared his throat and defaulted to his original programming. "However, this order comes from Council Leader Darby himself."

"Darby told *you* where my brother is, but he won't tell *me*?" She lowered herself into her chair.

What would Cath do? What would Cath do? What would Cath do?

It was impossible to think through the pain and the pealing.

Blair tucked her legs under the onyx slab and flattened her hands against the cool stone. "Major," she began, calm and collected and completely Cath-like. "I would like you to do something for me."

Rhett's brows arched. He'd done her favors in the past, and she'd made him the scapegoat the first chance she got.

"Please tell me when you and Darby have these meetings and what's discussed. As director, I must be kept in the loop. I'm afraid—" She frowned and stared at her hands as if her last thought was nearly too difficult to articulate. "I'm afraid that the Council Leader's personal feelings are clouding his judgment."

Rhett shifted, and his brows pinched. "I don't know if that would be appropriate. My duties—"

She closed her hand into a fist and slammed it against her desk. "Your duties are what I say they are."

The heat returned to his neck, stretching its fiery paws up to claw at his cheeks. "Of course, Director Scott." His gaze lingered on her as he turned to leave.

"And, Major," Blair spoke loudly, shouting over the ringing and the pain. "Don't come to my office without an appointment."

XIII

Elodie pulled Aiden down to her and pressed her mouth to his. Her throat tightened with a whimper, a growl, a need for more. Every day of her life she had given. Now, she would take.

She wound her legs around him and pulled him closer. Another moan pulsed against her lips, hot and warm. She didn't know if it was his or hers or where she ended and he started. His muscles were smooth slopes and ridges beneath her wandering fingers. She was an explorer. The first to the Americas. The first on the moon. Blazing a path for others to follow.

Aiden's lips left hers and trailed down her neck, exploring a new path of his own.

"Elodie," he whispered her name like a promise. It had never sounded so beautiful.

She tipped her head back and brought her hands to his chest. She traced the muscles tense beneath his rich brown skin. Her lips ached. Each pulse of heat called out his name. She guided his mouth back to hers and ran her fingers along his stubbled cheeks. Swimming in the waterfall was the best thing she'd ever done.

He pulled away, so quickly that the water that swirled between them and lapped against her skin felt like snow slush.

His eyes were nearly closed as he stared down at the ripples between them.

Elodie took a tentative step forward, silt squishing between her toes. "Aiden?"

Aiden stiffened, and his gaze snapped to the shore.

"Monster," he breathed.

Elodie clamped her jaw shut to keep her teeth from clacking as she turned to face the water's edge. Her breath escaped her in a trembling rush when she saw only swaying branches, sparkling water, and rocky shoreline.

"Where?" she whispered, squinting past the thick trunks of old pines.

"Stay behind me." Aiden held his arms near his side. His muscles were tense and at the ready, guarding Elodie against a monster she had yet to see.

Shivering against the wind, she followed him out of the water and again scanned the forest. "Aiden, I don't see anything."

His arm was rigid, elbow locked as he pointed to Elodie's discarded clothes.

"Put your shoes on." He shuffled backward until he reached his pile, his eyes fixed on a point in the distance. "When I say run, don't hesitate," he instructed, stuffing his feet into his boots.

She slid her feet into her shoes and grit her teeth as the sand and dirt and pine needles caked to her soles scraped and poked her skin. All the while, she surveyed the forest. Aiden saw a monster so clearly that the tendons along his neck bulged, but Elodie still saw only forest. "But, Aiden, I—"

"Run!" he shouted.

He was next to her in a second, grabbing her arm and hurling her in front of him.

Elodie ran. Slowly at first and then with more intensity, Aiden's footsteps chasing hers, urging her, challenging her to run faster.

Aiden's scream flayed her bare skin. Elodie skidded to a stop and whirled around as pinecones cracked and Aiden crashed onto the ground. He scrambled against the forest floor, scooping fistfuls of dirt and dried pine needles as he dragged his legs behind him.

She ran to him.

With a haggard scream, he flopped onto his back. He sucked in a trembling breath and went still.

Twigs jabbed her shins and dug into her knees as she knelt beside him and placed her hands on his chest. She shook him. He remained unmoving, no gentle rise and fall of his ribcage or steady thump of a beating heart within his chest. The wind has ceased blowing, too. The branches stilled and the birdsong vanished. Her world was nothing without him.

"Aiden?" His name was a sob that echoed around her.

"*I'm a soldier, El. I can't say no to the Key. No matter how much I want to.*" Rhett's voice hummed between her ears. "*You wouldn't believe what they want from me. Or maybe you would.*"

Beneath her fingers, Aiden's body shimmered. She yanked her hands away and scrambled backward as he dissolved into a thousand tiny pixels that blew away in the windless forest.

"Aiden!" she shouted.

Wet coughs erupted in answer.

"Momma . . . it hurts."

Aubrey's cry surrounded Elodie and another bout of coughs splintered against her back.

She scrambled to her feet and spun around. A sharp wheeze swept against her and more wet coughs exploded in the distance. She sprinted from the noise, from the memory of Aubrey in the MediCenter, from the invisible creature that had blurred the lines between reality and VR and broken Aiden apart.

Hadn't this happened before?

Tears blurred her eyes as she pushed aside the memories of Astrid. Elodie's lungs burned and her legs ached as she bolted through the forest. Twigs slapped her cheeks and her bare stomach, and her ankles screamed as she sped over rocks and fallen branches, but she didn't slow.

A shriek split the air, sharp and alive. It burrowed into Elodie and broke beneath her skin like a bruise. She'd heard it once before—after Cath and the gunshot. Elodie's chest shook and her eyes burned. She clamped her hands over her ears and squeezed her eyelids shut as the wail sounded again.

"Elodie, save me!"

INCOMING PRIORITY ONE ALERT FROM THE KEY CORPORATION

The Key Corporation has the great honor of bestowing the title of MediCenter Director to Ms. Blair Scott. From her work on the Zone Safety Committee and in the medical botany labs to being an important part of bringing Holly to each citizen, Blair has played an integral role in maintaining the safety of Westfall and the New American West Coast.

"It is my honor to serve Westfall and its citizens as the new MediCenter Director. I have always felt that it is my duty to continue to keep this city and the New American West Coast protected against viruses like Cerberus and terrorist organizations like Eos. Under my guidance and with my fortitude and dedication, our great city will only thrive.

"Thank you for putting your trust in me. I look forward to continuing my efforts and working to make Westfall the very best city in the world."

XIV

The door hissed open, and a blue, egg-shaped bot motored into the charging station, its charge indicator light flashing red. Sparkman shuffled from her place near the open port as the bot slowly backed into the bay. It whirred and clicked before going on standby mode until its battery had been fully recharged.

Sparkman shucked off her constricting lab coat, draped it over the ovoid bot, and checked the time on her cuff. The bot's entry had reset the door's ability to be manually opened. She didn't have the proper permissions to enter and exit the charging station, so passing her cuff beneath the scanner wasn't an option. Instead, she had to manually open the sliding door that hid her from the watchful eye of the Key as well as the few MediCenter employees whose careers placed them basement level. And it all came down to timing. In fact, timing held Sparkman's entire operation together. Just as she could only manually open the door to the room firmly inside the Dead Zone every four minutes, her trips to the basement would only go unnoticed by Normandy as long as her other tasks led her to the same floor.

Anytime she could, she'd been sneaking away to the bot charging station to stakeout the maintenance room Major Owens was so fond of. So far, she'd seen him enter seven times. There wasn't a pattern. At least, not one that she could decipher from the sporadic opportunities she'd had to descend to the basement with a reason other than the truth.

She hadn't attempted to enter the maintenance room since the first time when she'd scanned her cuff and was denied. The metal door was not in a Dead Zone, and repeated attempts to gain entry were logged in the Key's servers and reported to people she didn't want raising red flags. Gaining entry wasn't worth the risk.

Sparkman dug her secure communique device from the lining of her suit. Still no response from Echo.

Of the four Eos board members she had contact with—Echo, Whiskey, Delta, and Zulu—Echo was the one she reported to most often. Echo was creative, decisive, and intelligent. Sparkman sensed that, between the board members, there was an unspoken understanding that Echo had the final say.

Sparkman cursed under her breath and tucked the device back into its secure hiding place. There had been times when they'd each had to go dark, but Echo had always found a way to let her know. This time, nothing.

She pressed her fists together, cracking her knuckles as she shoved the foreboding that lingered just beneath the surface into a far corner of her mind. Emotions were warning bells that would drown out the facts if left to chime.

Sparkman glanced at her cuff. It was time.

She unzipped the chest pocket of her uniform and pulled out a heavy rectangular magnet. She took a deep breath as she pressed the first of the two buttons that sat flush against the metal. Activated, it hummed against her palm. She placed it on the door, pressed the second button, and stepped back. The gentle buzz grew in a crescendo before halting. A shot of blue light pulsed against the door and the heavy bolt clicked, unlocking.

Sparkman removed the magnet and dropped it back into her pocket before pushing open the door. Her braid swung back and forth as she peered out of the open doorway. Major Rhett Owens's broad back and red fatigues looked like a stain against the white wall as he waited outside the maintenance-room door.

Sparkman pulled the notepad from her pocket and licked the tip of her uncapped pen before charting the series of squares, circles, and triangles she'd created as a code for herself. If anyone were to locate her pad of Key secrets and Eos information, it would look like nothing more than doodles.

The elevator opened as the door to the charging room began to close. Sparkman slipped back inside the small space, tucking herself into a shadowed corner as she plucked her lab coat from the charging bot.

"Major Owens, glad you could make it." Sparkman tensed as the voice drifted to her from the bank of elevators. "We have much to discuss."

Sparkman jammed the toe of her boot in front of the door, stopping it before it closed and separated her from the world for another four minutes.

"Of course, Doctor. My duty is to the Key and Council Leader Darby," Owens said, his words nearly taken from a textbook.

"And our new director?" Normandy asked, fishing for the major's priorities and allegiances.

Rhett inhaled and paused before finally saying, "From what I understand, this director will not be director forever."

Sparkman's hand stilled over her notepad. Major Owens was smarter than she'd thought.

A faint beep sounded, followed by the gentle hiss of a door opening.

"I do see a bright future ahead of you, Major . . ." Normandy's voice faded as the maintenance room door closed behind them.

Sparkman receded into the shadows, letting her own door seal her in.

Once again, she pulled out her secure communique device. The lieutenant colonel set her jaw and took deep, even breaths, controlling her heart rate as she typed out a message to TFUJIMOTO.

SPARKMAN: Any update on MAINTENANCE?

XV

Not long after Rhett had left Blair's office, the ringing between her ears intensified, a sharp squealing of brakes that had made her stomach tighten and mouth water. She'd rested her cheek on her cold stone desk and closed her eyes. The ringing would stop soon or shred her to pieces. Either were welcome. At least it would be over.

A loud *slap* startled Blair, and her eyelids flew open. She lifted her head and blinked through her blurred vision as Maxine's palm again made contact with the top of the desk. Blair wiped the corner of her mouth and glanced at the onyx and the shiny puddle of drool.

How long was I like that?

Her vision swam and she listed from one side to the other as the ringing ebbed only to crash against her once more.

"I know someone," Maxine was saying. ". . . call them for help."

Blair wasn't sure she wanted help.

They think I killed her.

She was a murderer, and murderers deserved to pay.

She rested her head against the high back of her velvet chair and avoided the glare of the sun across the slick surfaces throughout her office. She didn't deserve mercy, but at least she wasn't alone. And with the violent ringing bleeding through her eardrums, her mind was finally blank. No more lies to sort through or angles to manage. Just the bliss of nothingness and the pain of consequence.

More time passed, although Blair had no idea how much, when her office door slid open. The joy of living as a raw nerve withstanding unending pain was not caring what people thought. No longer would Blair plaster on a smile or practice perfect posture when her door opened.

"This is Tyler," Maxine's voice was faraway and frayed around the edges like she was shouting at Blair through a layer of glass.

She squinted and peered up at her assistant. Blair didn't remember Maxine arriving.

Has she been here this whole time?

"They're going to help you," Maxine continued as she tucked her short hair behind pointed ears.

Tyler knelt next to Blair in a rush of green apple. Blair inhaled the sweet, fruity scent. Practically living in the Medi-Center had made her forget certain aromas. She knew only the comfort of bleach and antiseptic.

"You smell nice," Blair muttered. Her lips were dry and cracked around each word.

"She's way worse than you said. My normal kit won't fix this." Tyler scratched their bearded chin and looked up at Maxine. "What happened?"

"The ringing," Blair swallowed the bitter tang of bile that coated her tongue. "It won't stop."

Maxine blinked a few times, shifting her weight from one foot to the other. "She's overwhelmed. That's all. Getting such a huge promotion on the heels of a personal tragedy will do that to a person."

Blair's vision swam from Tyler to Maxine and back again. "Not overwhelmed." Another acrid swallow. "It's the ringing."

Tyler scratched their chest, their sheer, white tank moving back and forth, back and forth across tanned skin and toned muscles. "I have Poppy, but that's—"

"Give it to her," Maxine spoke in a rush.

Tyler stood, shrugging. "Look, Max, you're at the Medi-Center. They have to have something here that's not so—"

"This situation"—Maxine stabbed the air in front of Tyler—"never leaves this room. You hear me?"

They backed away, hands up as if Maxine held a gun and would pull the trigger any second, sending a bullet flying from her fingertip straight through their chest.

Blair couldn't keep bubbles of laughter from popping in her throat. If her assistant had truly had a gun, Blair wouldn't have been surprised. After all, what was one more murder?

"Make it stop," Blair pleaded, but Maxine stayed frozen in her threat while Tyler rummaged through the fanny pack buckled around their hips.

"I said, *make it stop!*" Blair was shouting now. Still, no one turned. Maybe she wasn't talking at all. Maybe she was locked inside herself, alone forever. The ultimate punishment.

Tyler's temples pulsed as they clenched their jaw. "This shit isn't a joke, Max."

Maxine glanced at Blair, her lips pressed into a thin line. "Does it look like I'm laughing?"

Long strands of dark hair escaped Tyler's messy bun as they shook their head. "You know what I mean. You have to work up to this, not just take it because getting a promotion made you comatose."

If she could have, Blair would have picked up Maxine's holopad and smacked Tyler across their bearded cheek. She wasn't so weak that a bump up to her rightful position would make her crumble. This was because of the never-ending gunshot. It was louder than she thought it would have been, the sound bouncing from one side of her office to the other, cutting her down a little more with each pass.

Red seeped into the edges of her vision. She closed her eyes, pulling the curtains on the memory of the blood and the shot that turned her adoptive mother from a woman into a paint smear.

The ringing intensified, and her eyes flicked back and forth under her trembling lids.

They think I killed her.

Guilt sang inside her gut, and she smothered it with another acidic swallow.

Green-apple breeze sent Blair's eyelids fluttering open.

"Drink this." Tyler set a vial on the desk in front of her.

Blair's hand shook as she reached out.

Tyler sighed, realizing Blair could no more lift the bottle to her lips than she could tell him what plagued her.

"Open your mouth," they instructed.

Blair did as she was told, her lips peeling apart like two pieces of tape. Liquid hit her tongue, bitter as blended kale. Her mouth tingled and smoke escaped her lips on her next exhale.

Warmth burrowed deep into her veins as the ringing faded and worry dripped from her pores.

"Blair?" Maxine chewed her lower lip, her gaze darting from Tyler to Blair.

Tyler was aglow in electric green as they watched Blair. "You okay?"

Blair wiped the crust from the corners of her lips and let it drift to the floor along with her guilt. She felt soft and fuzzy, warm and still. She felt like magic.

"Thank you, Tyler . . . Maxine." Blair's voice was a low purr that spilled from her lips in a waterfall of orange light. "I can take it from here."

For the first time in her life, Blair Scott desperately wanted to be alone.

Tyler didn't await further instruction. They zipped up their fanny pack and darted to the door without so much as a goodbye.

Maxine lingered, her mouth opening and closing, unsure of what to say to the woman who'd been a drooling mess and unable to speak only moments before.

"I'm fine, Maxine. You can go." Blair's smile swam against her lips like a school of fish. She felt like an angel and as if she had the knowledge of a god. Blair knew exactly what she needed to do. More than that, she knew her plan would work.

Blair waited for the door to close behind her assistant before she removed her holopad from the top drawer of her desk. She blew the dust from the screen and wiped her sleeve over the device before turning it on. The Key's logo spun in the center of the illuminated, paper-white screen as it powered up for the first time in months. Her stomach hummed as a red light reached out from the holopad's small camera. It scanned her face, and the screen unlocked.

WESTFALL HOLOGRAM UPDATE V4.4.1 COMPLETE

The notification box beamed.

Blair's throat dried even as her body tingled and her blood pulsed hot and wet through her veins. She hadn't been on her holopad since she'd completed her edits to the hologram that had become Holly. And was slowly becoming her.

She shook her head. Her efforts had gotten her this office and her new title. The rest? Well, Blair had an idea for that.

THEY THINK YOU KILLED HER.

The notification had morphed, and the new words glared up at her.

Blair cleared the box, her movements even and smooth, her breaths calm and deep, the blunt edges of her thoughts softened by the magic of Poppy. If only she could make Darby disappear as quickly.

Her fingers flew across the keys, swiftly and effortlessly, as she pulled up the list of networks stored within the device and switched from MediCenterSecure to CScottHome. Another scan of Blair's face, and Cath's personal home network password populated: SUNRISE.

Blair's heart shuddered within her chest.

After the storm comes the dawn.

This time, she didn't flinch when the sound of gunfire cracked between her ears. There had been signs there all along. Breadcrumbs only the starving could sniff out, and Blair had been sated—by her career, the constant trade of titles, each one grander than the one before, by the relationships with her brother and with Cath that she had convinced herself were strong and healthy.

Now, as director, Blair was ravenous. Hungry for answers. Hungry for revenge.

The Key had been in Cath's home network. *Was still* in Cath's home network. The corporation seemed to leave behind footprints everywhere it went, and it hadn't been so long since Blair had worked with the coding team that she didn't recognize them immediately. And if she could see the Key—

SECURITY ALERT

RESTORE DEFAULT FEATURES

"It's broken," she whispered. "Aiden did it. He—"

Her chest swelled with a stored breath. On his last visit to her office, the time before . . . *everything*, her brother had hacked into her holopad and cloaked her actions from the Key. She hadn't wanted it, but he'd done it anyway.

"It's fixed. Well, technically it's broken. You never know when you won't want someone watching."

He'd set out his own breadcrumbs, too.

Blair exhaled and the edges of her vision dimmed as she blinked away the clues her brother and Cath had laid out and let the Poppy sharpen her focus.

For hours she sifted through Cath's photos, spreadsheets, and saved articles. Long shadows stretched their fingers across Blair's desk as she pored over the digital remnants of her adoptive mother's life. For her plan to work, she needed something more—something of Echo's. But all she could find were leftovers of Cath's smooth edges and soft words.

There had to be more.

Cath was Echo, and from what Blair had learned, Echo was at the top of Eos. Yes, Cath had fooled them all, but Echo had had the real power. Echo was the one who stood to gain from the title of MediCenter Director. Echo made the plan. Cath simply followed direction.

Blair leaned back in her chair and drummed her fingers on her thick armrests. "Holly," she commanded, her own plan pivoting and adjusting, re-forming with each passing second.

"What may I do for you, Director Scott?" The hologram appeared on the other side of the onyx, all curls and slopes and fullness that hadn't been there previously.

Blair's lips thinned, but the headache and the ringing didn't return as they would have before Tyler and the gift of their medicine.

This was good practice. Blair needed to expose herself to and interact with the hologram, become desensitized to the way it resembled her.

"Call Councilwoman Robin Wilson. Voice only. And speaker mode."

If there was any chance of taking a bite out of Preston Darby, she'd have to dig into the softest piece first.

Holly blinked rapidly, and the phone rang through the speakers hidden in the ceiling and walls of Blair's office. Across the left side of her vision, a gray panel appeared as she waited for the Councilwoman to answer. Two white boxes illuminated the gray rectangle; VIDEO CALL and MAKE PRIVATE. Blair resumed drumming her fingers, her attention sliding from the white boxes to Holly and back again. She didn't want to take the chance of her headache returning with a call that streamed directly between her ears. Besides, she didn't have anything to prove or to hide from this hologram—the issue was with its creator.

"That'll be all." Blair ground out.

Holly's nod was slight, her curls bouncing a little too much with the movement, before she disappeared.

Robin chose that moment to answer, her whispery, featherlight words emptying in a rush of *congratulations* and *you poor dear*s for the *horror of the Council meeting*. Blair let the woman speak as she resumed pecking at her holopad, her fingers sorting through Cath's files.

"You know," Robin lowered her voice conspiratorially. "There are two different versions of what occurred in your office floating around, but neither of them mentions dear Cath." She sucked in a few breaths as if inhaling the words that rested on the tip of her tongue. "It's strange that, no matter how much I learn about her involvement with that *organization*, I can't help but think of her as *Cath*, one of my dearest friends. Did she ever tell you how we met?" Robin released a soft cluck of laughter. "We'd both just started at the MediCenter. That was back when we still wrote things down by hand, and you had to charge your cuff every night. There was one day, when your mother—"

"Councilwoman Wilson, I hate to stop you there."

Black. Blair thought as a final waterfall of pleasantries spilled from Robin's end of the phone. The impending trip down memory lane had dulled the sweet, pulsing waves of Poppy that rushed through Blair's core.

"Oh, my dear, it's Robin. We've known each other for far too many years for such formality."

Now, it seemed, that Blair was the new *dear*, replacing Cath without a second thought.

"Yes, of course we have. And what eventful years they've been." Blair exhaled a laugh even Cath would have been proud of. "So, *Robin*, I would love to continue this conversation in person. Are you available tomorrow?" she asked, her own version of Echo emerging, plotting, planning.

"My schedule is always clear for you, dear."

Whether or not this was because of Robin's emotions or Blair's new title, Blair didn't know. Either way, it didn't matter. Blair needed the majority of the Council on her side. No matter what Darby or Normandy believed, the women ruled.

"Great. I'll have Maxine send over details." Blair shook her head. "On second thought, I will send details over myself. Maxine doesn't need to busy herself setting a date between friends."

With a thought, Blair pulled up her calendar. Maxine had methodically color coded each of Blair's meetings either purple, green, yellow, or red. It was a code only the assistant understood. Blair didn't choose a color. Instead, she left Robin's name in the next open spot in her calendar.

"I look forward to it, dear." Blair could practically hear Robin swell with delight.

"See you soon, Robin," Blair said and ended the call.

She sighed and continued her hunt through Cath's digital belongings. Cath had never much been the picture-taking type. Those she did have, Blair swiped through quickly, glad that the Poppy was there to fill the aching hole in her heart and leave her numb to the emotions that could have swelled when reminiscing about the three of them, their smiling faces, and how Cath had lied the entire time.

There was one last file within the Photos folder. It was untitled.

Blair tapped on it. Small photo squares filled the screen, each alive with splashes of purple and green. She pressed on the first one. An iris bloomed in front of her, its delicate violet petals striped with a burst of yellow and framed by vibrant leaves and stems. Blair's heart climbed into her throat as she swiped once, twice, three times. Over and over again, her screen filled with a single iris. Finally, she reached the end of the album. The screen was white except for a small purple bud in the center.

Blair's breath hitched as a red beam reached out and her holopad scanned her features.

The flower bloomed, bringing with it four words, the sharp edges not even Poppy could soften.

FOR YOU, BLAIR IRIS.

The Key hadn't found this file. Not yet. Blair had kept an eye on their progress while she made her own. The corporation was too busy looking at the obvious when nothing about Dr. Cath Scott had been straightforward. Nothing could be when Cath had only shown them half of who she truly was.

Blair clicked on the words and the purple flower that loomed above them like a gravestone. The loading icon spun for a few agonizing moments before disappearing and taking with it the filename and icon.

Her skin cooled, and an icy chill crept up her spine as a transparent gray box appeared across the left side of her vision.

OPEN FILE FROM CSCOTTHOME NETWORK?

Blair shivered and accepted.

XVI

Sirens blared, stirring Aiden from the hazy space between awake and asleep where words were just a dull pulse over white noise and the creatures of nightmares merged with reality.

"Aiden?"

The voice was back, soft and lilting above the blaring alarm, pulling him into the light.

Pain burned beneath Aiden's skin slow and steady, but it didn't matter. He was flying, and it would all be over soon.

"Aiden, can you hear me?"

He tried to nod, but felt weightless, a cloud pierced by the burning rays of the sun.

"Can you open your eyes?"

He cracked open his eyelids. Light flooded his vision, and he pinched his eyes closed. Heat swelled through his head and neck so hot and fierce that the rest of him went cold. Saliva flooded his mouth and an anguished groan burbled past his dry lips.

"Slow and steady, Aiden. This is not a race. Take your time."

He felt the warmth of a body next to him, floating with him in the sky, too close to the sun.

Once again, he opened his eyes. This time, he didn't surrender. Tears slipped down his face and into his hair as he adjusted to the piercing light. But it wasn't the fiery orange of the sun. It was the sterile white of a building he knew all too well. The unblemished bleach-white walls. The smell of antiseptic that turned the air into a constant reminder of cleanliness and desolation.

"The MediCenter." The words slipped out a haggard whisper. He tried to sit up, but his vision swam, and his pulse beat against his ears.

"There you are."

Aiden's gaze followed the voice and the warmth that rolled from it in welcoming, hypnotic waves. The room had formed around him, complete with beeping screens and monitoring stations, but he couldn't trust his senses. He couldn't believe that the person standing over him was there, in the real. *Cath had died.* He'd seen it, smelled it, felt her blood and hair and skin coat his flesh like his own.

"I've been so, so worried about you." She stood next to the shiny metal chair at his bedside. She was more beautiful than he remembered, more perfect than when she'd opened her home to him and said she would take care of him forever.

A sob caught in the back of his throat.

"Am I dead?" If he was, he would gladly accept. He would have done anything to bring Cath back, but now he didn't have to. Now, *he* could look after *her* forever. No more guilt about his adoptive mother's end or the fact he'd lost more love in seventeen years than most people received in a lifetime.

Cath's blond halo of curls shook as she laughed. "You're not dead, Aiden." She grinned down at him, her soft skin creasing lightly around her eyes. "You were in an accident. But you're safe now. You're at the MediCenter."

An accident? A slow blink, and another, and another . . . He couldn't remember an accident. He could only remember Elodie and being taken from Wonderland by Key soldiers. Then, Blair and Rhett and the gun like a shining diamond on his sister's desk.

After the storm comes the dawn!

He flinched as the memory of a gunshot rang between his ears.

He and Elodie had run. They ran through destruction, through the zones, and into each other until the monster attacked. He winced as he struggled to lift his head from the pillow and look down at his leg, but his body still hadn't returned from the story his mind had convinced him he had lived.

"What happened?" he croaked. From the dryness in his throat and the pounding of his head, he could have been in this blinding-white room within the MediCenter for days . . . months. "How long have I been here?"

Cath stood and took the neatly folded fabric sheet from the metal table next to the bed. "Not long."

"How long is *not long?*"

"You need your rest." Another warm smile as she clasped her hands in front of her and stepped closer.

"The sirens are so loud." Aiden pressed his cold fingertips against his ears and gritted his teeth against the steady *thump thump* of the headache that pulsed behind his eyes. "I need to know what happened and how long I've been here." The thin sheet twisted as he moved, its stiff creases creating mountains of white fabric against his chest.

Cath studied him for a moment before sighing and giving in. "Several Eos members collided with Key soldiers shortly after Major Owens and his men apprehended you. There was an explosion. Thankfully, you weren't close enough to be irreparably damaged, but the force of it left you with a head injury. The nurse said there would be some effects, however fleeting, so I'm not surprised you're hearing things."

"*Irreparably damaged . . . however fleeting.*" The words fell in chunks from Cath's lips. She didn't normally sound so stilted and formal. Not with him.

"An explosion?" He didn't remember anything like that, but it didn't sound out of the realm of possibility for Key soldiers. The pit in his stomach filled with lead. "Elodie? Is she okay?"

Cath nodded. "She is safe and exactly where she needs to be."

"Am I—" His mouth went dry as questions spun through his head. Would the corporation send him to Rehab? Would they carry out his death sentence? "Am *I* safe?"

"The Council now knows that I placed you, *covertly*, within Eos and that you needed assistance with your mission and recruited Elodie as another operative working on the Key's behalf. Anything you did was to gain the organization's confidence."

Aiden's mouth opened and closed just as quickly. He would go along with the story she had told to save them. His mother was alive. Nothing else mattered. This time, Aiden wouldn't scratch the itch of doubt until it bled the truth. He would let it be, let it heal until it scabbed over and scarred itself in place.

"Now, put all your questions out of your mind. The medical team can only do so much. You must give yourself time to heal."

Aiden released a pent-up breath. He was safe from death but not free from the Key. He'd stay in this blinding-white room forever if it meant that everything he'd believed had happened in Blair's office had been nothing more than the result of a head injury.

"Promise me you'll rest and that I won't get a call saying that you're up to your usual antics." She hovered near the side of the bed and beamed that brilliant smile down on him.

"I promise." Aiden couldn't help but smile in return.

"I'll be back later to check on you." Cath leaned forward, her lips millimeters from his forehead. He closed his eyes, waiting for her to kiss him the way she had in Blair's office. His eyelids fluttered open. That hadn't happened. And they were in the MediCenter. She might kiss his forehead, muss his hair, and give him hugs when they were in the tunnels beneath the city or in the privacy of the Eos warehouse, but she wouldn't dare touch him here. Not with the Key watching. Instead, Cath took a breath and smoothed a wrinkle from her shirt.

He inhaled, but the bleach and alcohol that coated the inside of the MediCenter overpowered her scents of earth and honey. It didn't bother him. Not now. With Cath, Aiden was home, and he was going to stay.

"I missed you," he whispered into the golden curls that his nightmares had stained brilliant red.

"I missed you, too, my love." She walked to the door and paused, glancing over her shoulder as it hissed open and the Violet Shield streamed onto the floor in front of her. "I'm so happy you came back to me. Get some sleep and follow the medical team's instructions, and we will never be apart again."

"Yes, ma'am." He nodded, but no part of him wanted to close his eyes and drift back into the world in which his mother had died and monsters roamed. Not even to be with Elodie.

His vision blurred and his head pounded as he propped himself up on his elbows and tried to push himself to seated. He collapsed back onto his pillow and blinked past the bursts of white that glimmered against his vision like starlight.

"Mom," he called before the door closed. "Tell Blair I'm sorry and that I . . ." He trailed off. He wasn't sure what else he wanted Cath to say to his sister. He only knew he wasn't ready to say it to Blair's face.

"I'm sorry." He was apologizing to Cath now. He'd almost exposed her. He'd almost killed her.

She smiled that bright, cheerful grin that could fix anything. "I love you, Aiden."

His eyes burned as the door hissed closed behind the mother he'd had for more than half his life. He wiped his tears with the back of his hand then paused, holding his hands out in front of him. He squinted and brought his right hand closer to his face.

A crusted sliver of red stained his middle fingernail.

His nostrils flared and his chest squeezed as memories transported him back to Blair's office, surrounded by blood and his sister's high-pitched screams. Her screams morphed into sirens.

Sirens that were real, loud, and alive and happening now.

He clenched his hands into fists as his eyes searched the white walls.

It wasn't a dream.

This was the Key, he was back in the MediCenter, and the only thing Aiden knew for sure was that the Key could never be trusted.

EOS NETWORK SECURE COMMUNIQUE

RACER: Delivered. Should take less than a minute to worm through the Key's wall.

Unless I've miscalculated.

TFUJIMOTO: You? Never.

RACER: Appreciate the faith.

TFUJIMOTO: How long will we have to find them once we're inside the Key's system?

RACER: A few minutes. If we're lucky. The Key's always updating their bots.

They shouldn't see this coming, though. Brand new code. And I never share.

TFUJIMOTO: Should we wait? Gather more intel?

RACER: You mean, give the Key a chance to uncover our plan?

You want to get Wonder Boy out, this is your best chance.

But we can abort. Want to call it?

TFUJIMOTO: Never.

RACER: Knew you wouldn't bail.

TFUJIMOTO: You wouldn't let me hear the end of it if I did.

RACER: We're in.

Wonder Boy located. They've got his room buried under loads of traps.

TFUJIMOTO: All he needs is an unlocked door. He didn't get the name WB for no reason.

TFUJIMOTO: You there?

RACER: Super fckd. Got spotted. Had to jet. I had time to leave a hole. If they don't patch it, I can get back in when it's clear. Sorry to leave you with a heinous mess.

TFUJIMOTO: Is he out?

RACER: Got to him before I skedaddled. He knows.

                    I'm off. After the storm . . .

RACER LOGGED OFF

-:-:-

"Comes the dawn," Thea whispered against the wind as she balanced her broken and specially coded holopad on the white metal railing that protected the citizens of Westfall from the gray and churning waters of the Willamette twelve stories below the Tilikum Crossing bridge.

The screen flashed Key Corp red. *They'd found her.*

She pushed the tech over the railing and turned to the Max that had just pulled up to the Tilikum Crossing stop. Purple orbs bobbed along the pedestrian bridge on their way to and from the commuter train. Thea tightened the hood on her jacket and activated her Violet Shield. She didn't need it, but in times like these, it was better to follow the crowd.

She stuffed her hands into her pockets and squinted against the spitting rain as she trailed the line of fellow Violet Shield–protected citizens to the Max. With a thought, she pulled up the Eos network and the secure messaging system she and Racer had coded into her reprogrammed implant. There were perks to being from one of Westfall's golden families.

TFUJIMOITO: Did what I could.

                    Your turn.

SPARKMAN: Safe?

TFUJIMOTO: Aces.

Thea took a standing spot on the train and gripped the plastic loop still wet with disinfectant. Holly's voice chimed over the loudspeakers as the Max grumbled to life. Thea braced herself as the old metal auto lurched forward and sailed toward the east side of Westfall. As the train car left the bridge, Thea glanced over her shoulder. Rain always made the Willamette look like it was falling up, like gravity had switched and the steadily pulsing waters were draining into the heavens.

The Key would have to dive to recover her holopad. Even then, they wouldn't find much. Just proof someone had bested them. And, with any luck, they'd drown recovering it.

XVII

Aiden sat up, fighting through his swimming vision and pounding head as he squinted at his hands and the thin line of blood crusted under his fingernail. He'd suffered a head injury, Cath had said. That explained the headache and the neck pain and the dreams, or rather hallucinations, but the blood . . .

He ran his hand along his scalp, inspecting it for scrapes or gouges. There were none. He looked around the white room furnished only with the bed, side table, and chair. Maybe he'd been here long enough for his injuries to heal.

He turned his hand over, studying his fingernail from a different perspective. The time beamed up at him from his cuff; another minute ticked away.

My cuff?

He hadn't had a cuff—he'd gotten rid of it, smashed it beneath his boot after he and Elodie had fled the MediCenter.

He swallowed. That hadn't been real.

Had it?

"Hiya, slacker," a familiar voice shouted at him from the device. "Bet you thought getting caught by *the man* and locked away in the dungeon meant that you'd get out of taking your final."

Aiden's breath hitched in his chest as he stared down at the cuff, her words blaring from its small speaker and vibrating against his wrist.

"Tavi?"

She groaned, and he pictured her directing her cutting, brilliant-blue gaze at him. "Obvi. Who else around here expects you to actually learn something?"

"But you're . . ." He trailed off, unsure of what exactly he wanted to say. She wasn't there? Couldn't possibly be talking to him? Was a figment of his imagination? "I mean, why are you . . ." Again words left him, swept up by the cyclone of questions swirling through his thoughts.

"*So* articulate."

He heard the roll of her eyes in the stretch of her words. Tavi was still as bossy and curt as she had been the first day he'd met her when he'd arrived (on time) to his new position in the basement of the MediCenter at the End-of-Life Unit. A.k.a. the morgue. There was no point in trying to make it sound better than it was. Sixteen-year-old Tavi, with her helmet of neon-pink hair, glitter eyeliner, and pixie-like frame, had been his superior. Worse than that, well, worse for her more than for him he suspected, she had also been his instructor.

But what was she doing now, talking at him through his cuff while he was laid up in one of the MediCenter care units? She couldn't really expect him to continue his lessons after taking a blow to the head so severe that it had caused him to believe that he and Elodie had escaped Westfall and made it to the forests of Zone Seven, could she?

"This will go a lot faster if you don't think and just let me explain."

Aiden couldn't completely follow her instructions, he was always thinking about something, but he kept his ideas to himself and rolled his head from side to side, stretching out his stiff neck as he listened.

"I hacked the Key's network, got through to your cuff, and am in the process of finding you a way out, but, problem—the doors I can unlock the fastest aren't leading to any Eos stashes. I told Sparkman months ago that we needed to plant more but for some reason people always think they know better than I do."

He paused midstretch, unsure if he'd heard her correctly or if he'd dreamed that, too. "You're—"

"Eos?" She cut him off before he had time to formulate the sentence. "Yes."

"But you—"

"Follow the rules?" Again, she interrupted. "Turns out, toeing the company line makes it way easier to do my real job. You could learn a thing or two from me, if you ever paid attention."

"Tavi, this whole time you—"

"Knew you were a member?"

Aiden's lips thinned. She was most definitely the annoying little sister he never wanted.

"No, but I suspected," she continued, answering herself. "I was right, of course." She let out a self-satisfied grunt. "And call me Racer. I'm not Tavi. Not to Eos anyway."

"Tavi—"

"Racer."

"Whatever! Just let me get a word in." He pressed the heels of his hands against his temples. Now that it was quiet, he couldn't think of anything to say.

"So," she drawled, breaking the silence. "You had something brilliant you wanted to add?"

Aiden frowned. "Guess you already answered my questions."

"Good, now slide off that bed and get to the door. Don't worry about not having shoes, I'll find a stash for you soon enough."

Aiden stared down at his bare feet. "You can see me?" he asked, a little proud that he'd actually managed to successfully articulate his question.

"I can see everything," she whispered maniacally. "But seriously, it's the MediCenter. There's a camera in your room. Try not to be *so* dense."

Aiden grumbled something he hoped Tavi, er, *Racer* wasn't able to detect.

"Heard that."

Aiden winced, both from the pain that shot down his neck when he hopped off the bed and in anticipation of whatever witty insult she had at the ready.

"Fuuuudge." She sucked her teeth. "Waste of time."

He snorted. "Rude, but I definitely expected worse."

"Not you. Well, not currently." That was as close to a compliment as she was ever going to give. "I can't actually get you out. Sorry to get your hopes up."

The regret that softened her words surprised him. He deflated. It made sense that he would reach the precipice of rescue, of hope, only to be thrown back to the wolves. It was time to be punished for all his bad deeds, no matter how well intended they'd been.

"We call you Wonder Boy."

He blinked, feeling as if she'd skipped ahead without him.

"It started out as a joke, because you're, you know . . ."

Aiden didn't know, but he also didn't want to find out.

"But I realized that it's true. You do some wondrous things."

He'd been mistaken in thinking that she'd never offer him a real compliment. He'd been mistaken in believing that she never thought of him as worthwhile. As regular citizen Aiden Scott, who had trudged from one career to the next with no Match prospects or career advancements in sight, he hadn't been.

"What I mean, Wonder Boy, is that Eos has a purpose. *You* have a purpose."

His chest swelled as heat suddenly pricked his eyes. "Before you go, I do have a question: My mom, Cath, is she—"

"Yeah," she choked.

This time, he was glad for the interruption.

He wiped away the tears warming his cheeks. "Could the corporation have figured out how to bring her back?"

"She's in a box. I saw her myself." Tavi cleared her throat. "But there's some funky stuff happening with the Council Leader and Dr. Normandy. Like, mad-scientist funk. No one's figured it out yet. That part of the network is locked down so tight it almost doesn't exist, but if there was a way to make it look like the dead had risen, they'd be the two to figure it out." She paused. "Don't trust them. Don't trust anyone."

"I never have." But that wasn't true. He'd trusted Elodie and now he trusted Tavi, too.

"Did you get Elodie?" Guilt scratched at his chest. He should have asked about her sooner.

"I have to jet."

"A simple yes or no." He held his breath as he waited for her reply.

"Sparkman's on it."

He let out a relieved exhale. If anyone could save Elodie, it was the lieutenant colonel.

"Last thing, then I'm gone." Her words came out in a rush. "The Key will do anything to get you to break, and I'm not sure when I'll be able to get you out. *If* I'll be able to get you out. You're on your own."

Aiden had been on his own since his parents had died. Sure, he'd had Cath and Blair, but his sister had devoted herself to the Key, stuffing the void in her heart with career accomplishments and lies. Cath had shown him Eos and offered him stability. He loved them both, but he had always felt adrift, set apart from the strong women who knew themselves and what they wanted. The only ounce of direction he'd ever had had come from Eos.

"Tavi." This time she didn't correct him for using her real name. "They'll never break me. You have my word. *Eos* has my word."

She inhaled deeply and was silent for a moment before, "Never expected anything less, Wonder Boy."

The line went dead as Aiden balled his fists and charged toward the door.

XVIII

Elodie lowered her hands from her ears and opened her eyes. The scent of pine tickled her nose and mist dotted her lashes. She blinked and lifted onto her tiptoes to peer over the rock wall that guarded her from the steep drop-off into the Willamette River. Her dark, wavy hair, free from its ponytail, brushed against her cheeks and she tucked it back behind her ears as she stared at her reflection. In the surface of the rippling water, her full cheeks, round eyes, and square-tipped nose looked broken apart, pixelated.

How did I get here?

Again, her hair escaped from behind her ears and once more she forced it back. Threadlike fibers knitted her fingers together. She shook her hand. Corn silk glistened pale yellow around her tan knuckles.

"Do you love him?"

The words rode the misty breeze and brushed against Elodie.

"Aiden?" *He wasn't gone after all.* She whirled around, the hairs on the back of her neck bristling. The mist ceased and darkness met her vision. "Hello?"

The word echoed until it was nothing more than a knock in the dark.

A cone of light illuminated the space in front of her. Elodie shuffled backward and shielded her eyes. Her shoes squelched against the ground, and she squinted at the floor. An endless pool of red glimmered in the light.

Blood.

Her heart rattled inside her chest and adrenaline burned hot through her veins. She stumbled and slid in the glossy puddle of crimson. Her legs flew out from under her and she crashed onto the ground. Blood, warm as sunshine, coated her hands. Metal glinted in the light. She clamped one red-stained hand over her chest and reached out with the other. Her trembling fingers traced the silver point of Astrid's spear gun.

Elodie's blood-soaked shoes squeaked against the tile as she scrambled to her feet. She stared down at her trembling hands. This was Astrid. Elodie rubbed her palms against her thighs. Her best friend was everywhere.

"You can't die in VR, El." Astrid's declaration socked Elodie in the gut. *"It's not real."*

But you could die in VR. Astrid had.

Elodie screamed. This time, there was no echo. There was no sound at all. Only the burning of her throat and the rush of heat prickling her eyes.

The sugary perfume of flowers overtook the copper tang of blood as the floor beneath her feet softened into wet earth.

Welcome to Wonderland.

Elodie clutched her middle and sucked in a breath of air stained by the earthy scent of ripe tomatoes. She was in the Eos warehouse. She was safe. But Astrid . . .

Tears splattered Elodie's palms as she looked down at her hands. Clean.

It hadn't happened?

Her best friend hadn't died right in front of her in a virtual world that had spilled into the real?

"Aiden!" she called out again.

Wet coughs erupted in answer.

"Momma . . . it hurts."

Aubrey's cry surrounded Elodie and another bout of coughs splintered against her back. She spun around. The black curtains that shielded the doors into the Eos warehouse swayed.

The Key had come into the Long-Term Care Unit and taken Aubrey once before. They had killed the girl they'd labeled as Patient 92 and erased her from existence. Elodie wouldn't let them do it again.

She ran to the entrance and tore back the curtains. Ash rained onto the charred remains of the dense forest that had once stood watch around Westfall. Black stumps protruded from the earth like rotten teeth and shriveled ferns and ivy littered the ground in tangled gray clumps.

She was back in Zone Seven. *What was happening?*

A sharp wheeze swept against Elodie and more wet coughs exploded in the distance. She took off toward the noise, toward Aubrey. Plumes of ash coated Elodie's legs with each hammering step forward.

A glint of red amidst charred tree carcasses snagged her attention. Blair's shoes. The same pointed stilettos she'd worn to Director Holbrook's funeral. Elodie slowed and sucked in breath after breath, her mouth dry and chalky with ash and fear.

"Elodie, save me."

Elodie's feet cemented to the earth and her head swiveled to meet the small voice.

Aubrey's pale skin and delicate limbs were a nearly transparent film pasted against the forest behind her. The little girl looked the same as she had in the LTCU, all thin hair, round cheeks, and fragile bones covered in a paper-thin hospital gown.

"Aubrey . . ." Elodie clutched her chest as it rattled with a choked sob. "You're alive? How are you here? How—"

The little girl lifted her gaze. Her eyes burned bright violet.

"They haven't finished." Aubrey's lips remained closed as the words streamed between Elodie's ears. *"Save me before it's too late."*

Elodie reached out. Her legs burned as she clawed the air and tried to drag her planted feet forward.

Branches snapped and Elodie whirled to face the noise. Blair's shoes stained the forest floor Key Corp red, but Blair wasn't standing in them. The woman had the same slender, umber legs that disappeared beneath a perfectly tailored white pencil skirt, same red, fitted silk blouse that highlighted the smooth taper of her waist and broadness of her shoulders. Even her hair was the same, a beautiful storm of curly black that framed her face. But the features were wrong. They were thin and hollow and empty. Not smooth and full and alive like the Blair Scott she knew.

Elodie's breath hitched as recognition tightened her chest and the wail of sirens filled her ears.

Holly extended her hand, a hollow grin plumping her cheeks as the Key's red logo bloomed above her palm.

XIX

"Elodie, do you read me?"

Elodie's heartbeat raced as she struggled to open her eyes to the present and leave behind the twisted world of ash. She inhaled breath after breath and fought to pry her lids apart. Finally, she pressed the heels of her hands against her eyelids and rubbed. The plaster broke, and light bleached her vision.

The steady wail of sirens chewed on Elodie's nerves. Everything ached and tingled as if her whole body had been numb, fallen asleep and just now awoken. Was that what had happened?

Had it all been a dream?

Elodie's breath caught, her muffled cry swept up by the blaring alarms. She'd take this over the forest, the potential happiness of New Dawn. Whatever happened now was better than losing Aiden, watching him burst into pixels and blow away with dried leaves.

"Elodie Benavidez, this is Lieutenant Colonel Sparkman. We met at Wonderland. Are you able to hear me?"

Elodie peeled apart her dry lips. "Yes," she croaked. Her mouth felt full of sand as she dragged her parched tongue across cracked lips. "Yes, I can hear you," she said, a bit more firmly this time.

"Do you know where you are?" the lieutenant colonel asked, her voice vibrating Elodie's cuff as it streamed from the small speaker.

As she sat up, Elodie shielded her eyes against the harsh fluorescent lights pressing down from overhead.

"No." Another croak as she took in the white room marked only with a row of black Xs on the wall across from her.

"Understood." Sparkman said. "Only a few seconds until I can pinpoint your exact location within the MediCenter."

"The MediCenter?" Elodie shivered as she continued to take in her surroundings. A thin gown shuddered around her thighs as the air conditioning switched on. Gusts of cool, sanitized air rushed across her bare legs, leaving a sea of goosebumps in its wake. She squinted down at the stiff fabric of her MediCenter gown, her hands frozen as she gripped the sides of the metal gurney. She recognized the gown all too well.

"Located." The vibrations from Sparkman's voice against her wrist sent another chill through Elodie. "Ready to go?"

"This can't be real," Elodie whispered, dragging her fingers along the scratchy, paper-thin garment. "Why am I in the LTCU?"

"You're not in the Long-Term Care Unit. They have you in the basement." Sparkman was as clipped and firm as Elodie remembered from their introduction in Wonderland.

"*They?*"

Elodie's left hand throbbed, and her attention jumped

to the pain. An IV needle pierced the back of her hand, the clear tape holding it in place tattooed with the serial number of the bot that had injected it. Her heartbeat quickened as she followed the tube from her body to the small rectangular box attached to the wall—this room's hub for even larger tubes programmed to deliver an array of pharmaceuticals directly from the vials of medicines in the medi-pump lab. Clear liquid streamed through Elodie's IV and straight into her body. Her right hand shook as she grabbed the tube and tore the needle from her vein.

"They drugged me." She threw the IV onto the floor. Blood rolled down her fingers and splattered against the ground. "Zone Seven . . . the forest . . . New Dawn . . . they were all lies."

"The Key is good at that."

Elodie's stomach twisted and her vision swam as the sirens continued to peal. "Where's Aiden?"

"There's a door straight ahead. It's unlocked." Sparkman said. "Get up and go."

"*Where's Aiden?*" Elodie's yell cracked through the constant wail of Key Corp alarms.

"Not important. Leave now. East door."

Elodie's hands tightened into fists. "Not until you tell me where he is," she said, swinging her legs around and dangling them over the side of the gurney. "Is he—" She choked on the next word. Unable to ask if he was dead or alive.

"Another operative is working to get him out. We'll meet them at rendezvous. Now get up and go to the door on the east wall. It's unlocked but not for much longer."

Elodie's feet were like cubes of ice, heavy and cold, against the tile. They were pale, too. Her whole body was. As if the lights and the cold and the IV had steadily leeched her spark of life that had once shone through her skin as golden brown as heartwood.

"He's alive," she said, more to herself than Sparkman, as she forced herself to release the gurney and stand on her own.

The door was only a few paces away, but it could have been a mile, ten miles, the distance from the MediCenter all the way to the real New Dawn. Her trembling legs buckled beneath her, and her cold bones clattered against the tile.

"I can't," she breathed.

"They're coming for you, Elodie." Sparkman's voice was deeper, a gritty seriousness that made Elodie's teeth clack. "Key soldiers are on their way now. If they find you, they will take you away and bury you so deep that we'll have no chance of getting you out."

Elodie pushed herself to standing. Freedom was just on the other side of that door. She could make it. *She had to.*

She rushed forward, all knees and elbows, as steady as a marionette, and crashed into the door. It slid open with a groan, and violet light filled the space in front of her, staining everything in the shadowed room with crushed blackberries.

"There's a vent, a large metal grate, on the northeasterly wall," Sparkman guided. "I've unsealed it. Inside is a stash. Gather it."

The alarm sirens ceased, leaving a hollow shriek that still rang between Elodie's ears. Behind her, the door to her room beeped as someone passed their cuff beneath the scanner and was granted entry.

She rushed into the dark purple room, the door closing behind her before the other opened.

"Someone's coming," she whispered, her voice as shaky as her legs.

She'd waited too long. She was always waiting too long, always starting late and unable to reach her own happily-ever-after because of her inactivity.

"The northeast corner," Sparkman barked. "Pry off the cover and climb inside. Hide until the threat has passed."

Elodie's legs wobbled as she rushed through the dimly lit room, bumping and crashing into stored medical devices on the way to the wall and the large return vent that offered her sanctuary. Her bare foot slammed into the blunt edge of a parked gurney that held a large black rectangular box. She yelped and hopped toward the vent, falling to her knees in front of it.

Numbly, Elodie's fingers worked at the corner of the metal grate. Her nail beds flashed white as she dug her fingers under the metal lip to pry the vent away from the wall. It popped loose and hit the ground with a *clang*. The door to the room beeped as whoever tailed her was granted access to the purple room. Her hands shook and her heartbeat thundered between her ears as she crawled into the vent and secured the grate behind her.

"There are clothes and a new cuff. Put them on. Leave your gown behind and—"

Elodie clapped her hand over the speaker, muffling Sparkman's voice as the lieutenant colonel rattled off more instructions.

"Can't talk," Elodie said, nearly pressing her lips against her cuff as the door to the Violet Shield–drenched room hissed open. "I'm not alone."

Her trembling hands found the plastic bag that held the

stash of supplies Sparkman had promised. She slipped off her cuff and silently dropped it into the bag.

"El?"

Another shiver as she peered through the grate's narrow slats, searching for the owner of the familiar voice.

Rhett's white-blond hair blazed a deep blueberry in the shadowy glow of the Violet Shield. "Come with me," he said, craning his neck to see around stored equipment. "Turn yourself in. There are things . . ." He shook his head and cleared his throat. "I came to visit you while you were under. I hope you know I won't let them hurt you." He stilled next to the black box that sat on a rolling gurney in the center of the room. "Any of you." He placed his hand on top of the plastic, his gaze lingering on the container.

Elodie clutched the bag to her chest and scooted deeper into the shadows.

This was the Rhett from the forest. The medically induced VR forest where she'd believed she was free and trekking toward happiness. She'd told herself that her conscience had chosen the voice of her fiancé, but maybe she didn't have a conscience at all. Maybe she was destined to follow the conscience of others.

More boots thudded against the ground as the door unlocked and hissed open.

"Any sign of her?" Rhett asked the two dark-haired silhouettes in front of him.

"Nothing," said the first one with a shake of his head.

"And her implant's not responding, so pinging her location is a dead end," said the other.

Rhett ran his hand through his Violet Shield–stained hair. "Dr. Normandy said the meds would knock her implant offline for a while." He glanced down at his cuff and cursed under his breath. "The Council Leader . . . *shit.*" He cursed again, looking from his cuff to the shadowed box beside him and back again. "Unlock this and move it." Again, he glanced down at his cuff before jogging toward the door. "I'll send you the code and new coordinates."

"What's in it?" asked one of the soldiers.

Rhett stopped in the open doorway. "You do know how to take an order, don't you, Braggs?"

Braggs stiffened. "Sir, yes, sir."

Rhett nodded, and stepped back as the door hissed closed in front of him.

Elodie's sweaty palms stuck to the plastic bag as she sipped shallow breaths and watched the two remaining soldiers circle the shadowed box.

"Braggs, you are two seconds from getting reassigned," the other soldier said, crossing his arms over his chest.

Braggs blew out a puff of air, his shoulders relaxing. "Wouldn't be the worst thing. We went from searching for an escapee to lugging this hunk of junk around," he grumbled, kicking the gurney with the toe of his boot.

"Major Owens is in with Dr. Normandy *and* Council Leader Darby. For all I care, he could have us dropping off his laundry. I'm riding those coattails all the way to the top."

Braggs mumbled something unintelligible and gave the gurney another swift kick. "Holly, get the lights. I'm not doing this job in the dark."

Elodie winced as the violet lights paled and florescent white illuminated the space.

"He send you the code yet?" Braggs asked.

The other soldier removed his holopad from his duty belt and hammered in a few quick commands before reading off a series of letters and numbers.

Holly appeared with her familiar new curves and curls. Elodie pressed her lips tightly together to keep her anxiety from spilling out. It was only Helper Holly—the Holly who served as the MediCenter employees' search engine and programs assistant. This Holly would report back to the Key, but stay in line and there was nothing to fear.

"There she is, my sexy helper," Braggs hollered, rubbing his hands together.

"Dude, she's a hologram. Plus, she looks more and more like Blair Scott every day." The soldier shivered. "And that woman is terrifying."

"What can I say?" Braggs licked his lips. "I like to aim high."

Holly beamed her perfect smile at the men, seemingly oblivious to their remarks. "An identity check is required. Please state your name and rank before proceeding."

With a dutiful nod, the soldier said, "Lieutenant Ryan Foster."

"And Lieutenant Cutter Braggs." Braggs grinned, his voice a bit softer as he spoke to the hologram.

Holly blinked rapidly, her smile never faltering. "I'm sorry. You have not been authorized to unlock this package. Please exit the area and contact your commanding officer for further instruction."

Braggs stepped closer to the hologram. "Check again, sweetheart. Major Owens sent us to retrieve this, uh . . ." He glanced over his shoulder at the shadowed rectangle. ". . . *package*."

Holly's gaze locked onto his as she tilted her head and

wrinkled her brow in the way a mother might to a petulant child. "I'm sorry," she repeated. "You have not been authorized to unlock this package. Please exit the area and contact your commanding officer for further instruction."

Lieutenant Foster chuckled, tucking the holopad back into his belt and heading toward the door. "Looks like your girlfriend broke up with you, Braggs."

"Very funny," Braggs scoffed, turning his attention back to the hologram. "I'll be back, sweetheart, *with* authorization, so don't you go anywhere." He turned, mumbling to himself as he trailed after his comrade. "Fucking Owens."

"*Major* Owens," Foster corrected as he passed his cuff beneath the door's scanner.

"I'll call him *major* when he stops giving us bullshit tasks he can't even set up correctly." Braggs shook his head. "That fiancée of his really screwed him."

The door hissed open, and the soldiers disappeared back into the bleach-white room.

As the door closed, the faultless smile dropped from Holly's lips.

Elodie clutched the bag more firmly against her chest. This wasn't Helper Holly, the glorified computer tasked with answering simple questions and enacting even simpler commands, this was *the* Holly—the brain, watchful eye, and gatekeeper of the Key and its secrets.

Holly stepped closer to the package, her stilettos noiseless against the tile. "Major Owens sent two others to complete the task." She glanced down at the box, her head tilting side to side, birdlike. "Yes," she said in response to the conversation only she could hear. "Lieutenants Ryan Foster and Cutter Braggs. I made sure they exited." Holly reached out, her fingertips hovering just above the box. "No, it's undisturbed." She dropped her hand to her side, her gaze flicking up. It roamed the walls and stilled on the vent, on Elodie.

Elodie's teeth ached as she bit down, blocking even air from escaping her mouth.

"Understood."

Holly's voice speared the silence and made Elodie wince.

The hologram nodded stiffly, her attention darting back to the box a final time before she vanished.

Elodie held her breath as she waited, listening for footsteps, for more sirens, for Rhett. Sure she was alone, she peeled the plastic bag from her clammy grip and reopened it. She fastened the new cuff around her wrist and brought it to her lips.

"They're gone," she said, her voice remaining whisper soft.

"Good," Sparkman grunted.

Elodie dumped out the rest of the bag's contents. A Key Corp–red cadet uniform and hat spilled into the vent shaft along with a pair of shiny black boots.

"You want me to impersonate a soldier?" Elodie shook her head at her own question. Impersonating a soldier was not even at the top of the list of bad things she'd done already. "Won't people notice?"

"Most people are paying more attention to themselves than they ever will to you." Sparkman's voice thrummed against her wrist. "Especially since most citizens feel safe and protected by the Key."

Sparkman sounded like Aiden. Or maybe they both sounded like Eos.

"Remember to be quick," Sparkman said, continuing her

instructions. "Keep the hat on, and your head down. You'll make it to the rendezvous without issue."

Elodie shrugged out of her gown, bumping her elbows against the sides of the vent as she shimmied into the new uniform. "You're not going to be with me the whole way?"

"I can get you out of these sealed rooms. That's all. I've already been inside the network for too long. At any moment, the Key could find me."

The air vent hissed like a stuck balloon. Elodie finished lacing her boots before she kicked the metal vent. The cover clanged against the tile. Again, Elodie waited.

"You have to go now. I won't be able to unlock the door again. The Key is on my trail."

"Then what?" Elodie shuddered as she crawled out of the vent and back into the cold storage space.

"I sent rendezvous coordinates to your cuff. I'll meet you there."

With Aiden.

Elodie's new cuff lit up with directions as she replaced the vent and jogged to the door opposite the one to the room where she'd awoken.

Rapid beeping sounded behind her, and she stopped, frozen in her tracks. She turned, sure Rhett was back, sure she'd been spotted and would be taken away, never to be heard from again.

"Stop for no one," Sparkman continued. "Talk to no one, and make sure you're not followed."

Black shadows faded from the inside of the large rectangular box that sat upon the parked gurney. As the inside of the container cleared from storm-cloud gray to foggy sky, the shape inside took form.

Elodie blinked, unable to believe her eyes as she slowly made her way to the package.

"This isn't real," she muttered to herself.

"Elodie, do you copy?" Sparkman barked. "You need to get moving. They *will* be back. You don't have much time."

"It's Aubrey." Elodie pressed her hands against the plastic. The little girl's body was as slim and fragile as it had been in her dreams but much slighter than when under Elodie's care in the Long-Term Care Unit. But the Key had come into the LTCU and had taken Aubrey away, they had erased all evidence of Elodie's inquiries after the patient's whereabouts, and they had left everyone to believe that the little girl had died.

Perhaps *everyone* was too generous. Elodie seemed to be the only person who truly cared about Aubrey. And Elodie always would. After all, Aubrey had been the one to start her on this journey toward happiness and freedom.

Elodie's gaze traveled down the girl's thin arm. A small *92* had been tattooed on her wrist, the bold, black lettering in stark contrast to her sickly pale skin.

"I have to help her."

"You have to get out, now!" Sparkman boomed.

Aubrey's fingers twitched and her chest rose and fell in rapid succession. Elodie stared at the small girl's face, bony and thin. Her eyes tracked back and forth under her closed lids, rippling the delicate skin.

"You won't get another chance." Sparkman's warning vibrated against Elodie's wrist.

Aubrey's eyelids snapped open, and her gaze fixed on Elodie. Her irises were as purple as they had been in Elodie's dreams.

"Save me. Before it's too late."

The little girl's mouth hadn't moved, but the words scratched at Elodie's ears.

"I don't know how," she whispered, tears pricking her eyes. But she would figure out a way. Aubrey was her responsibility. It didn't matter that someone had taken her out of the Long-Term Care Unit. She wasn't safe within the belly of the Key.

"Sparkman, I can't leave her here."

"You can't help her if you don't first help yourself," came the Lieutenant Colonel's swift reply.

Elodie pressed her forehead against the case and looked down at the small child. Her heart squeezed. She was the only one who wanted to protect her, and she would. But right now, Sparkman was right. If Elodie got caught, it wouldn't matter whether or not she'd gotten Aubrey out of this box, they'd both be doomed.

Elodie forced a swallow past the hard lump in her throat. "I promise I'll come back for you."

A single tear washed down Aubrey's colorless cheek as she blinked, long and slow. *I'll be here.*

That was the troubling thing, Elodie realized as she ran to the open door. Aubrey had existed within the confines of the MediCenter her whole life. Her parents, if she had any, had never tried to get her out, and the moment Aubrey had been lucid and Elodie had tried to help her, the Key had made her disappear. How many others had they locked away?

INCOMING PRIORITY ONE ALERT FROM THE KEY CORPORATION

The new Key Corp Director has hit the ground running and has already made Westfall an even safer city. All citizens owe Director Scott and Major Rhett Owens a debt of gratitude for locating and apprehending the leader of the Northwestern faction of the Eos terrorist organization. The Key is keeping this traitor in containment and is one step closer to permanently defeating those who wish Westfall harm. Until then, the Key will keep you safe. Each citizen can do their part by staying vigilant and alert, and immediately reporting suspicious behavior or activity.

XX

Cath Scott's holographic curls were perfect. They bounced around her shoulders as light and fluffy as cotton. Preston rubbed his hands together, imagining the sunshine-yellow fleece of Cath's hair between his fingers. They were different from Blair's curls, of course. After all, the women weren't biologically related. Preston's lids hung heavy as he pictured Blair's soft, perfectly defined ringlets caressing her cheeks. How he longed to cradle her head in his hands, lay her down in his bed, press his—

Sirens blared, and the hall flashed violet, ripping Preston from his fantasy and throwing him into the present.

Wide-eyed, Cath spun around as the door to Aiden Scott's containment chamber slid closed behind her. With each step toward him, she shed a layer. First, her hair. Then, her skin, her clothes, and, finally, her voice. Gone were the golden curls, peachy pale skin, plain pantsuit, and voice as soothing as warm honey. In their place was a muted version of Blair. This new, updated edition of Holly reminded Preston of swimming, inching into the pool and sucking in short, staccato breaths when the water reached his waist. This was the current version of Holly—uncomfortable and only halfway there. Each time he looked at her he saw progress, but the end, the plunge into her fully realized version was still just out of reach.

"It's under control." Holly's voice was dampened by the blaring sirens that filled the MediCenter's basement lab.

"Someone turn the damn alarms off, now!" One of Preston's patients had already awoken, jarred from his VR program by what the reports had just revealed to be an error with his new implant. Preston didn't need the alarms waking up his other subject.

His fists hardened into granite as Holly strode to his side. His accomplishment had been extraordinary. She was simply pinpricks of light interpreted by the implant the Key had placed into each citizen at birth as a real-life form. With the latest implant update, Holly had changed from only a voice to a fully realized individual. At least, she was for those who still had a functioning implant.

Holly's throat pulsed with a swallow. "He believes Dr. Scott is still alive and that the events that he thought occurred were actually trauma-induced hallucinations."

"Great work," Preston said, more to himself than to her. He'd done an excellent job in programming the holographic version of Dr. Cath Scott. A version so lifelike no one would notice if he slipped her into the world outside of the MediCenter. He alone had the power to erase the rumors of Cath's death with a single command. "And the sirens?"

"The network was breached." Holly blinked rapidly, telegraphing her deep dive into the inner workings of the Key's systems.

Preston grimaced. It was the only one of her actions he couldn't control. No matter how hard he tried.

"Sixty-six percent contained and climbing."

Blink. Blink, blink, blink. Blink, blink.

"The location of the individual's device has been located."

Blink, blink. Blink. Blink, blink, blink.

"Alarm reset is imminent."

Her eyelids stilled and a smile glossed her lips. "Would you like me to send out a team to retrieve the—"

"No. I won't risk a leak of the true reason for the alarms," Preston interrupted, already pulling up his messaging screen. "I want someone I know on this."

Someone I can control.

As he closed his messages, an alert scrolled along the bottom of his vision. Blair had scheduled a meeting with Robin Wilson. The two had seemed chummy, but what did this mean? He kicked himself for not setting up the cameras in her office. That had been off-limits. Her apartment, too, not that she spent much time there. He hadn't wanted to destroy the mystery that engulfed their relationship.

Not knowing is part of the fun.

The reminder sent a shiver up his spine.

A call notification swallowed the alert he'd created after he'd mirrored Blair's planner. Preston answered, and Normandy appeared, transparent across his left eye.

"I received an alarm notification for the downstairs labs."

Downstairs labs. As if the word *basement* somehow tainted the doctor's precious work.

"Elodie Benavidez is missing," Normandy continued. "I suspect that's why." He leaned forward, tenting his fingers. "Was that also a part of your plan?" A taunting grin curled his thin lips. "Set her loose like a mouse in a maze?"

Preston felt choked by the purple-tinged air and stunned by the screeching sirens battering his ears. The Key had been attacked. *He* had been attacked. But Eos had failed to get the most important member of the young, traitorous pair.

Preston drew in a deep breath and mentally sorted through his list of priorities. Elodie Benavidez was nowhere near the top. She was just a girl. Sure, within his expertly designed VR program she might have been able to lead him to other Eos members, but she could also do that now, awake, loose. A mouse in a maze, indeed.

"I'm sure the Benavidez girl's escape is directly tied to the pharmaceuticals administered, which fall under your purview."

Normandy's eyes narrowed behind the small frames of his glasses. If they were keeping score, Preston would have been awarded a point.

"The alarms, which fall under my watch," Preston continued, "were alerting to a simple network breach. It was an overreaction, really. With the demise of their leader, no doubt Eos is poking around hoping to find a way in. Nevertheless, I've contacted Major Owens. After he's completed this task, he can help find the girl."

Normandy settled back in his chair, his grin deepening the wrinkles etched into his weathered skin. "I contacted Major Owens first thing." Again, the doctor drew his sword and advanced. "He's busying himself with my task as we speak."

"And Patient Ninety-Two?" Preston parried. "With the network breach, are you not worried about her security?"

"The good major is on it as well." Normandy adjusted his

glasses. "Did your *Cath* work as intended or did the youngest Scott see right through her?"

Darby's stomach churned, awash with acid. "Aiden Scott believes what I instructed—that everything after his capture from the Eos warehouse was a trauma-induced fabrication."

The alarm ceased and the Violet Shield was replaced by cool fluorescent light.

A loud *bang* made Preston flinch. His gaze swung to the metal door across from him. Aiden was out of bed.

Preston's heartbeat increased as Normandy's bushy brows lifted.

"The boy believed your version of Dr. Scott, did he?"

Another loud *bang*, and Preston's gaze snapped to Holly. She stared back at him, her eyes clear and bright, awaiting instruction.

Bang! Bang, bang! "I know you're out there!"

The corners of Normandy's lips slipped back into a smile as he slid his glasses down the bridge of his nose. "It sounds to me like—"

"Benavidez is your priority. I have a corporation to run." Preston ended the call.

You answer to no one, he reminded himself. *The day will come when Normandy is gone.*

"I know someone's out there!" Aiden's fists pummeled the metal. "If my mom is with you, send her back in. Prove that she's real!"

Holly stepped forward, her clothes already melting into Cath's sensible attire.

"Stop," Preston hissed. "He can't escape. He has no allies and nowhere to go."

In truth, other than gleaning Eos information from the boy, Preston wasn't positive as to his endgame with Aiden. Of course, it had something to do with Blair—most things did—but what? Maybe Aiden would be Blair's gift; the final prize after a long and thrilling game. Yes, Preston had sentenced Blair's brother to death, but that was all part of it. Tit for tat. This for that. The game they'd been playing since grade school.

Preston's heartbeat skipped as he imagined what Blair would exchange for the life of her brother and what dastardly scheme she had planned to get him back for toying with Aiden's life. Something with Robin Wilson, perhaps?

Blair's meeting with the council member flew to the top of Preston's priority list.

"I'll deal with him later," he said over another series of loud thumps. "I have another program in the works. One that is sure to get me what I want."

"I know that wasn't Cath! It was another lie! The Key is built on lies!" Aiden's shouts were muffled by the metal door and insulated wall that separated them.

Holly shook her head, her spiraled curls not moving quite as freely as Preston had wanted. "I'm sorry. I—"

He held up his hand. "It's my fault. I should have known you'd never be as good as the real thing."

He turned and stalked down the hall. He wouldn't look back. Whether or not Holly existed was up to him, and right now, she was useless.

Preston should have sent Blair in to see her brother. The real Blair. She would have done it. She would do anything for Aiden. And Preston had the sneaking suspicion that she would do anything for him, too.

XXI

An uncomfortable stillness settled over Blair like a wet rag as she read Cath's letter once, twice, three times before she was able to fully focus and understand the words her adoptive mother had left for her to discover.

Blair Iris Scott,

I hope this note never finds its way to you. I hope, before my time comes, I am brave enough to tell you these facts in person. You deserve to know the truth. You've been deserving your entire life.

I suppose it's best to start at the beginning . . .

Eos, labeled a terrorist organization by the Key, is far from evil and neither they nor any of their members have intimidated, coerced, or used violence to further their agenda. Eos's goal is to improve upon the old ways and take care of the land and its people. They want to see individuality, choice, and freedom at the helm, guiding us to a better world. They're not naive. Eos knows they face their own set of problems. No matter what the Key says, the issues of the past did not die by the hands of Cerberus. Hate, classism, greed, misogyny, racism . . . they are very much alive.

This brings me to my next point: Cerberus is no longer a threat. It hasn't been for decades. The Key Corporation is the true threat. They have and continue to use fear to maintain their rule. Dr. Normandy is one head of the beast, the Council Leader another, and until his death, Director Holbrook was the third. Without him, there's a vacancy. No doubt Normandy and Darby will fill Holbrook's seat with someone they believe they can control and one day convince to do their bidding. These men have a new plan to maintain power. The details are unclear, but I can tell you that there is no doubt that it is deadly.

And finally, Aiden—your curious, wonder-filled Denny. He's always been a bit at sea, and you have always been the lighthouse guiding him home. He suspected the lies of the Key and was on a mission to search out answers of his own. Under the Key's rule, the road to the truth only leads to one place. Every day I question whether or not I made the right decision in bringing him into this world of shadows and secrets. I suppose now I'll never know.

Trust that I only kept this from you to keep you safe. More than that, I have been a coward. With time, I hope you're able to forgive me.

I have always loved you, and I have always been proud of you. I was put on the earth to be there for you and your brother. Being your mother has been my greatest joy.

Take care of each other.

Forever,

Your mother

P.S. If you ever want to, if you ever need it, it's <u>here</u>.

Tears dripped from Blair's chin and splashed against her stone desk.

She ignored the last word *here* in hypertext the same blue as a spring sky. She didn't want to believe Cath's letter. She didn't want to believe that the corporation she'd spent her entire life following had lied to her and everyone else in the name of power or that Preston Darby and Osian Normandy appointed her with the belief that she would be their puppet. Blair had dedicated herself to their mission. She had abandoned her personal life in a determined quest to be the leader of the corporation that had saved them all.

Had everything really been a lie?

Blair's throat tightened as a headache sprouted behind her eyes. Not even the Poppy could stave off the flood of emotion that threatened to pull her under. Blair swiped the back of her gloved hand across her moist cheek. No, she wouldn't let herself drown. Cath had to be lying. After all, she had made a career out of being deceptive.

I have always loved you, and I have always been proud of you.

The words sucked the breath from Blair's lungs. What would

be the point in lying to her daughter from the grave? Cath no longer had anything to gain.

Could it be for Eos's benefit?

Blair bit her bottom lip. Cath hadn't said anything about needing to take action. She hadn't mentioned searching anyone out or that Blair should become a member herself.

Again, Blair's eyes roamed the note.

I was put on the earth to be there for you and your brother. Being your mother has been my greatest joy.

Blair's eyes burned as tears carved fresh tracks down her cheeks. She had known who Cath was all along. Her adoptive mother was grace and mercy and kindness. It wasn't power or domination that drove her to lead Eos, but truth. Even though she was gone, she still had so much to teach.

Blair hugged her legs against her chest and buried her chin between her knees.

Take care of each other.

"I love you, Mother," Blair whispered to Cath's memory. "And I will continue to make you proud."

XXII

Bang! Bang!

As the sirens faded, Aiden beat the metal door, giving voice to his agony.

He had failed his sister.

Bang!

He had failed Cath.

Bang!

He had failed Elodie.

Bang! Bang!

And Astrid, Sparkman, Thea . . . the list went on and on. And so did he, pummeling the metal door until his fists ached and his throat burned.

"I know that wasn't Cath! It was another lie!" Sweat dotted his brow and he pressed his cheek against the cold metal door. He'd wanted to believe that the woman who'd entered his room had been his adoptive mother, that he'd had an accident, and that his accident hadn't been her. He'd wanted to believe it so badly that he might have gone along with it, except for Tavi.

"The Key is built on lies!" he shouted a final time before going quiet. He pressed his ear more firmly against the metal and flattened his palms against the door as he held his breath and listened.

The voices were low, muffled by the layers of insulation and metal between them, but Aiden was sure there were two. The deeper voice was familiar, an oily slickness to it that he could almost place, but it kept slipping out of reach. The other was unmistakable.

"Holly," he breathed. Somehow the hologram had become Cath.

The voices went silent. Aiden waited, straining to hear more, but no other sounds came. Finally, he pushed away from the door. How long had he listened? How long had he been hidden away?

Within this white box somewhere deep inside the Medi-Center, there was no way to tell. That's how the Key preferred it. They'd try to take everything from him until his insides were blank. Then they'd replace his thoughts, feelings, hopes, and dreams with their own until the fresh white was stained Key red and the line between who he was and the corporation was blurred beyond recognition.

Aiden huffed as he massaged his stiff neck with his aching hands. No matter what the corporation did, it wouldn't work. His insides were too charred and twisted to wash clean. Even though his time in Zone Seven hadn't been real, everything else had been. Everything else was proof of his darkness, his evil.

The air-conditioning switched on and the pointed corners of

his crumpled bedsheet trembled in the cool breeze. There were only three things in this room: the bed, side table, and a single chair. The furniture was the harsh silver of cold metal. Everything else was white. Although, *white* wasn't the right word. This blinding, sterile shade that the Key coated most surfaces in should have its own label.

Hopelessness.

They should note its new name on the color wheel.

Aiden pressed his back to the cool metal door and slid to the tile. His heart still pounded against his ribs and his shirt stuck to his sweat-streaked chest as he focused on managing his breathing and steadying his heart rate. This barren room was similar to those mentioned in the horrific eye-witness accounts of Rehabilitation he'd been told by Eos members, but Aiden's experience had started differently. His entry into Rehab, if that's what this was, had begun in his mind. Instead of dealing with Aiden as a whole, mind *and* body, the Key had separated him into two. One, they left stretched across a MediCenter bed, the other was engulfed in VR.

But how?

Aiden winced as a stabbing pain pierced his neck. He dipped his chin to his chest and rolled his head from one side to the other and back again. The bots that had placed him in his bed could never be as gentle with an unconscious body as a human being could be. He grimaced, tracing the line of pain up the right side of his neck, to his jawline, and up to his ear—He froze, unable to inhale as his fingers struck the newly sutured cut just behind his earlobe. The wound itself was numb, his headache and neck pain the only evidence of the Key's actions.

Aiden released a trembling exhale. *The corporation had replaced his implant.*

Each citizen was given one at birth, and each Eos member had theirs removed upon initiation.

He'd been right. Holly had been in his room, beamed into existence through his new implant. While it was inside of him, the Key had the ability to make him see whatever images they wanted him to.

He had to get it out. He couldn't be certain of what was real until he did.

Aiden rose from the floor, slowly, deliberately, as his gaze lifted to the ceiling. His attention darted from one corner to the next until he saw what Tavi had proven was there: a camera. Its lens was a small glimmer against the hopelessness, like a drop of sunlight reflected off the smooth surface of a pond. The Key was watching—the corporation was always watching—and now he knew exactly what they could see.

Aiden reached the side of the bed and turned his back to the camera, its lens as wide as a pen cap. He dropped onto the edge of the bed, shoulders slumped in mock defeat. No matter what the Key thought they saw, if there was any way out, Aiden would find it.

"We call you Wonder Boy . . . You do some wondrous things."

The plastic-coated mattress crinkled under his weight as he leaned forward and reached for the side table. The handle jiggled as he opened the small drawer, its rounded edges a match to the rest of the furniture. The Key had made sure he couldn't hurt himself. But what did it say that they expected him to?

Aiden blew out a puff of air as he stared down at the drawer.

"Of course it's empty," he mumbled to himself. Left alone in here for too long, there would be a lot of that. "Think, Aiden, think."

Under his grip, the handle wobbled, its screw loose. He reached inside the drawer and searched its front wall with his fingers. He unscrewed the small bolt and hid it and the handle under closed fingers as he shut the drawer. He let out a long, defeated sigh and slid off the bed and onto the floor. From the angle of the camera, this was the only place in the room that the Key couldn't see.

He set the handle on the ground next to him and held out his hand. The screw rolled against his palm. Aiden winced as he pressed his thumb against its pointed end. It would do nicely.

Now, he could only hope that the implant hadn't had time to fully take hold. It was a small piece of gentech, but without the proper removal tools, it could take its host down with it.

Would it be so bad if this was the end?

He imagined the imposter Cath or a nurse bot coming in to find him sprawled out on the floor.

His thumb grazed the screw's metal point.

If he was truly a hero, he'd end it right now, jump on the grenade before he had a chance to blow up someone else. But he was a destroyer, and his darkness wouldn't let him out of life so easily.

"*. . . Eos has a purpose.* You *have a purpose.*"

No, it wasn't his darkness. It was that small fire of hope that Tavi had reignited. Eos needed him. More than that, his sister needed him. If the Key had turned Holly into Cath to fool him, what did the corporation have planned for Blair?

Aiden scooted to the bedside table and looked at his distorted reflection in the smooth metal.

"After the storm," he whispered and dragged the sharp point of the screw along the fresh sutures. A sharp gasp escaped his lips as the sutures popped and blood dribbled down his neck. The incision was still numb, but he felt the pressure of each stitch as it tore and heard his bloody flesh squelch as he forced the wound back open.

He dug his thumb and forefinger into the oozing sore. There it was. He could feel the slim foreign body hard beneath his fingertips. He narrowed his eyes at his reflection as he pinched the implant between his fingers and pulled. He ripped the device from his head. The implant's small, pill-like body pulsed Key Corp red and the two hairlike tentacles that grew out of each side wriggled and slapped against Aiden's fingers as it searched for its host.

He yanked the sheet off the bed and held it against the side of his head as he peered down at the implant. It was no bigger than a grain of rice—a weaponized water strider that the Key had outfitted with the power to control the citizen they had embedded into.

Aiden dropped the gentech on the ground and grabbed the drawer handle still resting by his side. He clenched the pull in his fist and smashed its metal end against the implant. The device cracked. Rapid spurts of red light pulsed through its body and down its feelers, and then it went dark.

The knot that had formed between his shoulder blades loosened slightly as he leaned his head back against the mattress. He could trust himself again. At least, he could trust what he was seeing.

Aiden wiped his hands off on the sheet, balled it up, and stuffed it and the rest of the evidence into the drawer. This battle was over. Now, he only needed to win the war.

XXIII

Preston passed his cuff beneath the scanner to the basement lab that housed his and Normandy's most promising experiments. To say access to the antechamber and the two labs that branched off it was elite was an understatement. Only four people in Westfall could access the lab. He and Dr. Osian Normandy were two of them.

The panel flashed green and the door slid open, revealing a small bubble of a room ablaze in purple light. From this vestibule, Preston had two options: the door on his right or the door on his left. Patient Ninety-Two was in the lab to his left. No doubt Normandy would be, too.

Another access panel, another green light, and another hissing door, and Preston was in a lab so white and bright that time lost all meaning.

Glass clinked as Normandy sorted through one of the cabinets that lined the wall opposite the entrance.

"Predictable," Preston grumbled, stepping across the threshold so the door could close behind him.

"You made it," Normandy said, his attention firmly fixed on the glass vial he'd removed from the cabinet. "I thought I'd have to send the soldier out to fetch you."

Preston's gaze wandered over the unconscious little girl. New IVs trailed from her bony hands and thin arms, a freeway of drugs that raced in and out with each beat of her heart.

"I came as soon as I was able." He frowned down at the subject, bypassing her on his way to the doctor. She didn't matter. Not to him, anyway. "Of course I had to finish up a few important items first. The corporation has many moving parts that I must attend to."

There was a new gurney in the room, a sheet stretched across the undeniable shape of a human form resting upon it. The gentle shudder of the cloth and the almost imperceptible rise and fall of the torso told Preston all he needed to know— this was a new experiment.

His fingers itched with curiosity and his pulse thrummed with a need he forced back until it was a mere rise of goosebumps on the nape of his neck.

In his personal life, Preston was loyal. He was devoted to Blair, to Westfall, to the Key. But when it came to his experiments, he was a beast, an insatiable devourer of flesh. There was no such thing as too many and never just one.

"Conducting a new experiment?" Preston cursed the slight tremble in his voice that betrayed the compulsion tingling against the back of his neck.

Normandy didn't respond. His movments were measured and methodical as he pulled a sterile syringe from a drawer beneath the hanging cabinets and opened the pouch. Plastic crinkled and the subject's heart rate monitor beeped slow and steady.

Beep. Beep. Beep.

Preston tapped the toe of his polished shoe against the tile as heat swallowed his stomach.

Beep. Beep. Beep.

It coiled around his throat and sat like an ember on his tongue, daring him to spit out the burning rage. But he wouldn't.

Beep. Beep. Beep.

With a thick swallow, Preston doused his anger. When it came to Normandy, a pregnant pause was never the simple absence of words or passive mark of disrespect. It was a minefield, and Preston would stay still and silent before charging in.

Normandy pierced the vial's rubber stopper with the sharp tip of the needle and drew out a small amount of clear liquid before he finally spoke. "Termination."

Preston's heart skipped. "Termination?"

The doctor sighed through flared nostrils. "That subject is no longer of value and therefore must be terminated." He enunciated each word as if Preston had never before set foot in a lab.

Preston squeezed his hands into fists and fought the urge to gaze at the covered, prone form. "I understand the meaning of the word. I do not, however, know why the termination of a subject requires my attention." He gritted his teeth as another surge of hunger brushed against his spine. He wanted to be there, wanted to touch and explore in the name of science, but he would never give Normandy the satisfaction of knowing his true desires. "Osian, I am very busy and—"

"Yes, you've said." Normandy peered at him over the rim of his spectacles as he capped the syringe and slipped it into the pocket of his pristine lab coat. "Moving parts, important duties, and so on."

Preston's eyes watered as a primal roar echoed between his ears.

"You wished to stay apprised," Normandy said, striding toward the gurney while nodding at the holopad that sat near the subject's blanketed feet.

A smile twitched against the doctor's lips as Preston approached the body a little too quickly.

He plucked the holopad from the silver metal. The back of his hand brushed against the person's still foot. Preston cleared his throat to mask the low groan that escaped his lips. "It's more than a wish, Osian. Our projects are connected. We must—" His words were lost, blown away by the cool air that swirled around him as Normandy yanked the sheet off the subject.

Preston's grip went slack and the holopad hit the gurney with a metallic *clunk*. He felt his heart beat in his stomach and each breath send a wave of chills through his core.

"You like what you see." Normandy released the sheet and it fluttered to the floor.

Preston couldn't take his eyes from the man's naked body, his chapped and slightly parted lips, the swirls of black hair that dusted his rising chest, his light skin blotchy with cold. The subject was unconscious, as pliable as clay, and Preston ached to mold him.

"You always were a deviant."

Normandy's cutting words halted Preston's reverie.

"Like you," Preston growled, grabbing the holopad. "I do what is necessary for science."

With a scoff, Normandy removed the syringe from his pocket and placed it on the gurney. "Your father—"

"Is this accurate?" Preston turned the illuminated screen of graphs and numbers toward Normandy, cutting the doctor off before he landed what was sure to be a devastating blow.

Normandy only stared back at Preston, the corners of his lips quaking with a suppressed smile.

Preston swiped through the pages, reviewing every last finding. "This is . . ." He shook his head. "It worked."

"You sound surprised."

Preston looked up. "It's taken you nearly five decades."

"Genius takes time," Normandy said, removing his glasses and wiping them on his lab coat.

"I achieved my goal in a fraction of that."

The doctor let out a brittle laugh. "As I said, *genius* takes time."

"Without me, you would have no hope of accomplishing this." Preston emphasized with a shake of the holopad.

Normandy blinked slowly as he replaced his glasses on the bridge of his nose. "Without you, I would round them up with a Cerberus booster. Have you heard?" His narrow features twisted, and his voice thinned with panic. "There's a new Cerberus strain, a *mutation*. It's back."

His cheeks flushed and his chest heaved in sharp bursts. "Remember before? Remember what happened?" His hands shook and his gaze fell to the floor. "Blood everywhere . . . 'Thank goodness we have the Key. They have a new vaccine. They will save us.'" He brushed a single tear from his cheek as he tilted his chin and pinned his gaze on Preston. "You think I need you to tamper with their implants and reprogram them to do our bidding?" His tone was steady again, breathing normal. "Oh, dear boy, this corporation coded its citizens long before you were even a thought."

"Bravo, Doctor," Preston said, setting the holopad onto the

gurney. "But you forget one thing. An entire race of immortals, scrubbed free of any genetic maladies and impervious to those that would invade from without, would not serve us." His heart skipped as his gaze brushed the man on the table. "You have made it possible to fool each citizen's immune system into believing that the implant is a part of the body, allowing it to migrate and gain an even bigger hold. Making the herd pure, only susceptible to diseases of our creation, is an impressive side effect, but we do not want them around forever."

"You think I desire immortality for *them*?" He took the syringe from the gurney and removed its plastic cap. "A few more tests, and then you, as a Darby, will be entitled to a dose as well."

Preston's breath caught. Normandy would dose himself, first. He would live forever, a buzzing gnat, chiding and chastising until Preston wished for death. He would never have freedom or peace. Not if the doctor reached his ultimate goal.

"Now, if you would stop fiddling with that hologram, I will make you my assistant for these final trials." The doctor peered down his nose at the graduation markings printed on the syringe. "Anyone with a science-based background will be more helpful than the major, and discretion is as important to you as it is to me."

Preston bristled at the passive insult. "Your science and mine go hand in hand, Osian."

"You manufactured a friend. No doubt, you wish she was more than that. Either way it is not where the power lies. Your playthings aren't even real."

"The Cerberus scare you've so dramatically enacted will cause panic. We want pliancy. Recoding the citizens' implants will do just that. They'll line up around the block for their new injection because they're willing drones. No chaos, no pandemonium, only a subdued and compliant flock," Preston responded, his brows knitted. The doctor's "genius" made him dense and unable to see that a submissive group was far better than one that had been coerced.

"The benefits to my next implant upgrade are tremendous. Each citizen is already a spy, passing information to Holly that she then brings to the Key. With this next step, we make them take action, and then, after they're each dosed and if it is necessary, we terminate them with a disease of our creation and hand the blame to Eos. It's perfect. But it's only perfect as a whole."

Normandy hiked his shoulders. "We will be in power until the end of time. What the masses do is of no consequence." His lips thinned as his gaze scanned Preston. "I see your true desire. You want a herd of clay soldiers that you can mold to your will. You want them on their knees. You want to be a god."

Preston ground his teeth until they creaked. "I heard something interesting the other day." He swiped his fingers along the edge of the gurney, outlining the man's supple skin. "Accusations from a narcissist are often admissions of guilt."

"Get out," Normandy spat before turning his attention back to the man's IV port.

"Osian, wait." Preston's words tumbled out on a breathless pant.

The doctor paused, the tip of the needle poised over the small scar, a peachy line against the subject's white flesh.

Preston fingered his tie. "Let me." His voice was heavy with desire as he pressed his fingertips against the tie blade, dragging them up and down. A steady hum pulsed behind his ribs. It filled him until he was nothing but vibrations, nothing but need.

Normandy tilted his head, and a knowing glint shone in his blue eyes. "I knew you couldn't keep it locked away."

Preston leaned in, hovering over the man's chest, each breath escaping in a quaking exhale that twirled through the subject's short, black hairs and sent goosebumps peaking across his pectorals.

Preston stuffed his trembling hands into his pockets. He wouldn't touch.

"No, doctor," he said, swallowing the saliva that pooled in his mouth. "This is in the name of science."

Normandy offered the syringe to Preston, pulling it back slightly as the young Council Leader rounded the gurney and reached for it. "Your father knew that, with time, you'd let it out again."

Not even Normandy's jab or the thought of his father could dampen the satisfying heat that yawned through Preston's chest. "My father never knew me."

And neither do you.

He took the syringe and dragged his fingers along the inside of the subject's arm. Preston's knees were softened butter as he stroked the soft flesh and pierced the skin with the tip of the needle. He depressed the plunger and continued to draw slow circles against the velvet skin around the IV port.

The steady beeps of the heart rate monitor blended into one long, piercing tone.

"Termination complete." Normandy typed a few notes in his holopad before taking the empty syringe from Preston and hurrying to Patient Ninety-Two's bedside. "Wheel that one over," he instructed as he attached a long, clear tube to one of her IVs.

Still adrift in the sea of pleasure, Preston didn't ask questions as he did as he was told, rounding the gurney to give the doctor space for the next part of his plan.

With brisk and practiced ease, Normandy attached the other end of the tube to a secondary port on the inside of the man's wrist. He turned back to the girl, his arms moving, the motions blocked by his thin frame. He nodded and stepped away as silver liquid flooded the tube, draining from the man and into the girl the doctor had gone through lengths to hide and protect.

"My pet," Osian murmured, stroking her sweat-streaked hair.

Preston had his own *pet*. His own love that needed to be seen to before he could continue with the process of turning Westfall into the docile herd of workers needed to keep their brilliant city operating at a high level.

He pressed his hip bones into the gurney and ran his fingertips along the cold skin of the subject's collar bone, down the shoulder, along the small dips and swells of the bicep and forearm.

Preston wanted Blair's approval. More than that, he *needed* her permission to move forward with this grand plan. After all, she would one day rule by his side.

He stilled at the man's wrist, trailing his fingers over the tendons corded beneath the skin.

He needed to feel her say yes.

His mouth watered and his eyelids hung heavy as he dug his fingers into the bands of tissue.

How supple she would be beneath his hands, how malleable. She would feel so good under his touch, bending to his will.

The subject's fingers curled.

Warmth flooded the pit of Preston's stomach and he couldn't suppress his moan.

XXIV

Fleeing the MediCenter had been as simple as Sparkman said it would be. After making it through the locked doorways of the basement, Elodie hadn't met anyone in the stairwell and had only passed a handful of people in the lobby. Each citizen had paid more attention to her uniform than the person wearing it.

Her escape out of the MediCenter and into the bustling Zone One streets had indeed been nearly as easy as last time, and that time had only existed in Elodie's mind. But this time was real, made obvious by the way her stomach growled and her legs burned from her brisk pace and their lack of use. There was also less promise here. Elodie had changed, but nothing else had. The Max still clunked along its tracks; people still marched ahead with blank expressions shrouded in the purple haze of their Violet Shield. The world had kept turning, exactly the same, while she'd been somewhere else entirely.

She pulled her red hat more snugly over her brow, glancing

around as she followed the directions blinking on the screen of her new cuff and turned down NW Everett Street.

Key Corp red was a bright, burning shade that could be seen from blocks away. Yet, the same way no one had really seen her as she'd forced herself to take measured steps through the lobby of the MediCenter, no one saw her now as she nearly jogged to the rendezvous point Sparkman had programmed into her cuff before she'd gone silent. The Key's red was electric, but it was normal. It was safe. The bursts of red that highlighted the various Key Corp buildings throughout Zone One were a comfort. The color signified health, happiness, and the brightness of the future. It was, in fact, the perfect disguise.

Elodie's cuff vibrated as she passed a brick storefront only a few blocks from the Willamette River.

She'd arrived.

The word SUDS was spelled out in large, bluish-white bubbles on the awning, and the neon OPEN sign that hung in the window was dark even though the hours of operation projected on the front door stated that Suds had been open since 10:00 a.m. Elodie checked the time on her cuff. Within the MediCenter it had been impossible to know what time it was. She glanced up at the cloudless blue sky and, for a moment, wished her vision was greeted by a thick blanket of pine branches swaying overhead. Inside the forest that bordered Zone Seven, happiness had never felt closer. She sighed, smoothing the stiff collar of her uniform between her thumb and forefinger. But the pine trees, crisp air, and warm touches hadn't really existed. In truth, she'd been cold and still and pumped full of drugs.

She took a deep breath and turned her attention back to

Suds's glass door. There was no use in aching for a bliss she could never truly realize.

The entrance chimed as the front door slid open and Elodie stepped through the Violet Shield. Suds's cheery, bubbly logo had been deceiving. Inside, the cramped entryway was littered with stacks of sealed cardboard boxes, and the long, narrow interior was divided in two by a yellowing counter that separated the front from rows and rows of plastic-covered clothes hanging from scuffed metal poles.

Like all Westfall families, Elodie's mother sent out their clothes to be laundered, but neither of them had ever stepped foot inside the laundromat. Elodie had always imagined clean smells and sparkling surfaces, not aging yellows and cluttered spaces.

"Fatigues are finished on Wednesdays," the guy behind the counter said without looking up as he typed on his holopad with one hand and twisted his mop of red curls around his fingers with the other. "A bot will drop 'em off at your place."

Elodie picked at the smooth edge of her thumb nail, which had grown out since she'd last been awake. "I'm not here for laundry." In truth, she wasn't exactly sure *what* she was here for.

He put down his holopad, looking at her for the first time since she'd walked in. He wrinkled his nose, his splash of freckles crinkling with the motion.

Again, her cuff vibrated. Her heart skipped as she glanced down at the new message. She'd gone to the wrong place. The Key was on her trail. They were about to—

Elodie's brow pinched as a message flashed bright white against the darkened screen.

WHAT A BEAUTIFUL SUNRISE.

She cocked her head.

What is that supposed to mean?

This whole thing would be a lot easier if Sparkman would have used the normal messaging app that was tied to each of their implants.

A bot emerged from around the counter. It whirred past, picked up one of the boxes, and disappeared back into the rows of hanging plastic-covered garments.

"You gonna tell me what you *are* here for?" His chair creaked as he leaned forward and rested his pointy elbows on the counter.

Elodie swallowed. "What a beautiful sunrise?" She tensed, unsure of what she'd unleashed.

He hopped off his chair, eyeing the empty street through the windows behind her, before asking, "What size are you?" He squinted at her, his smooth forehead creasing. "Large, prolly."

Rude. Gwen's voice tsked between Elodie's ears. *Say you're a medium. No, small!*

It didn't matter how much space Elodie took up. Her mother had always tried to make her littler.

A lump hardened in the back of Elodie's throat. "Y-yes," she said, choking on her reply.

As much as she didn't want to, Elodie missed her mom.

He peered at her a final time and nodded to himself before disappearing into the clothes. "You comin' or what?" he asked, poking his head out from between the plastic.

Elodie glanced down at her cuff. It was blank. No further directions given. She was supposed to be here. She was supposed to follow him. She cleared her throat and with it the pang of guilt for leaving her mother and the twinge of regret that Zone Seven hadn't happened at all, and charged after him.

Plastic brushed both of her arms as she sped between the rows to keep up with his long, ground-eating strides.

"Here." He plucked a bag from a rack and thrust it at her. A pair of jeans and a T-shirt peeked through the wrinkled plastic.

Elodie blinked from him to the wrinkled bag of clothes and back again. Running from the Key sure involved a lot of changes of clothes.

As they neared the end of the row, he motioned to a closed door in front of them. "You can get dressed in the storage room." He turned, staring down at her once again. "I can't fit into that getup," he muttered, jutting out his pointed chin. "But I have something similar." He reached around her and tugged loose another bag that covered the same kind of Key Corp—red fatigues she currently wore. "They won't notice we're not the same size."

"Who won't notice?" Elodie asked, her own plastic bag crinkling in her hands.

He rolled his eyes. "*Newbs*," he groaned. "They don't teach you anything anymore." He tore the plastic from the fatigues and slung them over his shoulder. "I'm a runner," he said matter-of-factly.

She bit her bottom lip. Except for what she'd seen of Eos through the very small lens Aiden had provided, she knew nothing about their organization. Clearly, she had much more to learn.

With another beleaguered groan, he dragged his palm down his smooth cheek. "You change into those and disappear into the tunnels." Brows lifted and lips pursed, he stabbed the wrinkled plastic bag of clothes with his finger. "*I* put on your clothes, or in this case *these clothes*," he said, jostling his shoulder, "and leave the store. To, you know . . ." He waved his hand in the air as if the simple gesture could explain more than words. "*Run* somewhere. A Dead Zone, actually. Although, I don't literally run." He wrinkled his freckled nose. "But I guess *walker* doesn't sound as great as *runner*." He shook his head, and his red curls brushed his forehead. "Either way, the overlords won't know that *you* didn't leave, and they'll never suspect that this simple drop-and-wash is run by Eos."

Elodie felt like Holly, blinking rapidly to sort through all the new information. "Dead Zone?"

With a sigh, he pressed his palm against his forehead. "*Newbs.*" He spat the word like a curse and pointed to the closed door in front of them. "Leave your getup in the storage room. The access hatch to the tunnel is behind the boxes."

Elodie was tired of being pushed around by people who knew more, knew better. She'd been herded from event to event, crisis to crisis, without proper time to plan or readjust.

She tore the plastic from her newest outfit, discarding the crinkled mess on a heaping pile of plastic as she neared the storage room.

"And this is an exit only!" he called from within the racks behind her. "You can't come back this way. It doesn't work like that."

This time, Elodie groaned. She had no desire to revisit this confusing place.

The storage-room door slid open an inch before stopping. The seamless hiss and quick slide she was used to had been replaced by a mechanical grinding that stopped and started, opening the door inch by inch until there was enough room for her to wiggle through.

Like the entrance of Suds, the storage room was filled with sealed boxes, some labeled with the corporation's red logo, others labeled by hand in tall, squiggly letters that got smaller as the word got longer.

Elodie shuffled away from the door as it struggled to close. Once again, she was changing clothes in a cramped and unfamiliar space.

She hurried out of her uniform, folded it, and placed it on top of a short stack of nearby boxes before tugging on the high-waisted jeans and plain blue T-shirt the grumpy attendant had given her. She pulled her hair tie from her sloppy ponytail and scooped up her stray strands, tying them in a high and tight bun.

"The access hatch is behind the boxes." She clamped her hands on her hips as she turned her attention to the cardboard stacked against the back wall. Where was that bot when she needed it? She sighed, staring at the floor-to-ceiling piles of boxes. "The sooner you get this done, the sooner you'll get to Aiden, and the sooner you'll get to relax and be happy."

Even though it wouldn't be as sweet as what she could have found in New Dawn, the reminder that happiness was just ahead brought goosebumps to her arms and heat to her cheeks.

Her future with Aiden was somewhere in the tunnel on the other side of these boxes.

She reached out for the first box. Cardboard-brown pixels burst against her skin. She sucked in a breath and yanked her hand back. A smile plumped her cheeks as she reached through the wall of boxes, her hand disappearing into the projected image.

No heavy lifting required. Elodie stepped through the hologram. She glanced over her shoulder, through the rainbow of light that hung in the air around her, at the dingy, cluttered storeroom.

"Goodbye," she whispered. Not to Suds, but to the life she was leaving behind. She had made it out of the MediCenter, but she could go back now, exchange what she had learned for leniency, and get most of her old life back. She turned to the concrete wall in front of her and the hatch pressed into its center. It was dull black metal—exactly like the one Sparkman had disappeared into in Wonderland. Elodie turned the handle and lifted the door.

She was never going back.

Dank air met her skin as she peered into the dark maw of the tunnel. Aiden was in there, waiting for her. Elodie pressed a small button on the side of her cuff. Light burst from the plastic piece she'd followed to find this Eos secret spot. Metal steps glinted in the light as she shined the cuff into the tunnel. She climbed in and closed the door behind her.

Water splashed beneath her boots when her feet hit solid ground. "Hello?" The word echoed through the tunnel.

Elodie jumped as light flashed a few paces ahead.

Illuminated by the light from her cuff, Sparkman adjusted her cap and rested her hands on her hips. "You made it."

If the lieutenant colonel was surprised that Elodie had successfully freed herself from the MediCenter, made it through the odd experience that was Suds, and into the tunnels beneath Westfall, she didn't show it.

"Where's Aiden?" Elodie panted, suddenly breathless with the realization that this was it. They'd been separated, but now they'd be together. Did he remember what had happened in VR? In the lagoon in Zone Seven?

An orb of white light bobbed from the other end of the tunnel as footsteps rushed toward them. Elodie stared at

Sparkman, gauging the seasoned soldier's response. Sparkman brushed her long braid from her shoulder and stared ahead, as unreadable as stone. Elodie held her breath as hammering foot-steps splashed through unseen puddles.

"Runner's out," Thea Fujimoto breathed, emerging from the dark. "Said everything is clear."

Elodie's heart squeezed. Thea looked so much like Astrid. She had seen the oldest Fujimoto sister in Wonderland, but she hadn't thought she'd see her again. Not after what had happened with her best friend. Elodie choked back a sob as the light from Thea's cuff highlighted her pointed chin, sharp cheekbones, and shiny black hair. This was as close to Astrid as Elodie was ever going to get.

"Glad you got out." Thea hooked her thumb around the strap of her crossbody, a hollow smile ghosting her lips.

"Is Aiden coming?" Elodie blurted out, afraid that any other comment would end in a sob. "You got him out, didn't you?"

Thea's gaze slid to Sparkman, and she gave a stiff shake of her head. "He'll be fine." She blinked at Elodie, her face as placid as the soldier's.

"*He'll be fine?*" Elodie couldn't keep the anger from her voice.

If Aubrey was proof of anything it was that, if left in the hands of the Key, *fine* was a far cry from how Aiden would fare. Elodie had to get them both out and away from the corpora-tion. A task which seemed impossible when Thea couldn't be bothered to give her a real answer.

The light from Sparkman's cuff danced against the craggy roof of the cave. "He's been an operative working within the Key for many years. He knows what to do and how to stay safe."

Water splashed as Thea tapped the toe of her shoe against the ground. "The next chance we get, we'll get him out."

"*The next chance you get?*" Elodie couldn't stop repeating Thea as if the second time she heard the words, their meaning would stick. "It was your job to get him out the first time just like Sparkman got me out."

Thea's eyes narrowed and her face contorted as she crossed her arms over her chest, the light from her cuff shining directly under her chin. "Sparkman got you out because I made a choice. I chose you. And, believe me, it wasn't because I wanted to."

The words stung, and Elodie took a step back. She'd always thought Thea liked her, and she assumed that Thea would like her even more after learning about her involvement with Aiden and Eos. "Try again. We're hidden right now." Elodie's gesture took in the darkness of the tunnel around them. "Hack into his cuff the same way Sparkman hacked into mine and get him out."

Sparkman took a step forward. "It's not about where or how we're positioned. Not anymore. The Key is on high alert. If they see anything in their system that is outside of their parameters, they'll attack first and ask questions later."

Thea's stance loosened as she agreed with the lieutenant colonel. "And we can't afford to take that risk right now."

"Then you should have done a better job the first time! You shouldn't have had to choose between us. You should have been able to free us both." Elodie's chest burned, and her vision swirled with tears. They should have left her in VR. At least there she could have been happy.

Thea's hands were tight fists at her side. "I chose you to honor my sister!" The words splintered and cracked in her throat. "It's what she would have wanted."

"Astrid would have wanted both of us out!" Elodie couldn't swallow the anguish that flooded her chest. She'd never before been this alone. She'd always had Astrid, and then she'd had Aiden. Now, she only had herself. "There has to be something you can do."

"Stop," Thea croaked.

But she couldn't. There was too much fire within her, too much pain that had been locked away for too long. "There has to be!"

"El, stop." Thea's voice was barely a whisper.

"You're just not thinking hard enough," she said, the words continuing to tumble from her lips. "If you did it before, you can do it again."

"Stop!" Water splashed onto Thea's bag as she slammed her foot against the ground. "I won't let you make my sister's death about your boyfriend. There's so much more going on, and none of it has anything to do with him," she thundered. "Grow up Elodie! First Rhett and now Aiden . . ." Thea shook her head. "Stop picking a man and following him around thinking that he'll be the one to change your life. He won't," she spat. "You're the only one with the power to change your future."

Elodie's throat burned, stuffed with emotions at war with her mind. She'd always belonged to someone other than herself. First her parents. Then Rhett. And finally, Aiden. Of them all, she'd only been allowed to choose one. Rhett would have led her to the life she was supposed to have, and Aiden to the life she truly wanted.

Sparkman cleared her throat, breaking the silence. "We need to move, regroup, come up with a plan."

Thea's gaze bored into Elodie.

Elodie opened her mouth to speak, to apologize, to say that she had loved, *still loved* Astrid like her own sister, but no words emerged.

A small sound came from the back of Thea's throat as she relaxed her hands and brushed past Sparkman.

You're right.

It sat on the tip of Elodie's tongue, but she couldn't push the phrase past the pride that hardened her lips into stone. She had never considered that she could make her own way.

Her breaths erupted in quaking pants as possibilities swirled and adrenaline surged.

Now, she was being given the chance, and she didn't know if she was brave enough to take it.

XXV

Normandy pushed the electric tea kettle along the slick white surface of his desk until the long black cord had fallen over the back and the metal pot sat in the upper right-hand corner. There were many newfangled ways to make a cup of tea, most people had it brewed by a fancy machine that infused the hot water with the tea leaves, sugar, and milk without human intervention, but even the best machines made errors. There were many things the doctor preferred to do himself or leave as they were. He'd been called *old fashioned* many times and had always taken it as a compliment.

Normandy wiped the lenses of his glasses as he waited for the water to boil. He stared down at the tortoiseshell frames he'd had patched and mended over the past fifty years. They were another thing he couldn't let go of—remnants of a past life he'd carry with him to the grave.

Although, death may now be quite a way off.

He wrinkled his nose as a foul, fuel-like odor struck him.

He pinched the bridge of his nose and took focused, measured breaths through his mouth. He'd carry this to the grave as well—in more ways than one. The fact that, since the age of twenty-three, he hadn't been able to taste or smell anything outside of these polluted, mechanical experiences was something no living person knew, and it would stay that way.

After surviving Cerberus, he vowed that no one would learn of how he suffered, how he'd almost lost his life to the virus that had burned through so many. It may have been five decades since hospitals had been overrun and infected bodies burst in the streets, their blood streaming into the gutters like rain, but Normandy remembered it all too well. He remembered how the survivors had been rounded up and carted off to safe houses for fear that Cerberus rested dormant within their veins and would eventually emerge and slaughter everyone who'd made contact.

Normandy had heard tales of these so-called safe houses, an ironic name for such horrifying places, and he'd decided right then and there that to truly remain safe, he would act as if he'd never been infected. With the hospitals in disarray and society struggling just to feed and clothe those in need, it was an easy enough task, an easy enough lie. And it had stuck. For fifty years his denial had worked, and it wouldn't stop now.

The kettle's bell chimed, and Normandy settled his glasses back onto the bridge of his nose before pouring himself a mugful of steaming hot water. He pulled the wooden box of tea sachets from the top drawer of his desk. The old hinges creaked as he opened the lid and brushed his fingers over the delicate, hand-packed tea bags. It was not a difficult choice. They were all the same, each a mixture of dried herbs, flowers, and berries that settled his grumbling stomach and warmed him from the inside out.

He placed a bag into the hot water, enjoying the sleepy way in which the plants surrendered to the liquid and settled at the bottom of the mug in a cloud of their own dissolution. He took a sip, closing his eyes as the warmth washed over his tongue. He swallowed, and his mouth was devoid of taste. He had yet to find another drink or food that left him without the acrid aftertaste he'd never become accustomed to.

Years ago, when survivors first emerged with the symptom, it was said to be the palate resetting as if the body had rebooted a part of itself and was now able to smell and taste the chemicals that had been in their meals from the beginning. That hadn't been truth. It had been hope. And hope always burned bright until it ran out of fuel.

The overhead lights flashed, signaling that there was some-one requesting entry to his office. Most offices were equipped with a bell, but when he worked, he often became so entranced not even the sirens that had blared through the lower levels of the MediCenter could disturb him.

He pushed one of the buttons under the curved lip of his desk, and the door hissed open.

Major Owens entered and stood awkwardly in the center of the room, empty except for Normandy's desk and chair. After all, his office was not a place for social calls. His office was a place of work, and he only ever worked with himself, or at least he did now that he'd found out the truth about Sparkman. Uncertainty wiggled in the back of his throat, and he forced it back with another sip of tea.

"There are rumors," Normandy began, staring up at the soldier from behind the rim of his steaming mug. "Have you heard them, Major? They're swirling about like a cloud of gnats."

Rhett Owens tapped his meaty fingers against his thigh and his throat bobbed, working on an answer.

Perhaps cutting to the heart of the matter wouldn't work with the young soldier. Normandy set down his mug. Getting to know someone new was a terrible thing. "Major Owens, you know that my previous associate was found to be working for Eos. We found traces of the lieutenant colonel—I should say *former* lieutenant colonel—in the recent network breach. She had released a virus we know to have been developed by the terrorists." His glasses slipped slightly, and he adjusted them back to their proper place. "It's getting more and more difficult to trust people, don't you think?"

"Lieutenant Colonel Sparkman was my superior." Owens's gaze fell to the floor. "You never really know some people," he mumbled, and Dr. Normandy was quite certain he was no longer referring to the ousted officer.

"Then you also agree that we must keep focus on what truly matters—the continued strength and prosperity of the corporation. Without either, where will we end up?" Normandy's brow furrowed, a putrid taste coating his mouth. The worry had returned; climbed up his throat and nested on his tongue. Sparkman knew too much. What she could do with the information she'd learned about the Key and Normandy's *experiments*, or what she had already done with the knowledge, made his flesh sticky with sweat.

Owens shifted his weight from one foot to the other. "But I don't think I know which rumors you're referring to. There's always something floating around the MediCenter."

Normandy tugged on his earlobe. His ears tingled with the soldier's inability to come right out and say what he was thinking. Sparkman was indeed superior. But then the lieutenant colonel had been steeped in lies.

"You work for me now," Normandy said, leaning back in his chair. "And, aside from completing your assignments, all I ask of you is to be honest. You understand as well as I how important the truth is."

Normandy settled into the moment between breaths. That still space that held absolutely nothing but promised everything. It was a bit like his work, still and empty, and then *poof* . . . the magic of new life. History books would call him *creator*, would use phrases like, *against all odds* and *changed the world.* Major Rhett Owens and Lieutenant Colonel Sparkman wouldn't be mentioned by name. Instead, the two of them would be *hurdles* or *obstacles* faced by the *visionary.*

Owens's fingers continued their steady dance against his leg. "People are worried. Dr. Scott's death, Blair's promotion, the change in Holly's appearance, the—" he paused and cleared his throat, "—*incident* at the fair. The alarms that went off in the basement but were never explained or officially reported . . ." He hiked his thick shoulders. "To some people, it feels unsteady."

Normandy stiffened, the movement slight enough to not betray the unrest that rippled through him. "Unsteady enough to warrant change?"

The major's gaze flicked to the tile floor and back up again. His lips parted, and he took a breath to speak, but reconsidered.

Normandy narrowed his eyes. "Coups have arisen from less."

This time, Owens tensed, a sharp, jarring movement that telegraphed his thoughts.

"I asked you a simple question, Major." Normandy leaned forward, pressing the young soldier. "A question you, as a protector of this corporation, have a duty to answer. More than that, you should desire to report any malfeasance and do away with traitors before they're able to infect the population with their lies. However, it seems as if you would rather protect these insurrectionists." Normandy placed his elbows on his desk and tented his fingers. "If I didn't know better, I would think you were one of them."

"I would never betray the Key." Rhett's Adam's apple bobbed with a tight swallow as he fixed his attention to a point behind Normandy. "Director Scott met with Councilwoman Wilson. A few others were brought in, though I don't have names." His icy-blond temples pulsed with a clench of his jaw. "I was informed that they discussed the Council Leader." A reddish flush spread up his neck. "There was mention of him not being fit for the job." Heat stained the tips of his ears cherry red. "There are people who feel the same. Of course, I am not one of them."

Normandy's lips twitched with a smile. He wasn't shocked. No, *amused* was more fitting a word. Blair Scott's appointment to director might as well have come with a death warrant. He'd known it was only a matter of time until she signed it herself. As for her thoughts about Preston . . . Well, it would do the depraved, petulant brat to get knocked down a peg.

The doctor picked up his mug and took another drink. "Fortunately, these *rumblings* are not concrete facts, but more propaganda."

The major's amber eyes finally settled on the doctor. "I'm sure people throughout the MediCenter are jealous of Blair— *Director Scott's*—quick rise."

"Yes," the doctor mused. "That must be it."

Heat had engulfed the young soldier and turned his cheeks

crimson. It was a wonderful tell. Normandy made a mental note to add it to his collection.

"But do keep tabs on the matter," Normandy instructed. "If the rumors hold any ounce of truth, we should like to remind the new director exactly who she's working for."

Owens's nod was tight. "If that's all—"

"You do not relieve yourself, Major," Normandy said, wagging his finger in the air. "Only I give you permission to go." He held up his bony hand as the major opened his mouth to retort. "Nothing is more important than the tasks I have for you. The first being one you seem to have misunderstood." Normandy quelled his rage with a deep inhale as he dragged his finger along the rim of his mug. "You had two of your . . ."

Goons.

"Men," Normandy said, camouflaging his first choice with another, "attempt to move the package."

Owens cocked his head. "The girl?"

Normandy blinked. "What other package have I left in your care?"

"I thought—"

"That was your first mistake," Normandy interjected. "You're not here to think. Leave that to me."

The major nodded in the tight, soldierly way Normandy appreciated more than any words the young man could have uttered. Believing words mattered more than actions was a flaw. A flaw he would one day correct.

"When I give you a task, no one else is to know about it much less complete it on your behalf."

Again, Owens opened his mouth to speak and again Normandy's gesture silenced him.

"Major, what was it that I said earlier about trust?"

This time, Major Rhett Owens remained silent.

Normandy smiled. Owens may not be the brightest soldier, indeed he was not as intelligent as Sparkman, but he got the point eventually.

"That brings us to the Benavidez girl."

Another tight swallow and uncomfortable shift as Owens resumed staring at the wall behind the doctor.

"We need leverage," Normandy said, scooting his mug over to the kettle. "A way to push her in the right direction."

Owens's gaze cut to the doctor. "We can track her through her implant. Leverage isn't needed."

"It's not about where she's located." Normandy steepled his fingers and rested them against his chin. "The Council Leader's first virtual program ended . . . *unsuccessfully*. He's begun another round with a different subject, but it will most likely end the same, and it is still imperative that we learn everything there is to know about Eos and what information Miss Benavidez is harboring."

And what they have discovered from the lieutenant colonel.

He wouldn't share that worry with the soldier. If Major Owens did his job, Normandy would soon find out what information his former assistant had leaked.

"Then we bring Elodie in and question her. I can get her to talk. We don't need—"

"*We?*" Normandy spat. "You throw the word about as if you and I are on the same playing field. I assure you, Major, we are not even participating in the same sport. You do what I ask, when I ask. That is your duty. Leave the thinking to me."

Major Owens offered another submissive nod.

"I'm surprised you have not yet learned that coercion is a delicate art best achieved without the use of brute force." The room was silent for a moment as Normandy mulled over his options. He was the most intelligent man he knew, and the absolute best at hatching a plan. A grin tickled the corners of his lips as a plot unfolded in front of him. "Miss Benavidez's mother."

Rhett's brow furrowed. "She doesn't know where Elodie is. Besides, we can track El's implant."

"But a daughter would do anything she could to save her mother." Normandy removed his glasses and buffed slow circles along his lenses with the corner of his lab coat. "And if Mrs. Benavidez is left shunned by her daughter, or even if using her to reach Elodie goes as well as I desire, she will be the perfect candidate for my next round of trials. Everyone will assume that she, the mother of a traitor, is missing because of her daughter's dealings with the Eos terrorists." He nodded to himself. This ordeal would end up producing an even better result than he'd expected. "No one will miss her. Especially not her husband. He's been regretting their Match for years."

Owens's cheeks paled as he took a step closer to Normandy's desk. "Doctor, I understand you want to take down Eos. We have the same goal. But you don't have to bring Gwen into this. She's not responsible for what Elodie did. *I* didn't even see it coming. She doesn't deserve—"

Normandy slammed his fist against his desk. The kettle shook and his tea sloshed over the edge of his cup. "Do what I say or answer to the Council for your insurrection. I'm sure they will not look so favorably upon you during a second trial, especially since Blair Scott made such a mockery of your abilities."

Owens stepped back, his arms rigid at his side. "Yes, sir. It won't happen again, sir."

"Good. Now leave. Fetch Mrs. Benavidez and bring her to me." His nerves settled as Owens nodded. "And won't it be so nice for her to see a familiar face?"

The major's cheeks flamed again as he offered another rigid nod and made his retreat.

Normandy set his glasses on the table and rubbed his eyes. He was so close to creating the perfect soldier. He would only have to suffer fools a bit longer.

XXVI

The gauzy pinks and blues of twilight cloaked the sky as Elodie emerged from the tunnel. Sparkman and Thea each engaged their Violet Shields before they pushed forward. Elodie did the same, the protective light encasing her in a bubble of purple as she followed the pair whose footsteps were featherlight against the pavement while they silently wove around stocky apartment buildings. Gone were the tall, gleaming buildings of Zone One and the sprawling suburbs of Zone Two. They had made it to Zone Three. The living quarters clustered together like beehives made that much clear.

Elodie had only visited this zone once. When she was little, Gwen had taken her to one of the many beige-brick apartment buildings to visit an old friend. She had waited on the swing set in one of the small playgrounds peppered throughout the complexes while her mother went inside. Not long after, Gwen emerged, her eyes puffy and red. She'd said they would never come back to the disgusting and cheap hovels of Zone Three, and they hadn't.

"This one." Sparkman motioned to the closest building.

The color of the brick was just as Elodie remembered, but that was the only thing that matched her memories of Zone Three. In her mind, the brick was crumbled and weathered and the grass patchy and brown. But this building—Elodie turned and her attention floated from one building to the next—*all* the buildings were well cared for with verdant lawns, rows of budding roses, and benches shaded by the delicate purple leaves of plum trees.

It was interesting how her mother's opinion and the sharp words she'd used that day had eaten away at the truth until it was tattered, dirty, and damaged.

Elodie chewed her bottom lip as she followed Thea through the sliding glass door and into the high ceiling and polished concrete interior of the apartment lobby. Keeping her muddy shoes in mind, she carefully stepped around the plush rugs and honey-gold furniture that filled the space with warmth and comfort—a far cry from the sterile whites, cheerless grays, and cold porcelains of her mother's home.

The elevator opened as they approached, and Sparkman lowered her cap, casting an even deeper shadow over her eyes.

"Six," she instructed the machine.

The doors closed, and the elevator whirred to life, depositing the trio on the sixth floor. The same rich hues and soft carpeting spilled into this level as well, and Elodie took care not to leave behind a trail of grime she'd collected on her shoes while tromping through the wet, dirty tunnels that ran under the city.

When they reached the end of the hall, Thea scanned her cuff beneath the reader for apartment 6116. It flashed green, and the wood-paneled door opened with a soft *hiss*. The three clicked off their Violet Shields as they entered. The high ceilings continued inside, exposing wooden beams and metal pipes that snaked above the single open room. In the far-left corner was a small kitchen with steel cabinets and appliances. A large steel table with matching chairs and a cot were the room's only furniture. Thea turned on the overhead lights as Sparkman walked to the back wall of floor-to-ceiling windows and closed the burlap drapes.

"Is this your apartment?" Elodie asked Sparkman as she gave the drapes a final tug.

The lieutenant colonel pressed her finger to her lips and nodded to Thea who pulled a clear plastic ball from her satchel. She tossed it into the air. As it neared the ceiling, it let out a shrill ring and a blinding flash of neon-green light.

"Buffered," Thea announced as she opened the mouth of her bag and caught the orb as it fell. "If the Key has any mics or cameras nearby, they won't be able to see or hear us. For all intents and purposes, while within these four walls, we don't exist."

Elodie had spent time in VR not existing to the outside world, and it had been the best moments of her life.

A chair scraped against the floor as Sparkman took a seat at the head of the table. "This is one of Eos's safe houses. No one lives here, but anyone can stay or come for help if they're in trouble."

Thea dropped her satchel onto the table. "Let's not waste time with details," she said, eyeing Elodie as she sat.

Let's not waste time with me.

That's what Thea had meant by *details*. She'd honored her sister, done what Astrid would have wanted, and now she had no more energy left for the girl who'd blown up everyone's life because she was too busy following one guy's promise of happiness instead of creating her own. Elodie didn't blame her. It sounded as pathetic as she felt.

Elodie smoothed the collar of her T-shirt between her fingers as she walked to the other side of the table, sliding into the cold metal seat across from Thea. She hadn't wanted to sit next to the eldest Fujimoto and feel the waves of hate shoot from her skin like quills, but she instantly regretted sitting opposite her. Hostile energy was better than the resentful gaze Thea currently pinned her with.

Thea's bag vibrated, and she dug through its contents, finally releasing her scowl to focus on her holopad. "Just got a note from Racer." She swallowed, glancing up at Sparkman. "You were made."

The air thickened as Sparkman inhaled deeply and pressed her fists together, cracking each knuckle.

Elodie felt the weight of the words, but their meaning took a moment to click. "You can't go back." Her fingers flew to her lips as she took a sharp inhale of her own. "Not to the Medi-Center, or Zone One, your home . . ."

Sparkman took off her cap and set it on the table. "It was a matter of time," she said, her throat tightening.

"Where will you go?" Panic sharpened Elodie's voice. She'd had momentum, someone pushing her forward, but now . . . Now she had time, stillness. Her thoughts swirled, and her heart raced. She couldn't go back, either.

Sparkman brushed her braid from her broad shoulder. "One step at a time, Elodie. Each move forward sheds light on new opportunities."

Elodie couldn't imagine any step would lead them back into the Key's favor. Even if it did, she wouldn't accept. No matter how much she missed the comforts of the life she knew, she couldn't go back into the dark after bathing in the light.

Sparkman rapped her knuckles on the table as if signifying the close of that topic and the beginning of a new one. "Any luck finding Echo?"

Thea's dark hair brushed against her collarbones as she shook her head. "Racer's on it, but she hasn't found anything yet. I'll know the second she does." The bright screen of her holopad gleamed in her dark eyes as she typed out a message. "The Key has buried Echo deep."

Each of Elodie's breaths was a rainstorm against her eardrums. "Echo—" Her throat constricted, and her tongue felt like paste as she forced the words out. "Echo's dead."

Sparkman's gaze snapped to her. "Where did you hear that?"

Elodie wheezed, strangled by the memories flashing behind her eyes. "I saw it. I was there when Cath confessed to being Echo. I was there when—" The words caught in her throat as the memory of gunfire cracked between her ears. "I was there when she died."

The legs of Sparkman's chair screeched against the floor as she shoved back from the table. "Cath Scott was Echo," she murmured, bracing her hands against her thighs.

"You didn't know?" Elodie croaked, anguish burning her throat.

Thea sniffled and cast her gaze to the ceiling. "No one did."

"It's part of what keeps everyone protected," Sparkman said, her head hanging like a wilted rose blossom. "No one member of Eos knows the names of all the others, and only those with a certain clearance level know who sits on the Eos board."

Tears stung Elodie's eyes, and she flinched with the memory of Cath's blood splattering against her cheeks. "She died protecting you. Protecting everyone in Eos."

It didn't make Cath's death any better or the loss hurt any less. There was nothing she could say that would.

Sparkman cleared her throat. "We have to keep moving forward."

That seemed to be the lieutenant colonel's answer for everything. Elodie understood. Life was less painful when barreling ahead.

"There is a plan in place," Sparkman continued. "We just have to follow it."

"It's too late for that." Thea flattened her hands against the table and stood. "Last year alone, eleven of our members had *accidents*. Now Echo is dead, you've been made, no one knows the status of Normandy's project, and Aiden Scott is trapped inside the MediCenter." She paused, pinning her dark gaze on Sparkman. "You know as well as I do that it doesn't matter how strong he is. It's only a matter of time before they get him to talk."

Elodie's chest squeezed, and she swallowed the wail that scratched at her throat.

"We don't have time to stick to a plan that will take another year to achieve." Thea crossed her arms over her chest. "Not to mention that that was the timeline that Echo had set. Without her . . ." She let her words trail off, shaking her head. "Power is supposed to belong to the people, not to a corporation. We've been lied to for far too long. It's time to take our city back."

The sentiment was thrilling, but *back* implied that the people had had Westfall to begin with. *Back* implied that there had been a before—a time when citizens were in power and designed a city, a country, a world that served them best—but that had never been the case. Not for all people.

Elodie waded into the charged silence, unsure if she'd earned her place within this conversation. "How? The Key is powerful.

You can't just go outside and tell other citizens that the corporation they've relied on their entire life is evil. Without proof, no one will believe you. Plus, the Key will have you arrested—sent to Rehabilitation—or worse."

Sparkman crossed her ankle over her opposite knee and mirrored Thea's folded arms with her own. "There are many ways to make things known. Give the citizens *proof*, as you said," she mused. "If anyone can get people to listen without putting a target on her back, it would be Thea."

"I am a Fujimoto, after all. Any doors the Key has closed, my name can open."

The glint in Thea's eyes warmed Elodie's chest. She knew it well. She'd seen Astrid's eyes light up the same way countless times. Thea had come up with an infallible plan.

"And even better than opening doors, being a Fujimoto has taught me the art of opening wallets. Closing them, too." She lifted her chin, stretching her long, slender neck. "As my father says, *control the money, and you control the beast.*"

Elodie joined the duo and crossed her arms over her chest. "But cut off the money, and you'll kill it."

For the first time, Thea smiled. It was mischievous and daring and sparked deep within her eyes. "It's time that they knew. It's time that *everyone* knew." She tossed up her hands. "It's not like we have anything left to lose."

Elodie's gaze swept over the women who had saved her, given her a second chance. Their losses hadn't made them bitter. They had shed their grief until there was nothing left to hold them back. There was a type of freedom in only having yourself to look out for. A power that stared caution in the eyes and knew it would win, despite the warning.

"We still need a figurehead—someone like Echo for the elite to divert their funds to," Sparkman said, resting her wide chin on her fist. "None of your contacts will be willing to pull their support from the corporation without putting it behind someone they believe will serve them better, no matter how impressive your argument or true your facts. A new leader . . ." Sparkman's brow furrowed with silent contemplation. "That's the only way a coup will work. After that's in place, we focus on Cerberus."

Elodie's gaze bounced from one woman to the next as she waited for them to elaborate. But the two remained silent, pondering next steps.

"What about Cerberus?" she asked in a rush.

Thea blinked at her. "It no longer exists," she said matter-of-factly. "The Key eradicated the virus decades ago."

Elodie wasn't surprised. Aiden had told her a version of this after he'd kissed her, when his hands had roamed over her skin like the thirsty in search of water. If Cerberus was still active, still spread by touch, she would already be dead.

"That day at the fair . . ." Elodie's brow wrinkled with further realization. "I expected the Key to come arrest me, but they didn't. They waited until the next day to find me. When Astrid and I were in VR and—" She stared down at her hands, unable to look at Thea.

Sparkman cleared her throat, saving them from the memories and the awkward words that weighed down Elodie's tongue. "They were never concerned with Cerberus. They were worried about control."

"The corporation has to keep its citizens scared so they stay docile," Thea added, her voice a little more fragile than it had been before. "They want us to feel like we can't survive without them."

Elodie picked at the jagged edge of her fingernail. "How many people know?"

With a shrug, Thea glanced at Sparkman. "Not enough."

And out of those, how many actually cared?

Not everyone wanted the same kind of freedom. Certain people thrived under the weight of the Key. The corporation had given its citizens structure and rules. They had eliminated the critical thought and responsibility required to live a life of choice. In erasing the power for each person to make their own decisions, they'd also taken away hope and desire, spontaneity and the thrill of not knowing exactly what waited ahead. Some people didn't need those things to feel complete. Some people . . . like her mom.

Elodie swallowed back the waves of guilt that surged up her throat as she thought about her mother. Gwen was probably worried sick. And real worry, too. Not some fabricated tizzy that she performed for attention.

The Key was shrouded in lies. Which of them had they told Gwen about her daughter?

Thea scooped her bag off the table and slung the strap over her shoulder. "The loss of Echo is too big. Someone will step in to fill it. Until then, I can get the word out." She gave Sparkman a tight nod and didn't look at Elodie as she turned and headed toward the door.

"Not everyone will believe you." Elodie couldn't keep from calling after her.

Thea's determined footsteps halted. "It's not about that," she said over her shoulder. "It's about doing what's right."

"You sound like Astrid." Elodie winced, wishing she could catch the words as they fell from her lips.

Thea brushed her hand along her cheek and cleared her throat. "I like to think that Astrid sounded like me."

The door opened, and Thea activated her Violet Shield as she disappeared into the hall.

The safe-room door slid shut as a gray messaging box formed across Elodie's vision. She hadn't wanted to send a message to anyone. In truth, she had no one left to talk to.

The Key's red logo unfurled, and Holly's face filled the vidlink screen. The hologram's hair was as curly and full as it had been when Elodie had spied her at the MediCenter, but up close, she looked more like Blair than she ever had before. Maybe Aiden had been right when he'd said that Blair only cared about her job. She had to be obsessed with the Key and its power to slowly transform Holly into herself.

"Hello, Elodie."

Elodie's heart slammed against her ribs as the hologram unleashed that perfect, unassuming grin she used to dazzle the masses and put everyone at ease—almost everyone.

"The Key would like you to come home."

Elodie tensed her jaw to keep her teeth from clacking.

Sparkman tilted her head, her long braid swaying as she squinted at Elodie. "Are you okay?"

Elodie couldn't tear her gaze from Holly. The corporation had invaded this safe space. They hadn't found her—they couldn't after what Thea had done—but they were still with her.

Holly blinked slowly, calmly, as if waiting for Elodie to drift off to sleep and return to the dream of New Dawn. "There's someone else who would like you to come back, too."

The hologram stepped to the side, and Elodie's breath escaped in a strangled cry.

Even though Holly was in the room, it didn't seem as if her mother could see her. Gwen's expertly coiffured hair didn't budge as she shook her head and wrung her hands, and her sky-blue pantsuit was crisp and clean and perfectly pressed as she sat in a metal chair in the middle of a stark-white room, a row of black X's on the wall behind her.

Elodie stiffened. Her mother wasn't in just any room. This was the room where Elodie had awoken in the basement level of the MediCenter. Unless employed by the MediCenter, people who were taken downstairs didn't usually come back up.

"They have my mom." Elodie's voice was a dry, shaky bark.

"The Key?" Sparkman shook her head. "She doesn't know where you are. The corporation wouldn't apprehend her without—"

"I'm looking at her."

Sparkman's green gaze took in the room around them. "Right now?"

"Holly called me." Elodie's swallow clunked within her throat as she watched Holly, as still and lifeless as a bot. "The Key has my mom."

Holly glanced at Gwen before turning back to Elodie. "Everything can go back to the way it was. No one else has to get hurt. You only have to come back home."

"Don't hurt her!" Elodie's lungs squeezed as she shouted. "She doesn't know anything."

Sparkman was talking, shouting, but her words melted away, turning to thunder as they reached Elodie.

Holly pursed her lips and they thinned into a straight line.

"You know as well as I do that this is about so much more than what your mother does or doesn't know." She clasped her hands in front of her and reaffixed her placid smile. "Every action has a consequence."

The hologram disappeared, leaving Elodie to watch her mother rise from the chair to pace back and forth.

Sparkman's boots pounded the concrete in perfect time to Elodie's hammering heart. Calloused fingers grazed her neck, brushing back her hair and gliding over the scar behind her right ear.

The lieutenant colonel spoke again, her words booming like a storm against Elodie's ears as she again focused on her mother. The door to the white room slid open. Elodie's breath caught as Rhett strode in.

"The doctor is on his way." He didn't look at Gwen as he spoke. Instead, his chin tipped down and his gaze roamed the pristine floor. "I'm sorry."

Gwen took a tentative step forward. "Sorry? For what?"

Rhett didn't look up as he stepped back through the open doorway.

"For what?" Gwen's shout was punctuated by the sharp *click clack* of her stilettos against the tile as she hurried toward the closing door. It shut before she could reach it, sealing her inside the same room Elodie had woken up in.

"You told me I would see her!" Gwen's palm slapped the door. "Where is my daughter?"

"Mom! I'm right here!" Elodie's chest tightened with a sob. But it was no use. Her mother couldn't hear or see her and had been kept so far away from the truth that she might as well be on another planet.

"I trusted you, Rhett!" Gwen shouted, pummeling the steel with open hands. "But you're a coward. Elodie saw it in you. You never would have made her happy." Her voice cracked as her anger shattered. "I should have listened." She sagged against the door, but it didn't keep her from sliding to the tile. "And now she's gone."

The feed cut out.

"No!" Elodie surged to her feet as the gray box dissolved and her vision cleared.

Sparkman was next to her, steadying her as she swayed on her feet.

"They're going to do something terrible." Tears fell hot against her cheeks as she clung to Sparkman's outstretched arms for support. Elodie hadn't thought her mother would be in danger. Gwendolyn Benavidez always followed the rules—she didn't have anything the Key wanted. "We have to get my mom out of there. Her and Aiden."

"First, we have to correct one of Aiden's mistakes," Sparkman ground out.

Elodie stepped back, brows pinched. "What did he—" Elodie swallowed the rest of her question as light glinted off the sharpened point of the knife Sparkman clutched in her hand.

"When you join Eos, your implant is supposed to be removed so you can't be tracked or manipulated by the Key."

Elodie's calves hit her chair as she took another step back. "I didn't join Eos." She felt foolish saying it aloud while in an Eos safe house with a woman so deep within the organization that she could no longer go back to her old life.

Sparkman ignored Elodie's comment, saying, "The implant isn't there to keep tabs on your health and make your life easier.

It never has been. It's there to give the Key control. With it, they can monitor your every move. They can track you. No doubt they're trying to right now. It's a miracle they haven't found you already. But they will."

Elodie's chair scraped against the floor as she waded backward, unable to take her eyes from Sparkman's blade. "There has to be another way."

Sparkman shook her head. "There isn't one. The only solution is to remove your implant. With it in, we have no hope of ever saving your mother or Aiden from the Key."

Elodie rubbed her finger along the X-shaped scar that had been with her since she was delivered from the gestation pod. "Will it hurt?"

Sparkman said nothing as she walked to the kitchen and removed a handful of dish towels from a drawer before tapping the faucet to turn it on.

Elodie swallowed. There was no way around it. She was either committed, truly committed, body-and-soul committed, willing-to-die committed, or she might as well deliver herself to the Key.

"You can always go back," Sparkman said, as if she could read Elodie's thoughts.

Elodie stared at the blade as Sparkman passed it under the stream of steaming tap water. A sudden rush of calm washed over her—the serenity of making a choice and knowing it was right.

Her breathing steadied and her heart relaxed back into its normal rhythm as she dragged her chair over to the sink.

"Can't say you're not one of us now," Sparkman said, drying her hands.

Elodie fisted her hand over her chest and bowed the same

way the Eos soldiers had outside of the ELU on the day that had changed her life forever.

Sparkman returned the gesture with a nod, her mouth sliding into a crooked half smile.

Elodie sat down and stared at a thin crack on the opposite wall, and when the knife pierced her skin, she didn't even blink.

XXVII

Preston didn't bother using the button that would flash the lights inside Normandy's office. Instead, he passed his cuff beneath the access panel and let himself in. After all, there were no offices or rooms within the MediCenter that he wasn't allowed access.

The door slid open, and Normandy didn't look up from the holopad on his desk or the glossy printed photos that surrounded it. The doctor was lost in his own world.

Preston crossed his arms over his chest and leaned against the metal doorframe. Cocking his head, he studied Normandy as his fingers pecked the hologram's keys as if it was his first experience with a keyboard. The old man had an aversion to technology that Preston would never understand. It was one of the reasons Normandy no longer fit with this world.

Too bad he hadn't been with my father at the end. Maybe Clifton would have pulled the doctor down the stairs with him.

Then again, Preston's father would never have done his son such a favor.

"If this is the way you enter a room, it's no wonder you have so few friends." Normandy spoke without looking up or changing the pace at which he worked.

Preston pushed himself away from the doorjamb, his annoyance with Normandy's quip easing as he envisioned the old man tumbling down the marble staircase of his Zone One estate. "Aiden Scott's implant is irreparably damaged."

Normandy released a beleaguered sigh and turned his attention to the printed photos, stacking them into two neat piles. "Why don't you do as before and replace it with one that is functioning?"

"With the recent breach, moving him to a surgical suite is too much of a risk," Preston said, flicking a speck of lint from his sleeve.

"Then bring the surgical suite to him." Normandy finished sorting the pictures and leaned back in his chair. "Honestly, Preston, it's concerning that you're unable to come up with these solutions on your own."

Preston's jaw hardened. "I'm not looking for your assistance. I have it quite under control."

Normandy removed his glasses and carefully set them between the two stacks of photos. "This new virtual reality session was supposed to be *the one*. Or is that not how you phrased it in your most recent message?"

Preston's stomach heated. He should have known better than to come here. He was a fool for believing that inspiration would strike while in the doctor's presence, but he'd needed a distraction from Holly and the basement labs and the frustration of half-completed projects. "As with any science, there are setbacks."

"This is not a setback. This is the end." Normandy tented his fingers and nailed his gaze to Preston's. "What more can the boy offer you?"

Blair.

Preston's stomach squeezed.

He would never allow Normandy to know that she was his motivator, his endgame, his reason for being.

Preston crossed his arms over his chest and leveled his own stare at the doctor. "He has answers about Eos. Their leader was his mother. No doubt she's the one who got him involved. I'm sure he was privy to all types of important information."

"There are other ways to get answers," Normandy mused as he glided his fingers along the edge of a stack of photos. "I myself have found one."

The doctor narrowed his eyes. A challenge that made Preston's toes clench in his boots.

"Give the boy to me. He can be of use in testing the final updates to the dose."

Preston's mouth went dry. Releasing Aiden would be giving up his advantage over Blair, the best one he'd ever had. "I only came to update you on my progress as you have done with yours."

"You came for more than that." Normandy lifted his glasses and wiped the lenses on the arm of his lab coat. "A simple update such as this could have been done via message, yet you came to deliver the news, or lack thereof, in person." He settled the frames on the tip of his nose and continued to glare at Preston over the lenses. "You want me to tell you that you haven't made a mistake, that everything will be okay as long as you stay the course." He pushed his glasses into place. "I do not give out awards for participation. You failed. However, your failure can be remedied. Simply turn the boy over and see your embarrassment transformed into success."

Preston's fingers itched to snatch the doctor's spectacles and crush them in his grip. "Aiden Scott is mine."

His sister, too.

"I have not failed." Preston lowered his arms to his sides, clenching his hands into fists so tight his knuckles ached.

And I'll prove it.

Before Normandy had the chance to respond, Preston stormed from the office. Visiting the old man hadn't been a waste of time, after all. Indeed, it had been just what Preston needed to spur him forward.

As he waited for the elevator to arrive and return him to the basement, he brought up the latest series of messages he'd received from his special team within the Research and Development Lab.

The Key had apprehended Eos members in the past and Preston knew that each traitor had had their implant removed upon joining. He also knew that the reimplantation process was costly and came with its own set of complications. To be most effective, the gentech device needed time to grow into its host and learn the brain's neurological patterns. Without the proper amount of time, the implant faltered, sending incomplete or incorrect information to both the host and the corporation. That had happened with Aiden, and Preston couldn't run the risk of it happening again.

"Holly." He paused, stepping into the open elevator and waiting for the hologram to materialize by his side. Although she was nothing more than light and a manipulation of the mind, he swore he felt her form next to him. "Have R&D prepare the device for its first test subject."

The device discussed within the messages was still unnamed and would most likely stay so until he revealed it to those within the MediCenter deserving of the knowledge of his latest achievement.

"In Dr. Tetch's last report, he stated that it would not be ready for human testing for at least ninety days," she said.

Preston closed his eyes and listened to the *whoosh* of the elevator and its soft metallic creaks as it descended to the base of the building. The hairs along his arm rose. She was staring at him, soaking up the information that rolled from his skin in waves of heat.

"I will contact R&D and have them prepare it straightaway."

The elevator stopped and Preston opened his eyes. Holly was gone and an incoming call notification from Dr. Tetch scrolled across the bottom of his vision.

XXVIII

Aiden ran his fingernails along his neck, scraping the dried blood from his skin. The Key had yet to try any new tactics since his implant malfunctioned and Eos had found a way to pull him from his drug-induced trip to VR. He relaxed against his stiff mattress and clasped his hands behind his head. Somewhere within the walls of the MediCenter, frustrated lab coats rushed around trying to figure out precisely why his implant wasn't working and exactly what they could do to get it back online.

"You'll have to come force it back in yourselves," Aiden grumbled and cut his gaze to the camera installed in the corner of his room.

There was a quiet *click* and then a hiss like a thousand Medi-Center doors opening.

His lungs itched and he coughed as he bolted from his bed, his gaze narrowing on the closed door. Fog rolled into the room, a mist that rose from the floor. His vision blurred and the floor seemed to fall out from under him. He was on his back, staring up through the gas that hovered above him like puffy white clouds.

A shadow approached, its face distorted by a shiny plastic mask. It crouched next to him, its tie grazing Aiden's cheek like a cold hand.

"He's ready." The voice was a muffled shout underwater as Aiden succumbed to the waves of unconsciousness pulling him under.

XXIX

Preston stepped back as two bots motored into the room, scooped Aiden up, and deposited him onto the gurney waiting in the hall. Preston followed them out, removing his gas mask and tossing it onto the metal cart next to the unconscious body as the door to Aiden's room closed behind him.

The walk to the private R&D lab was short. In fact, if it wouldn't appear like a demotion, Preston would move his office down to the basement with the rest of his secret projects. Although, close proximity might not keep his experiments secret for long.

The door to the lab opened, and Dr. Tetch turned his attention from the massive three-wall control panel to the bots that wheeled Aiden into the room.

The still unnamed device sat in the middle of the space like the pilot's seat of an old passenger airliner. In fact, that's where the skeleton of Dr. Tetch's device had taken its inspiration.

"They might as well fly in style while on their VR trip."

He'd made the whole experience sound like a vacation when, in fact, any person unlucky enough to be strapped into the padded chair would end up wishing for death.

"It's ready." Dr. Tetch dug his fingers into his unkempt beard and tugged on a few unruly strands. "Or as ready as it can be this early and on such short notice."

Preston straightened his tie as he waited for the bots to place Aiden in the seat and fasten his restraints. "The Key appreciates your efforts, Doctor."

"I have to admit I am a little jazzed to see it in action." The dark shadows beneath Tetch's eyes were like bruises in the bright fluorescent lights as he squinted at the bots and their metal pincers busy positioning the test subject. "Like, twenty percent jazzed and eighty percent terrified."

Preston was one hundred percent intrigued. "You don't think it will work?"

"No, I know it will. I just don't have confidence that his brain won't leak through his nose after we're done." Preston cast him a sideways glance, and Dr. Tetch hiked his rounded shoulders. "Yeah, that's not real science, but you know what I mean. This could go . . ." He stuffed his hands into his lab coat and pooched out his soft chin. "*Badly* is the only word that's coming to mind."

Preston stiffened. "Could the subject expire?"

As much as he wanted to prove Normandy wrong and suffocate the old man with his findings, it all meant nothing if he lost Blair's brother in the process.

"He won't die, if that's what you mean." Another shrug. "But there's a chance he could be left as a wet noodle of a person."

The bots finished, and the empty gurney creaked as they wheeled it from the room.

"Let's proceed." The only thing Preston needed from Aiden was for him to be alive.

Tetch clapped and waddled to the middle wall of the control panel. His hands flew across the keys and Aiden's vitals appeared on the wall to the left as a diagram of the device took up the space in front of the doctor.

A series of beeps sounded, and a ceiling hatch opened. Preston's pulse sped as a mechanical arm unfolded and reached down until its oval tip, the size of Preston's shoe, was in line with the back of Aiden's head.

"Let's get this show on the road!" Tetch cheered as he entered another series of commands into the control panel.

Two tentacles sprouted from each side of the oblong device. They slapped the air like wild snakes until one found Aiden's shoulder. It calmed the others, calling them to the test subject. They slithered up his neck, along his cheeks, and paused beneath his nostrils. Key Corp–red flashed from the body and tracked down each feeler. They shivered, receiving instruction, and then plunged into Aiden's nose.

XXX

Aiden's head felt fuzzy. He rubbed his eyes with his left hand and blinked back the cloudy film that coated his vision.

Blair's office.

He sucked in a breath as his gaze settled on the gun and his right hand wrapped around its grip.

"Please, Aiden." Tears glossed Cath's cheeks and her gaze frantically searched Blair's office, landing on Elodie then Blair. The two wore similar twisted expressions of terror as they cowered next to Blair's solid stone desk. "I'll tell you whatever you want to know. You don't have to do this."

"I don't?" He'd been here before with Cath and Blair and Elodie.

Is this how it ended?

His left hand flew to his forehead. His brain was stuffed with cotton. He couldn't focus, couldn't remember, couldn't think.

A whimper escaped Elodie's lips, and she clapped her hands over her mouth to quiet her cries.

"No." Cath's tangled curls shuddered as she shook her head. "I love you, Aiden. We can figure this out."

No matter how hard he tried, he couldn't move his right arm or lower the weapon. His darkness had taken hold and would destroy them all. "I don't deserve your love."

Cath stepped forward and extended a trembling hand. "Oh, my boy—"

"*Wonder Boy . . .*"

"You do."

"*You have a purpose.*" Tavi's voice clattered between his ears like armor. "*Don't trust them. Don't trust anyone.*"

"This isn't real." He blinked, and the gun vanished. "None of this is real."

Cath's features twisted and the room around him quaked before folding in on itself like a crumpled sheet of paper.

White light burned his eyes and a heavy slickness glided across his upper lip.

"A few kinks to work out," came an unfamiliar voice.

Aiden squinted and a floor-to-ceiling control panel came into view. "Where am I?" His head pounded as he took in the three walls of tech and the portly man who seemed to be in control of it all.

"Not a noodle person." The man's brows lifted as he scratched the stomach of his lab coat. "So, I'd call that a win."

Footsteps clicked on the tile behind Aiden. He tried to turn, but the plastic restraints over his wrists and ankles kept him in place.

"It most definitely was not a failure." The Council Leader came into view, a smile playing at his lips.

Aiden's heart slammed against his ribs, but he managed to

keep his voice steady as he spoke. "Guess I beat another one of your VR traps. You really need to up your game."

Cocking his head, Darby adjusted his tie as he took position directly in front of Aiden. "You could always save yourself and tell me what I want to know."

Aiden swallowed. This wasn't Rehabilitation. This was a fact-finding mission. As soon as the Key got what it wanted, they would dispose of him.

They might as well get it over with.

He'd keep his promise to Tavi, to Eos. He would never tell the organization's secrets. Not in this life or a virtual one.

"I don't answer to you."

"No, you answer to Eos, correct? To Echo?" The Council Leader stepped closer, and Aiden had to look up to meet his gaze. "Only, she's gone. But you remember that, right?"

Aiden's jaw tensed and his grip tightened around the chair's cushy armrests.

"You have to, with how much of her the bots were forced to scrub from your skin. Is that what pulled you out of this round?" Darby stared down at him, his dark eyes shining in the bright lights. "Dr. Tetch needs to catalogue all the information he can if he wants it to be perfect next time."

The restraints groaned, straining to keep Aiden in place as he flexed beneath them. He could tear through the plastic and through Darby as well. Not because the Council Leader was short and Aiden tall. No, Darby's height was misleading. It was clear from the tight fit of his suit and the thickness of his neck that he was built solid. But Aiden was a bullet, on a single trajectory to protect Eos and the people he loved. And he would use his last ounce of goodness to rip Preston Darby to pieces.

The Council Leader's nose wrinkled as an empty chuckle clanged in the air around him. "I know what you're thinking. You better be sure you can finish the job before Dr. Tetch alerts the soldiers."

Aiden's gaze flicked from Darby to the doctor and back again. Without a weapon, did he have enough time to end Preston? Did he even have what it took, or would his darkness abandon him, only unleashing itself when it sensed goodness nearby?

Darby bent over, his face inches from Aiden's. "Keep in mind, little brother, if I can do this to you, imagine what I can do to Blair." His tongue slid across his bottom lip. "With my VR programs, I could make her open to just about anything."

Anger and fear swirled into one and settled like a steel ball in Aiden's stomach. He might not be able to stop Darby from hurting him or his sister, but he could buy them both some time.

He halted his struggle against the binds and leveled his gaze at the Council Leader. "You want info? You'll have to work for it."

XXXI

The Poppy had worn off hours ago. The fuzzy warmth that had wrapped everything around Blair in its own neon glow was now replaced with the cold chill of the truth—she had loved Cath, and Blair had sold her life, her soul, to a corporation and all she had to show for it was lies.

She clasped her arms around her torso, shivering as she stared out the floor-to-ceiling windows of her office and down at the street below. Citizens walked along the brick-lined pavement, their Violet Shields bobbing with each step.

How many of them know?

The thought sent another gush of ice water through her veins, and she hugged her arms tighter around herself and squeezed.

Blair had sped through life, trying so hard not to be reminded of the past that she had missed what was in her present. She was a smart woman. She could have figured out the Key's lies, but she had made sure she was closed off to anyone's truth. She'd only ever had time and space for her own. That's why Cath had let her stay alone in the dark, her only comforts the accolades and advancements that were now as hollow as a dried bone. Her adoptive mother had known Blair wouldn't believe her. She had also known what Blair was only beginning to figure out—power didn't come from stubbornness and ire. Power, *real* power, was born from knowledge. The knowledge of the truth, knowing when to use it, and who to entrust it to.

She eyed her reflection and tentatively pressed her palm to the glass. She'd never touched another person, never thought she would. What would it be like?

Behind her, the door hissed open.

Blair sighed. Next time, she'd have to remember to lock it.

"Sorry for the intrusion, Director Scott."

Rhett's introduction struck her back as she stared at his reflection in the window.

"I don't have an appointment," he continued, combing his fingers through his closely cropped hair. "Ms. Wyndham wasn't at her desk, and your door wasn't locked so I . . ."

He trailed off as Blair drummed her fingers against the window. "Let's hope this isn't the start of a bad habit."

He stepped forward and the door closed behind him. "This couldn't wait. It's too important."

Blair narrowed her eyes at his image ghosted against the glass. Messages weren't often as important to someone else as they were to the person relaying them. There were also a hundred ways to send information. Barging into her office was at the bottom of that list.

"Go ahead, then, Major," she said, turning to face him. "What is so important that it can't wait for a scheduled meeting?"

His Key Corp–red blazer was rumpled, the arms wrinkled, and the front creased as if he'd worn it to battle. "Dr. Normandy knows that you met with members of the Council."

Blair blinked long and slow. Robin wouldn't have said a word to anyone, neither would the other women who were later in attendance. It wasn't worth the risk.

"And who told him that?" She clenched her teeth, trying to hold on to the anger that she was too exhausted to carry and now seemed to drain out of her body, pooling around her feet like a shadow. Rage felt good, intoxicatingly so, but after the quick flash of counterfeit power, it morphed into chains slung around her neck like an albatross.

Rhett's eyes were the sharp gold of a rising sun as he stared at her.

"I did." He stepped closer as if offering himself as apology. "I had to. It's . . ." His gaze roamed her face, peeling away a layer with each smoldering glance. "It's complicated with the doctor."

"You've been spying on me?" Her question came out breathier, more shocked, abandoned, betrayed than she would have liked to reveal.

They hadn't had the best relationship, but she'd felt like they'd reached an understanding. She'd thought they'd shared a mutual attraction. Her heart stuttered as she remembered the last time they'd been in her office together. He'd been so close, so hot and strong. They'd ached for each other. At least, she believed they had. But then, Blair had done her fair share of teasing and misleading to get ahead. Perhaps Rhett had learned something from her after all.

"I haven't." He took another step forward. "I wouldn't." He shook his head. "The MediCenter isn't the best place for secrets.

People talk. When I heard the rumor, I knew it was true. It sounded like something you would do." He inched closer, filling more of the space between them. "Something strong and deliberate that needs to be accomplished."

Rhett was correct. The MediCenter was only good at harboring its own secrets, but the rest, well, Blair didn't know what to say to that. She shifted under his heavy gaze and stared back at him, waiting. For what? She wasn't sure.

Rhett's jaw tightened and his temples pulsed. "There's so much you don't know. Nobody knows. I can't keep—" He stopped. His nostrils flared and the tendons in his neck went rigid as he stared at a spot past her head. "As you're the director, I thought it best to inform you."

He'd transformed right before her eyes. The bits of light that had shined through his cracked facade were again filled with shadows as he reverted to being Major Rhett Owens, the unreachable Key Corp soldier.

"You deserve to know the truth. You've been deserving your entire life."

Cath's words fluttered to life between Blair's ears. No more manipulations. No more tricks or webs or traps. She needed to know the truth. She could handle it. What's more, she could do something about it, because she was exactly what he believed her to be—strong.

Her curls brushed her shoulders as she cocked her head. "Tell me what's wrong."

It wasn't a command or even a request. It was an offering.

Rhett's gaze again found hers. Desire lit his amber eyes, but not the carnal thirst that had burned there before. This was a new kind of ache.

"Blair," he breathed, an offering of his own. Another pause as his mouth moved, searching, wanting, before he said, "I'm a soldier. I'm supposed to protect." He glanced down, motioning to his uniform. "I'm supposed to safeguard Westfall and its citizens from anyone who might do them harm. But Westfall is the Key."

Rhett's breaths were charged heaves, as if he had to wrestle with the air to get it to go down.

"And I don't know how to protect the city from itself."

Her fingers tingled to reach out to him. She could now. She knew that, but how much did he know?

"That's the problem, isn't it?" she asked. "There is no end to one and beginning of the other. They are one and the same, an ouroboros."

They stood in silence for a moment as the weight of their exchange settled around them. They were on the precipice of treason.

Shadows stretched long fingers across the puffy rug as clouds covered the sun.

"That's why you met with Robin Wilson and the others," Rhett said, breaking the silence.

Nodding, Blair smoothed her gloved hand along her arm.

Rhett shifted, his mouth creasing into a thoughtful line as he moved his weight from one foot to the other. "Does she know about the girl?" He swallowed, a heavy clunking noise against the silence of the office. "Do you?"

Her brow wrinkled as she squinted up at him. "What girl?"

"Patient Ninety-Two." He shook his head, his attention falling to the floor. "Elodie tried to tell me about her. I didn't listen. I never listened." He let out a bark of laughter. "Why would I? I thought she was supposed to listen to me. We were supposed to get married, and she would do her job and then come home and wait for me until I got there."

He paused, working his bottom lip between his teeth.

"I would have made a name for us. I would have put us in Zone One. If we could all just follow the rules, we would be happy. Follow the rules and nothing will go wrong."

Was he telling her or reminding himself?

Blair didn't have anything to add. Nothing constructive anyway, nothing he wanted to hear. For her entire life she had followed the rules. It had gotten her a hollow position and an even emptier life. And the bits about Elodie? Well, that they would never agree on.

"It's not supposed to feel this way," he whispered. "*I'm* not supposed to feel this way. It isn't natural."

He blinked up at her, and her heart tripped within her chest. There was fire there, an intensity she had never seen before.

"But when I'm with you—" His breath hitched, and he cleared his throat and took a step back. "These things aren't supposed to happen," he said firmly. "I'm not . . ." His voice trailed off and he shook his head as if the motion was enough to rid himself of feeling.

"The Key," he began again. "They're not supposed to experiment on little girls. Keep them in a box blacked out to the world."

Regardless of her emotions, her need, she couldn't keep quiet. She wouldn't let him get away with his hypocrisy simply because her body warmed and her pulse quickened with desire whenever he was near.

"But that was your plan for Elodie. You wanted to put her in a box and blot out the rest of the world, erase all of her possibilities until the only thing she saw, the only thing she *had* was you."

Blair cocked her head, amazed that he hadn't seen it, afraid that he didn't want to.

"The Key and Westfall share the same sickness, so how can you expect the corporation to act differently from the society who taught you that who you are and what you want matter more than a woman's aspirations?" The blasphemy spilled from her lips like mercury. "The corporation's goals far outweigh the damage they can inflict on one little girl. Like you are valued more highly than Elodie, they have more value than any other citizen."

No matter Blair and Rhett's undefinable connection or the way the air thickened between their hot bodies, she wouldn't be surprised if he took out his cuffs and led her to the Council Leader. As he'd said, he was a soldier of Westfall, of the Key.

"I don't think I'm a good man."

Her heart squeezed. She wasn't sure she'd been a good woman.

"I've been a good soldier," he continued. "But I'm learning that that's a different beast." He paused and stared down at the toes of his shoes. "Do you think she'll forgive me?"

"Elodie?"

He shrugged. "All of them."

"Do you think you'll forgive yourself?"

He looked up at her. "Can you?"

Tears pricked her eyes, and she glanced at the ceiling. Her chin trembled, and her legs itched to bolt from the office and never look back. Not at Rhett or the Key or the mistakes she'd made with her brother and Cath.

"I'm sorry," he whispered, closing the distance between them.

Tears rolled down in hot streams against her cheeks as he stood in front of her, warm and solid. She wanted to collapse against him and share the burden she'd been carrying for so long. With Cath's death and revelations, it had only gotten heavier.

"For so many things. I'm sorry."

Me too, she mouthed, but the words remained unsaid, resting on her lips.

They stood in front of each other, nearly touching. His ragged breaths brushed her cheeks as the heat from his body caressed her skin.

"I can't—" His voice broke, and he shook his head. "I don't want to do this anymore."

Neither do I. Blair trembled, a raw nerve yearning for the safety of his tenderness and warmth.

This world had beaten them until their skin had calloused into a rough shell. But they were soft in the middle, just like the rest. They needed love and patience and kindness. Perhaps that is why they had each developed armor. Not to keep others out, but to keep the dying embers of themselves safe from the blustering winds of the lives they each lived.

Silence wrapped around Blair and Rhett, a velvety cloud that lifted them up and away if only for a moment. She studied him. His eyes glistened with unshed tears and his throat worked to break up the lump that she was sure had formed there. She had one, too. It was a dam that kept the swells of emotions from drowning her. If they both released the boulder barricading their feelings, perhaps they could cling to each other and survive the flood.

"Rhett . . ." Her hand reached for his chest, for any part of him that she could hold on to.

"Blair," he growled, inching closer, tilting his face down to hers.

She closed her eyes and leaned into him, stretching up, up like a bloom to the sun.

She had been wrong before. *This* is what it felt like to fly.

XXXII

Blair had never been kissed. She'd seen it once, in an old magazine that a classmate had smuggled into one of their lessons. The photo had been an advertisement for a watch. Blair and the other students had only been able to stare at the people, their bodies pressed together, arms tangled, parted lips touching. The man had been looking at the camera—looking at her. It had made her stomach swell and flutter in a way that wasn't bad exactly but wasn't good, either. Or rather, wasn't *appropriate*.

She'd reported the rule breaker to the instructor. The next day, the student was gone, shuttled off to a school in Zone Four that was better equipped to help young people in need of a bit of extra guidance, and Blair was named class leader. She'd managed to keep that title nearly every quarter since.

That feeling in her stomach was back. Heat poured down her hips and into her legs, softening her knees.

"Kiss me," she felt herself whisper.

Rhett let out a moan, his hot breath singeing her lips. He

licked his own while his heavy-lidded gaze brushed over her. As gently as the sea laps against the sand, he pushed back her curls and traced her round cheek with his fingertips. "Are you sure?"

She nodded and the motion buried her cheek against his palm. "Yes." She shuddered. She had never been so certain in her life.

He cupped her chin and tilted her face to his. "Blair," he murmured against her lips. "I—"

Behind him, the door hissed open.

Rhett stiffened, and his hands snapped to his sides. He jetted backward as if her office door had opened onto the void of space.

Blair's gaze shot to the door, to the person who had entered. Fear sliced through her like a guillotine.

Preston Darby's glossy black hair didn't move as he tilted his head and furrowed his smooth brow. "I hope I'm not interrupting." His voice was a summer storm—calm but churning with the threat of something more.

"Not at all." Blair cleared her throat and took her own step back. "Major Owens was just leaving. Weren't you, Major?"

Rhett was the perfect soldier, stiff and rigid, staring intently at the spot behind her head. "Yes, Director Scott."

"Thank you, Major." Blair groped the air behind her until her fingers grazed the firm slab of onyx. "I'll take what you mentioned under advisement," she said, leaning against the lip of her desk to keep her knees from buckling.

Rhett nodded, his shoes squeaking against the tile as he spun around and marched toward the exit, his gaze never once landing on the Council Leader.

Blair's attention was also far from Darby. Instead, it roamed Rhett's sturdy shoulders, muscled arms, and strong hands. Her fingers grazed her cheek, still warm from his touch. They'd shared something, not only the forbidden touch, but something she couldn't quite explain. It had crept into the room, hidden in the corners, scared and timid, until it had felt safe enough to step into the light. It was indefinable, and they could never share it with anyone else.

Darby cleared his throat, his arms firmly crossed over his chest.

Blair dropped her hand from her cheek and settled it onto her hip. "What can I do for you, Council Leader Darby?"

She'd proceed as if nothing had happened. Rhett was tall and broad and had easily hidden her from Darby's sight. He could speculate all he wanted but confronting the director of the MediCenter about those speculations was another thing entirely.

Darby walked to one of the two black velvet chairs opposite her desk. "Did he hurt you?"

Blair jerked backward. "What?" She shook her head. "No, of course not. Major Owens had some information to share with me. He did and then he left."

Darby's fingertips dug into the chair's high back, dimpling the fabric. "He was so close to you."

Blair's mouth went dry. Her swallow caught in her throat, turning her tongue into a rigid plank.

"No one else should be that close to you." His voice trembled, and his dark gaze pressed her more firmly against the edge of her desk. "That man forgets his place."

"Major Owens works for the Key. Therefore, he works for me," Blair said, regaining her composure. "He seems to know his place exactly." She crossed her arms over her chest and settled back into familiar power. "I appreciate your concern, but I assure you, I have the situation under control."

Black.

When with Rhett, Blair was anything but in control. That was part of the thrill.

"Now, Council Leader, was that what you came to see me about, or—"

"Preston," he grunted. "Call me Preston."

"Okay, *Preston*," she said, dramatically, and a bit immaturely, stretching out his name. Dealing with Darby was always tedious. "What brings you to my office unannounced and unscheduled? Gathering more data for your precious hologram?"

She bit the tip of her tongue, silently scolding herself. Bringing up Holly would do her no good. She had a plan and was going after the Council Leader in the best and most effective way she knew how. Antagonizing him wouldn't help no matter how much he deserved it.

Darby loosened his grip on the chair and glided his palm back and forth across the soft velvet. "I know you met with Robin."

Blair didn't react. She wouldn't show her cards until he showed his.

"It was wise of you to get a jump on the rumors." He tilted his head, blinking at her like a bird. "She is the source, is she not?"

Blair took a deep breath, filling her lungs with the pieces of a new plan. "I had hoped to put an end to them before they reached you."

"I thought as much." He drummed his fingers along the back of the chair. "We must put a stop to any rumors of a coup. The corporation can't appear to be unstable."

"Of course." Blair nodded. "Let me know what the Key needs, and I will be happy to do whatever's necessary. As director, there are many who will stand by my side and fight for what's right."

"You are perfect." Darby cleared his throat. "Perfect for your current position."

Blair unleashed a coy smile. He was exactly where she wanted him. "Councilwoman Wilson did say something else. Something about a girl." She squinted and tapped her finger against her full lips. "Patient Ninety-Two, I think it was."

He said nothing, his black eyes fixed on her mouth.

"Council Leader?"

He dragged his finger along his tie, his attention still resting on her bottom lip.

She quelled the disgust that tightened her stomach. She would get what she wanted and then she would send him on his way.

Resolved, Blair glossed her fingertips over her jawline, down her neck, and rested them on the collar of her blouse. "Yes, that's what she said, Patient Ninety-Two."

He stared at her fingers as they smoothed down her silk collar and circled the top unbuttoned pearl button.

"Preston," she purred, tracing her bare decolletage. "Have you heard of Patient Ninety-Two?"

He rounded the chair, still gliding his fingers up and down the blade of his tie. "I am not at liberty to discuss the experiments conducted in the basement labs."

"Not even with me?" She dipped her finger behind the edge of her silk blouse and drew slow circles against the hidden mounds of her breasts. "I am the director. Does that not entitle me to certain . . . favors?"

He sauntered closer, a sickeningly sweet grin playing at his lips. "I know this isn't truly the information you seek."

Blair stiffened and her fingers stilled. "It's not?"

"No. I know what you want." His voice was gravel, husky while his black eyes roamed her body. "I can see it clearly."

"Very perceptive of you, Council Leader." An attempted smile wobbled on Blair's lips as she crossed her arms over her chest. "I actually wanted to ask you about my brother." She glanced down at her cuff. "Maxine should be back now. I'll call her in so she can take notes." She moved toward the door, but Darby was there, cutting her off.

"Don't do this to me, Blair." He scrubbed his hand down his smooth cheek. "Not now. Not when we've almost made it."

She scooted backward, flinching when the backs of her legs again met her desk.

"I know you're scared. We've been playing these games for so long that it's difficult to stop."

Her heart pounded a warning against her ribs as he moved closer, the tips of their shoes touching.

"You're too close," she said, her stomach seizing as his trembling exhale blew in quaking gusts across her skin.

"As close as the major." He licked his lips. "I should ask him if you like it."

"No, that's not—" The edge of her desk dug into her flesh as she struggled to increase the distance between them. "Step back, Preston."

His teeth dug into his bottom lip as he inched forward, pressing the front of his body against hers. She forced her hands between them and shoved, but he was firm, unmoving, rooted into place.

"You want this." He moaned and crushed his body against hers, slamming her back against the slab of onyx in every way she'd wanted Rhett to, but this was wrong. *He* was wrong.

"You're touching me." She tried to keep her voice from shaking as she stared into his dark eyes.

"I am."

Blair's stomach lurched and her mouth filled with saliva.

He snaked one hand around her back and flattened the other against her neck as he pressed his lips to her ear. "Now swallow."

She did, forcing the bile back into her stomach.

He shuddered against her, the evidence of his excitement pressing into her hip.

"Stop." She'd meant it to be a command, a clap of thunder, a storm, but it came out as mist.

"It's okay, my love." He nuzzled her neck, his stale coffee breath hot and sticky against her skin. "I promise it is. I'll explain everything, I just have to—"

"Stop." A bit louder this time.

"You don't have to be nervous. You won't catch the virus." He kept his hand against her back, fingers splayed and digging into her flesh as he lifted his head to stare into her eyes. "And now we can begin. You were the last piece. I needed you with me. I needed your approval." He rubbed his hips against her. "Imagine ruling by my side. The world pliant under our fingertips after each citizen is dosed and upgraded. Thank you, Blair. Thank you for permission."

"Let me go." She didn't recognize her voice as it tripped past her lips. "Please, Preston, let me go." She closed her eyes and tried to twist out of his grasp as he dragged his calloused fingers down her neck.

"You're so innocent," he breathed, tracing the same path with his fingers as she had moments before. "So much you don't know."

"Stop." It was a cry now, hot tears tracking down her cheeks.

"Your modesty is—" He leaned into her again, pressing his nose against her hair as he inhaled. "Intoxicating."

Another wave of nausea as she pawed at the desktop behind her.

He tugged at the fastened buttons on her blouse. They popped free easily, and his body quaked as he brushed his palm over her bra. "You don't have to play coy with me, my love. There will be no repercussions for our actions."

Her heart squeezed as her fingers found cold ceramic. She moved her hand up the vase to the five sharpened pencils that rested against its rim. "Preston," she said, her tears drying as she tightened her grip. "Get the fuck off me."

She slammed the pencil into his thigh. Fabric tore once, twice, three times as she repeatedly stabbed the sharpened point into his leg.

"Get off me!" she screamed, landing a final blow. Blood seeped between her fingers as she snapped the pencil, leaving inches of it buried in his flesh.

He howled and stumbled back, clutching his leg, the splintered end of the wood jutting out between his fingers.

"You bitch!" he spat.

Blair dropped the makeshift weapon and swiped a trembling hand across her cheeks. "Get out."

Darby's shoulders shook as he pulled the pencil from his leg. "I should have expected nothing less." He laughed and tucked the bloody pencil nub into his pocket. "You never cease to amaze me."

Blair ran to the door. Darby's shoes clicked unevenly against the tile as his limping steps ate up the ground behind her.

Please be there. Be there. Be there.

The door slid open, and Blair gripped its frame to keep from collapsing.

"Maxine!" she shouted to the young woman busily typing on her holopad in the small glass office across from Blair's.

Maxine shot to her feet, holopad in hand, and rushed from her cubicle and down the narrow corridor outside Blair's office. Her face twisted with concern as she took in Blair's tear-stained cheeks, blood-streaked hand, and unbuttoned blouse.

"Council Leader," she said, her lips tightening as Darby, with his ripped pants and bloody leg, filled the open doorway next to Blair.

"Lovers' quarrel," he explained and wiped his red-streaked hand on his pants before straightening his tie. "You understand."

Maxine only nodded.

"I need you in my office, Maxine." Blair's smile bared teeth. "The Council Leader is leaving."

Darby stepped back, motioning for Maxine to enter. She did so, the smallest savior in the world.

"Blair," he whispered, filling Maxine's empty space on the other side of the doorway. "No matter how fun this was, do not think you can test me again."

Fun. Tears burned her eyes, but she did not let them fall.

"Say you understand me."

She swallowed. He was almost gone. She was almost safe. "I understand."

"That's my girl." He brushed his bloody thumb across his bottom lip and smiled. "Blair, you've made me the happiest man in the world," he said as the door hissed closed between them.

Blair doubled over. Clutching her stomach, acid washed up her throat as she retched on the floor.

Maxine ran to her side.

This was too familiar. Too much like Cath's death. Too much like Rhett. Too much . . .

Blair stood. Her arm shook as she passed her cuff beneath the door's scanner. "Lock."

The lock slid into place with a *click*, and Blair released a trembling exhale.

"I'll get a bot to clean that up right away." Maxine said.

Blair smoothed her hands down her skirt. This office had once been her fortress. Now, it seemed to be her punishment.

"What happened?" Maxine's question hung in the putrid air.

What had *happened?*

Blair had been a huntress, all power and guile, and then, suddenly, prey.

How had he done it? How had she let him?

She stiffened, dabbing her lips with the sleeve of her blouse. "Come along, Maxine, we have work to do."

XXXIII

The knife clanked against the steel sink basin as Sparkman set it down and turned on the faucet. Elodie blinked, her gaze finally relaxing, drifting away from the thin crack in the safe-room's wall. A cabinet door creaked open and bottles clinked as Sparkman pawed around inside, but Elodie didn't turn to look. She remained cemented in place, wary of her movements and certain that any one of them would obliterate the control she had over her body and mind.

She feared the pain that would come crashing through her head and the anxiety of what waited back in Zone One. Sparkman said that the headache would take time, that shock would make her numb, a lie before the agony. But perhaps Elodie could hold on to the numbness, will away all other feeling. With the overwhelming task of prioritizing and rescuing three different people from the Key, desensitization was welcome.

There was also the matter of her implant. It had been with her since she'd been delivered from the gestation pod and into this world of deception. It had grown with her, learned with her, and now Elodie knew that it had also been watching her and reporting back to the corporation.

The hairs on Elodie's arms stiffened. She could feel its carcass staring at her.

Her eyes slid to the corner of the counter where Sparkman had smashed it until its long tentacles had ceased twitching. It was curled in on itself with its long, hairlike feelers tucked against its narrow body.

There weren't many bugs in Westfall, but Elodie had once seen a dead spider in the back of her closet, its legs kinked and bent, closed in on itself. She had shouted for her mother who then promptly sent out all of Elodie's clothes and shoes to be relaundered. All of that over an insect.

This creature had been inside of her.

Bile burned the back of her throat and stained her dry mouth.

Sparkman rescued Elodie from the nausea that clenched her stomach, holding out a towel, the middle of it dark with liquid.

"Press this firmly against the site," she instructed.

Elodie did as she was told, wincing when the stench of alcohol reached her and the liquid made contact with her flayed skin.

"And take these." Sparkman set three oval pills on the counter next to a glass of water. "You want to get in front of the headache."

One of the pills stuck to the tip of Elodie's parched tongue. She shivered against the bitterness as she took drink after drink before finally washing it down. The MediCenter didn't give out pills. Doctors ordered shots to be administered by bots or vials of liquid that dissipated into puffs of smoke when ingested. She'd heard of people taking pills to relieve aches and pains, but she'd only ever taken what the Key prescribed—content, food, supplements, her Match. She'd strayed with Violet Royale, thinking that doing so made her unique, the kind of rule breaker who was edgy and impressive. She had been so naive.

"And you'll need to change this," Sparkman continued, a wrapper crinkling as she removed a large bandage. "I'm not sure if I'll be with you or where exactly we'll find ourselves, so you should keep a clean one with you," she said, sliding two fresh bandages next to the expired implant.

Elodie removed the alcohol-soaked towel as Sparkman applied the dressing to the spot behind Elodie's right ear where the body of her implant had been. Her gaze fell to the blotch of red in the center of the cloth. Her breath hitched as images of Astrid and Cath filled the blank, dark space within each blink.

"You should eat something."

Elodie jerked free from her thoughts. "Yeah, that would be great," she said automatically as her stomach rumbled in agreement. It had been ages since she'd eaten.

Sparkman opened another cabinet and pulled out two transparent gray pouches the size of Elodie's nursing textbook. A thick stream of water flowed from the tap when Sparkman touched the faucet. She held the first gray pouch under the water, waiting a few moments before folding the plastic lip down and doing the same to the other.

As Sparkman carried them to the table, Elodie stood. She closed her eyes and gripped the edge of the countertop as a wave of dizziness washed over her. She took a few deep breaths and waited until she was certain the ground wouldn't disappear from beneath her feet before stuffing the bandages into her pocket and dragging her chair back to the table to join Sparkman.

The lieutenant colonel shook the gray plastic pouch, brushing away the stray water droplets that had condensed on the outside of the bag and now leapt onto her khaki suit with each brusque shake.

"Three-bean stew," she said, holding the bag out to Elodie. "More like chunky tomato mush, but you get what you get."

With a grimace, Elodie took the gray pouch and tore it open. Warm air rushed out, tinged with the sharp scents of plastic and canned tomatoes. Elodie jiggled the bag and the reddish-brown stew sloshed from side to side. Nothing could taste as bad as the beige protein shakes her mother had made for her, and at least this meal of clumpy mush was served without any passive-aggressive jabs.

She tipped the bag up to her lips and slurped in a mouthful of three-bean stew.

It's better than mom's beige shake.

She paused, the bite hardening in the back of her throat.

"We have to get my mom," she said, finally able to swallow the pasty clump of beans. "We have to save Aubrey, too."

Sparkman paused midchew. "Aubrey?"

"One of my patients in the LTCU. She's who I saw when I was leaving the Key. She's just a little girl, Patient Ninety-Two. She needs me, and she's my responsibility. I was supposed to—"

"The girl with the violet eyes," Sparkman's jaw hung slack. "The last one of Normandy's experiments that I assisted was Aubrey. I led Eos soldiers to the ELU to retrieve her body." Looking up at the ceiling, she shook her head. "She's alive."

Barely. Elodie swallowed.

"First," Sparkman began with more vigor, "we have to locate Aiden. We've left him behind for too long already. Then your mom and Aubrey."

Elodie opened her mouth to argue, to say that saving her mom was more pressing than rescuing Aiden. That he knew the truth and how to survive the Key's fury, but her mother was oblivious and unequipped. But she didn't need to prove her case. Saving any of the three was impossible if they couldn't get back into the MediCenter.

And a part of her was scared.

She was trying to be a better version of herself. One who could stand on her own two feet and dictate the terms of her own life. It was easy to aspire to and achieve when alone or book-ended by strong, independent women like Sparkman and Thea, but what would happen when she again faced Aiden? She had a fear of slipping backward, of shrugging off the weight of her life and laying it in his arms to carry how he wished.

She could no longer afford to give away her power. It had cost her too much already.

"How do we get inside the MediCenter to save anyone?" Elodie asked, deciding to use her energy on current problems instead of those well into the future. "You were found out, and I . . ." She shook her head. "Unless I turn myself in, I can't go back, either."

Sparkman set her empty pouch on the table and leaned back in her chair. "We could amass our soldiers and take the MediCenter by force, but there's no guarantee we could hold it long enough to get everyone out." She rubbed her chin, her brows knit in contemplation. "It would also destroy the plan Echo put in place and all that Thea is working toward. We can't expect citizens and benefactors to believe us when we tell them that Eos is not a terrorist organization if we lay siege to the most iconic and important building in Westfall." She reached out and mindlessly glided her fingers along the red stitching that rimmed the bridge of her cap. "We have soldiers on the inside. However, I don't know of any to contact. Echo always had that info . . ." Sparkman trailed off, lost in thought, her gaze fixed on a point across the room.

Elodie set down her meal and tilted her chin. "We do know one person."

Sparkman brushed her braid from her shoulder and shook her head. "Even if we could get a message to Aiden there's no way—"

"Not Aiden." Elodie stifled the urge to pick at her nails and apologize, sink into herself until the moment passed and Sparkman came up with the idea herself. "Rhett is on the inside. He works with Blair Scott and she's now one of the most powerful people on the West Coast."

It felt good to come up with a plan of her own. She had a voice, and it was time she used it.

"Major Rhett Owens?" Sparkman crossed her muscled arms over her chest. "He's been working with Dr. Normandy." She opened her mouth to speak, but paused, frowning. "He's lost to us."

"He's not." It didn't matter who else Rhett worked with. She knew him. Not as well as she would have liked for the person she was supposed to spend her life with, but she knew him better than Sparkman. "I saw him with my mom. And he talked to me while I was in VR." She leaned forward. "He's always been the same—focused and flat and unapologetic—but he was different with her. He was different with me."

A lump lodged in the back of her throat.

"It's a risk worth taking. And, like you said, we don't have any other options."

Sparkman tilted her head back and forth before giving one stiff nod as if settling a disagreement with herself. "I trust that you know Major Owens better than I do, but without your implant, we have no way of reaching him."

Elodie sighed. "Another problem Echo would have solved." She was beginning to understand why capturing Echo was so important to the Key.

A muffled *buzz buzz* emanated from Sparkman's uniform. "That'll be Thea with an update," she said as she reached into her pocket and removed a small rectangular device. She stiffened and set the gadget on the table, motioning for Elodie to take a look.

EOS NETWORK SECURE COMMUNIQUE

ECHO: I'm not sure who this message will reach, but I need your help.

ECHO: You need mine, too.

XXXIV

Blair buttoned her blouse all the way up to the hollow of her throat as she walked back to her desk. It felt like a choker, but at least she was certain it was there and she was no longer exposed. She sat on the edge of her chair, her knees bouncing. She couldn't keep still. Every inch of her buzzed and crackled with apprehension. She wanted to flee. But where would she go? Home? Alone with only her thoughts and the memory of Preston Darby's hands on her skin to keep her company?

Her swallow lodged in her throat.

No, she couldn't do that. If she went home now, she'd crawl beneath her mound of perfectly pressed blankets never to be seen or heard from again. Darby . . . what had happened . . . it would be the anchor that would drag her under. She couldn't drown now. Westfall needed her. Her brother needed her.

The bitter stench of stale coffee washed against her senses. Her stomach lurched. Preston was on her, burned into her flesh.

She squeezed her lids shut. She wouldn't think about what

had happened. She would file it away along with her lies and the memories of her birth parents, of Cath. She would deal with it later. If she was lucky, she wouldn't have to deal with it at all.

The slight *clink* of glass broke through Blair's thoughts, and her eyelids fluttered open.

"You should take it." Maxine nodded at the vial of Poppy she'd set on the corner of the desk. "Go home. I can see to the rest of your meetings."

The reflection of the clear liquid-filled glass reached toward Blair. Her hands itched to grab it and her heartbeat thrummed inside her chest with anticipation. Poppy would help her. It would take the pain away. It would wash her clean of the filth that clung to her like a second skin. But the drug wouldn't last forever. And then she'd be back here. The only difference between now and then was time.

"I'm fine."

Red.

The lie pierced her gut. Blair clapped her hand over her stomach, sure that fresh blood would spurt between her fingers. But nothing came. She was still intact. Just as she had been after losing her mother, and then the next one, and then her brother. This time, she'd lost a piece of herself. No, she hadn't *lost* it. It had been taken. But she couldn't help but feel like she'd offered it up on a platter.

Maxine plucked the bloody pencil from the rug and dropped it into the trash bin. "What happened?" she asked, staring down at the fresh stain on the newly cleaned carpet.

There was that question again. As unanswerable as ever.

Blair shook her head. "Nothing."

Another bloodless stab through her gut.

She winced. "It's not worth discussing."

Maxine glanced down at her holopad, frowned, and looked back to Blair. "You're not Matched, are you? The Council Leader did say you had a lovers' quarrel."

Bile washed up Blair's throat. She tensed her jaw, unable to open her mouth without the contents spilling out into another acidic puddle.

"Not that being Matched to Preston Darby would be the worst thing. I mean, he *is* the most powerful person on this coast." Maxine's lips formed her signature O.

Could he force our Match? Of course he could. He's the Council Leader. But will he?

Blair's thoughts flew and her heart raced as she choked and sputtered on the sour liquid that coated her tongue.

Blair, you've made me the happiest man in the world.

Her chest rattled with a muffled sob. Had that—what he had done—been a proposal?

"He's not bad to look at either." Maxine shrugged. "If you're into dark and brooding. Although, he is kind of an ass."

"We're not Matched," Blair snapped.

Maxine recoiled, her lips parting as if she had a biting retort but quickly thought better of it.

Blair's gaze found the Poppy. It would make everything so much easier . . .

Maxine slid the vial closer. "Whatever's going on"—she sighed, a long release of breath that carried more weight than any words—"it'll make you feel so much better."

Blair smoothed her palms down her thighs and squeezed her knees, a command for her feet to stop bouncing. "Pity someone else, Maxine. As I said, we have work to do."

"I wasn't—" Maxine clamped her mouth shut as Blair held up her hand.

"Save your explanations as well."

Maxine nodded and picked up the vial.

"Leave it."

Another nod, and Maxine returned the Poppy to the corner of the desk. Blair wanted the temptation. She wanted to face it and win.

"Would you like to review your calendar?" Maxine asked, breaking her subservient silence.

"There's something else I need your particular brand of help to accomplish."

Maxine's brown eyes sparkled. She was good at most things. After all, she was the only assistant Blair had ever had for longer than a few days. Maxine Wyndham was a tenacious little monster frightfully adept at getting exactly what she, or in their case, *Blair* wanted. And, if she didn't already know the answer to any given question, she knew just where to find it.

"There are various medical offices in the basement level," Blair continued, relaxing a little as the lies took hold and the visions of Darby pressed hard against her temporarily withdrew. "The Council Leader asked me to look into one of the patients being cared for: Patient Ninety-Two. Her name is Aubrey." She waved her hand dismissively. "Darby didn't mention her last name or date of birth, but her patient number should be enough."

Maxine cleared her throat and tucked her blond hair behind her ear. "And the Council Leader asked *you* to look into this patient?"

Blair took her holopad out of her desk drawer and studied

her assistant's reflection in its darkened screen. There was something there, in the way Maxine held her mouth. Not in the gossipy little O that had the power to sink ships before they'd even set sail or the firm line or slight smile—both of which conveyed her annoyance. This look, the way her lips stretched thin, bunching in the corners as if closing her mouth around too big of a bite, Blair had never seen it before.

The hairs on the back of her neck rose as she swiveled her chair to face Maxine. "I have many more responsibilities now than I did prior to becoming director." She softened her gaze and frowned in an approachable and compassionate way even Cath would have had trouble seeing through. "If you're not comfortable with these new duties, I will miss you, but I will also understand your need to find a more suitable position."

Maxine's expression smoothed. "You and I connected so well because we have the same goal: to be at the top." The screen of her holopad flashed, but she didn't take her eyes off Blair. "I only meant that checking in on an experiment seems like a waste of your time."

An experiment?

"You're probably right." Blair rested her chin on her hand as she powered on her holopad. "No one said being director wouldn't also come with busywork."

Blair was good at concocting plans. In fact, she'd come up with two that very day. Her throat tightened with the memory of Preston's hand against her neck. Sure, they didn't always follow the exact path she expected, but very few things in life ever did. There was, however, one thing that remained constant—Blair Iris Scott never went down without a fight.

Maxine grinned, flashing a row of perfectly straight teeth.

"Then it's settled. I'll look into the girl while you focus on more important things." Her gaze flicked to the vial of Poppy. "I went ahead and cleared your schedule for the rest of the day."

"Maxine." Blair caught the petite woman as she made her way toward the door. "You're always the first to know, well, anything really."

Maxine straightened, lips tightening, O forming. "I've been told I have a face people can trust."

"You sure do." Blair's smile was as warm and playful as a summer brunch date. "Then I know you've heard that the Council Leader is holding my brother in one of the basement labs."

The O vanished, replaced by the look that brought goosebumps to Blair's flesh.

Blair's curls bounced around her shoulders as she chuckled. "And to think, I used to hate predictability."

Maxine's jaw worked on an answer before she gave up and instead returned Blair's smile and left.

The door closed and the lock clicked into place as Blair found the edge of the gloves that had blended into her skin so well that no one would have noticed had she never removed them. Cool air met her hands and wrists as she stripped them of the gift Maxine had given her. Her knuckles popped as she stretched her bare hands. Her skin was chalky and tight, but the ripped skin around her fingernails had healed and her gnarled, too-short, sensitive nails had grown into white crescents. Now, there was no difference between her true hands and their gloved appearance.

She pinched the moist, gelatinous gloves between her thumb and forefinger and dropped them into the trash. They landed on top of the bloody pencil with a wet slap. The Poppy was next.

She stared at the bin, shame nipping at her heart as memories flashed behind her eyes, each in a battle to be the one traumatic moment that would finally bring her down.

"Aiden." Blair blinked back the tears that pecked at her eyes. She had promised to take care of her brother. She had promised to make Cath proud. And she had promised to protect Westfall.

With a thought, Blair pulled up the letter Cath had left her.

P.S. If you ever want to, if you ever need it, it's here.

She accessed the final hypertexted word.

EOS NETWORK SECURE COMMUNIQUE

ECHO:

The curser blinked next to her adoptive mother's alias, and Blair's adrenaline pulsed as she entered her first message.

XXXV

Elodie's gaze found Sparkman's. "How—" Her lips continued to move, but her words were swept away by her tumbling thoughts.

The lieutenant colonel's reddish-blond temples pulsed as she clenched her jaw, her eyes darting back to the device as it let out another burst of vibrations.

ECHO: I know how to free Westfall.

And it starts with saving my brother, Aiden Scott.

Elodie's heart skipped. It was Blair.

But Blair Scott was firmly aligned with the Key. She had had her brother arrested, had tried to turn her mother in to the corporation, had accepted the title of Director even after all of their lies.

Could she not have known?

ECHO: I don't know who within the
                  MediCenter I can trust, but I know
                  that I can trust you because Cath
                  did. You might not think that you
                  can trust me and that's fair. I can
                  only tell you that I now know things
                  that I didn't before. Things, I'm sure,
                  you've known for years.

                  Whether or not you believe that
                  you can depend on me, know that I
                  would die for my brother.

Like everyone else, Blair had been duped. She had followed the rules and succeeded at the life the Key had laid before her. That success had to have its advantages. There must have been a way for Blair to rescue Aiden from the clutches of the corporation without contacting Eos and outing herself as a sympathizer.

"This doesn't make any sense." Elodie winced as she scratched at her bandage. "She has a better chance of getting him out than we do."

"It's a lead in," Sparkman said without taking her eyes from the device as she waited for the next series of messages. "Whether or not she needs our help for this particular task doesn't matter. She's showing us that we're on the same side, making us more comfortable before she informs us of the true objective."

ECHO: Aiden isn't safe.

                  Neither are we.

Dr. Osian Normandy and Council
Leader Preston Darby have a plan.
It will destroy us.

It's happening now, and we have
to stop it.

Sparkman was right. Elodie's cheeks heated. She felt foolish for believing that, besides the dissemination of information,
their only real problems revolved around her. She couldn't see
the forest for the trees; meanwhile, the woods were burning
down around her.

ECHO: Are you with me?

Elodie didn't have to think about her answer or look to
Sparkman for guidance before typing in their reply.

SPARKMAN: Where can we meet?

XXXVI

Westfall was on a new trajectory. One that Osian Normandy's latest discovery had cemented in place. The final pieces of the puzzle had been snapped together inside the basement lab that Preston now stood outside of.

He ran his fingers through his hair, digging his nails into his scalp. Goosebumps sprouted along the back of his neck as he dragged his fingertips through his gelled strands once, twice, three times. He exhaled sharply, shoved his hands into the pockets of the new, crisply pressed pants he'd changed into, and resumed pacing outside the door.

Preston couldn't go in. Not yet. Not since he knew the doctor was inside. He couldn't bear to face him. In his current state, Preston wasn't sure that he wouldn't do something he would later regret. He had so many feelings to sort through. Feelings he hadn't anticipated would ever again rear their ugly heads. But they had, and it had all been because of Blair.

He narrowed his eyes and smoothed his hand over the three

puncture wounds he'd had stitched up and numbed before heading down to the basement.

Jealousy had been the first feeling to come on scene, awoken as soon as he'd walked into her office. That man had been there—Major Rhett Owens. He'd been close to her, *too* close, a giant planet blocking out the light that was Blair Scott.

And she had allowed him to eclipse her.

Bewilderment had been the next to arrive. If she had been any other woman, Preston wouldn't have been surprised that she'd fallen for the major's charms. Rhett Owens was hardly the first man of means to force himself onto an innocent, but Blair wasn't any other woman. She was Preston's equal. So, why, or rather *how* could she have lapped up Owens's bait?

Jealousy had scalded his tongue and turned each breath into fire, but she had quickly extinguished the flames with the sort of teasing ways she saved only for him.

Cue lust, desire, longing, devotion.

His pace increased, his boots smacking against the tile as he marched from one end of the hall outside of the basement lab to the other.

It had seemed like Blair saved that particular brand of tantalization just for Preston, but what if she had used it on Rhett as well? What if that was why the major was so close to her? Not because she had taken his bait, but because he had taken hers.

What if he touched her . . . first?

Now, rage entered, clanging through Preston's thoughts like a gong. He tightened his hands into fists and thrust them deeper into his pockets as his vision blurred with a silenced howl.

And then she had mentioned Patient Ninety-Two. He should have seen it for what it was—an attempt to withdraw information he had yet to make available to her—but she had started to drag her fingers along her silky-soft skin. She had known what she was doing. He understood that now. At the time, he'd thought it was a reflex, her subconscious conveying that she thought about him the same way he thought about her. That she wanted her fingers to be his, touching, caressing, exploring.

He had accepted her invitation. Yes, she had resisted, but that was all a part of this game that they played. He hadn't yet realized that she had changed the rules.

Even though she'd stabbed him—an action so completely Blair that even he couldn't think of a better way to characterize her prickly brand of charm—he hadn't felt rejected. She was always surprising him and her action was just another example.

Pacing back and forth down the hall, he dug his teeth into his bottom lip. The hum of the fluorescent MediCenter lights grated against his nerves.

His intrigue had only lasted until his adrenaline had worn off. The barbed spurts of excitement that had shredded his veins and made his insides fiery hot had allowed his hopes and expectations to get the better of him. He saw that now. He saw what she had done. And that it had not only been with him.

For years she had played with him, made him love her, obsess over her. After all this time, she hadn't returned his affections. She had made his every waking thought about nothing but her. She had ensured that he wouldn't be happy unless he possessed her. And for what? To feign modesty when he finally called off their game? Had he not come to his senses, she would continue her efforts to extract information while leading him on.

An inferno raged behind his ribs, scorching his lungs until

each breath was a haggard gasp. He clapped his sweating palms against the painted concrete wall, steadying himself as the ground tilted beneath his feet.

He would have laid down his life for her, would have taken someone else's, done anything had she only asked. Instead, she had kept *him* as a pet, strung him along until she was director, until he professed his devotion to her, devotion she had manufactured.

Heat bubbled beneath his skin and screams echoed between his ears. He slid down the wall, his legs like lava melting beneath him. The part of himself he'd locked away shrieked and rattled rusted cage doors.

It was as if she had drugged him, been his dealer, addicting him to the possibility of true love and a lifetime together.

Preston had only ever loved one person as much as he loved Blair. He would have thought that, after being broken by his father's disdain, he would have been better equipped to stay in one piece this time.

Preston stared ahead, his vision blurring into white nothingness.

His mother didn't love him, either. That betrayal didn't hurt as much. Hating herself made it easy for him to hate her, too. But his father . . .

One of the cage bars snapped.

Clifton Darby had been there for his son, affectionate and attentive, until one day he wasn't.

While on their last family visit to their country house before it had become his primary residence, Preston had caught a toad. Since most wildlife was thought to have been exterminated, the whole event had been quite a surprise to the five-year-old. And that this toad not only existed but was thriving had been even more fantastical. It had also been deserving of closer inspection. He had wanted to see how the creature worked, and there was really only one way to do that.

His father had come into his room and sucked in a breath so deep that Preston had felt lightheaded. Later, he'd realized that it hadn't been the air suddenly leaving the room but the feeling of bliss, a euphoria that arose when discovering one's true purpose in life.

Preston had held out one of the legs he'd ripped off, its slimy skin hanging in tattered flaps around what Preston had assumed was its femur. The rest of the toad was laid out on his desk. He had torn off the amphibian's arms and legs and carved out each bulging eye with a teaspoon he'd taken from the kitchen.

It had all been in the name of science, but his father didn't want to hear Preston's explanations. Clifton had called his son disturbed and never again listened to anything he had to say.

If my father wasn't able to stomach who I am, how could I believe that she would?

The rest of the bars that surrounded the *disturbed* part of himself he'd locked away turned to dust, choking out the version of him that had been in control.

The fire raging inside of him cooled and the tips of his fingers went numb. He took a deep breath, resurfacing after a deep dive.

He was back, fully together, and now he would take what he deserved.

XXXVII

Preston passed his cuff beneath the scanner to the door of the basement lab. The burst of cold air and violet light that washed over him as he entered the small, sterile antechamber was near to a baptism (if the history books could be trusted). He felt purified, reborn, his purpose strengthened and reaffirmed. As he gained entry to the lab on his left-hand side, Preston couldn't help but smile.

The door slid open, and Normandy glanced up from Patient Ninety-Two and the holopad propped against the side of her clear enclosure. His blue eyes took in Preston's disheveled hair and broad grin. "What's wrong?"

"Everything is perfect."

Normandy continued to eye him suspiciously. "I doubt that's the case."

Of course, nothing can be perfect without your say-so.

Preston's smile stretched wider, curling up at the ends until his cheeks ached. "I need your help."

Normandy adjusted his glasses, peering at the Council Leader from over the thin rims. "As I suspected."

There's no way you could have.

Preston felt cool, empty. He should have rid himself of the shackles years ago. "I've decided that we need to act now rather than later."

Normandy crossed his arms over his chest, his chin tilting up ever so slightly.

Preston drummed his fingers against the top of the plastic box and stared down at the drugged girl whose veins coursed with the silver-colored solution the doctor had pilfered from a now expired subject.

"You said you needed to run more tests to make sure the doses are ready to be widely administered. I can help you to that end if you help me to mine."

Normandy huffed. "I do not need your assistance in procuring more specimens."

Preston's hand stilled. "How long do you expect me to wait?"

The doctor opened his mouth to speak, but Preston cut him off. "Allow me to put it more plainly—you have been taking Eos members, citizens who seemed *off*, citizens whose disappearance could be easily explained away by their nefarious dealings with the terrorists. This was not a bad plan. However, it's a slow leak. You need another subject now. Not in a month, not in a week, not in however long it will take you and your *shifty soldier* to find a new quarry. I have such a person."

And when it works, she will freely give me what I desire.

"I have already found such a person. My *shifty soldier*, as you so eloquently put it, has taken said citizen into custody."

Preston's fingers twitched.

"For what the young have in stamina, they certainly lack in patience." Normandy plucked his holopad from the gurney, the paper-white pages reflecting in the lenses of his glasses. "It may not be moving as quickly as you would like, but as I've said before, genius takes time."

Time was the one thing Preston didn't have.

"Then you will dose both subjects, yours and mine."

Normandy's chest rose with a deep intake of breath. "This is not an open trial. This is science. *My* science. I did you a favor by including you and your ideas about the implant you're so fond of." He paused, his fingers pecking the keyboard, before he continued. "I have one opportunity to make this everything it needs to be without causing catastrophic side effects that can and will keep citizens from trusting the corporation. I will not waste it in an attempt to satisfy you." He slid his glasses down and flicked his gaze to Preston. "Besides, any attempt would be futile. You are a black hole, inhaling everything, twisting and distorting it into a perverse mockery of what it was before. It is a good thing I have discovered a way to be here forever. No doubt, left to your own devices, you would do the same to the Key."

Preston pictured the doctor as that toad splayed across his desk, insides leaking out from the tears in its flesh. The undeserved response from his father and the subsequent scolding had kept Preston from fully exploring what made the creature tick, but that curiosity never left him. It had been chained up but never vanquished.

"I expect a dose to be prepared today. If you're not willing to administer it to my subject, I will do so myself," Preston said. "One side will not work without the other, so we must move forward together."

Normandy remained silent. The only sounds in the room were the steady beeps from the girl's monitor and the light taps of the doctor's fingers against the holopad.

As Preston turned to leave, the doctor cleared his throat. "*Preston.*"

Goosebumps washed down Preston's arms.

"My goal can be accomplished without yours. I have no desire to completely control the citizens through their implant, but to make them pure, open to my designs . . ."

Preston recognized that pause, that slow inhale. This fantasy was the doctor's euphoria.

"That is my goal. It may take time, but I will soon have all the time in the world."

So, Osian would move forward at his own pace and without him. Well, that would never do. Preston needed Blair. His endgame, the final picture he'd painted of his visions of the future had her by his side, willing, loving, open to him in every way possible. Normandy was decidedly absent from his future, but as long as he had Blair, Preston could figure out a plan to do away with an immortal Osian Normandy.

Preston sauntered back over to Patient Ninety-Two and the doctor who had gone back to making notes and viewing findings. There was a deal to be made here, a deal that he could now suss out, devoid of the fiery emotions his former, incomplete self was prone to. Everyone had that one thing that made their insides purr and tremble. For him, it was Blair. But for Normandy—

The girl's fingers twitched, and Normandy's gaze roamed her, his breath quickening almost imperceptibly. If Preston hadn't released the cooler, more scientific version of himself, he would have missed it all together.

"I have a lot of power at my disposal. As Council Leader—"

"Your *father* was Council Leader."

With the mention of his father, a frigid glacier formed in Preston's stomach.

"You, *Preston*, are a child. A petulant one at that."

Icebergs splintered from the glacier, spearing Preston's insides. "If you don't do your part, and do it now, I will end the girl."

Normandy's fingers halted their fluid motion across the holopad's screen.

"Excuse me?"

"What part did you not understand?" Preston's tone remained level, empty. "If you do not do what I ask, I will remove her from this case and kill her where she lays." He cast an assessing gaze down at her and shrugged. "It won't be hard. It's not like she'll fight back."

Normandy's swallow was audible. "Your father was right about you."

Ice water seeped from Preston's pores, gluing his shirt to his back. He wasn't angry that the doctor continued to summon his father's ghost. No, that emotion was for the past, fractured version of himself. Excited anticipation, that's what he currently felt. Either way, the girl would die. Preston had already decided that much. There was no turning back now. Not when his interest was piqued and his insides thrummed to see if, when he sliced her open, her blood ran red or silver.

"You disgusted him."

"As I said." Preston suppressed an anticipatory shudder as he slowly keyed in the code that would remove the clear box and give him access to the girl. "I only need one dose."

Holly appeared, all smiles and soft curves.

But this wasn't *his* Holly. His Holly would know him by the sound of his breaths. She would analyze the air in the room and determine that he was present by his scent, the beat of his heart, the electrical impulses that radiated from him. This was the hologram that came standard in every Westfall building. It was there to help, a face for the common computer, but nothing more. Nothing like his real creation, which possessed millions of tentacles, each snaking through a citizen's implant.

"An identity check is required. Please state your name and rank before proceeding."

The hologram was only a shadow of Blair, the chalky outline of Preston's desire. It reminded him of what he wanted, what he was so close to obtaining, but what Osian Normandy stood in the way of him possessing.

Preston's stomach tightened and the splinters of ice punctured deeper. His hand stilled over the keypad, but he couldn't keep his fingers from twitching. He wanted to reach out and touch the beams of light, smooth the errant strands of hair from her round cheeks. He had had a taste of the real thing, and now he wanted to feast.

"One dose for Blair Scott?" Normandy asked, trying another weapon in his arsenal.

Preston's jaw hardened, but he pushed through. "Council Leader Preston Darby. Remove the case so I can access the patient."

The hologram blinked rapidly and the keypad flashed green beneath his hand. A moment later, the clear rectangle dissolved into four lines of hardened plastic that bordered the girl. There, it would wait until Holly instructed the molecules to once again form the protective cover Normandy had installed.

The doctor's throat worked as he set the holopad next to the little girl.

Preston's lips stretched into a grin. He hadn't had to pull Normandy apart to find out how he worked, but he couldn't wait to do so to Patient Ninety-Two. She was different, new. And new inventions deserved proper dissection.

Normandy gripped the edge of the gurney, his skin paling to an unnatural shade of ashy gray. "You're obsessed with her, the new director."

"One dose, Osian. One dose and I'll return your pet, locked up safe in her precious trophy case." Preston brushed the back of his hand against the little girl's cold cheek. "Wouldn't that be nice?"

"Your feelings for Blair are clear to anyone with a brain." Normandy had regained his composure. His words moved more smoothly now, but his fingers twitched like the legs of a spider next to the girl's bare arms.

Preston didn't respond to the old man's flaccid attempt to regain control. Instead, he moved to the cabinet nearest the doctor. It was the same one Normandy had gone to when he'd gathered the drug to terminate his previous subject. Preston would end this life the same way. He wanted to preserve the girl's porcelain skin and fragile bones, for now at least, and an injection was the best and easiest way for him to do so.

Preston opened the cabinet door and peered up at the rows of glass vials.

The doctor didn't realize how simple he had made this task. Had Osian lived by the same work habits as the rest of the Medi-Center's medical professionals, Preston would have had to resort to strangulation, which would have marred the specimen before he even began his study of it.

He grabbed the glass container of potassium chloride and paused.

How long would it take to wake her?

It would be so much more satisfying if he could watch the fear, the light fade, the curtains close.

And Osian said there was no satisfying me, he thought, a chuckle itching the back of his throat as he turned to face the doctor.

"The way you leer at Blair, what you've done with that"—Normandy aimed his sneer at Holly—"*thing* you created. Blair Scott is your weakness. A cancer. She is—"

"Do not speak of her," Preston spat as he yanked open the drawer at his hips. He pulled out a sterile, packed syringe and slammed the drawer closed.

He could abide Normandy slandering his name, bringing up his father, and even stating the obvious about his relationship with Blair, but he would not tolerate Osian's attempts to drag her through the mud.

"As I said," Normandy continued, and Preston could hear the smile slither against his lips. "She is your weakness."

Preston uncapped the syringe and stabbed the needle into the metal-rimmed rubber stopper on top of the vial, emptying the glass into the barrel.

"And she is yours." Liquid rained onto the floor as Preston shook the syringe in the girl's direction.

"And what happens after her death?" Normandy asked, removing his glasses and wiping them on the sleeve of his lab coat. "I murder Blair and we call it even?"

Preston's fingers twitched.

"We both know these theatrics are for show." Normandy's

nod took in Preston and the dripping syringe dangling from his spasming fingertips. "A tantrum, if I'm honest," he said, placing his glasses back on the tip of his nose. "You have proven your point. You are in charge."

"You will give me the dose?"

Normandy's laugh froze Preston's veins, and his fist tightened around the syringe.

"Put down your toy weapon and go play with your holographic doll, *Preston*," he said, pushing his glasses up the bridge of his nose. "I am very close to the end. My ultimate goal. I will not destroy my years of hard work so you can force a Match to an opportunistic slut like Blair Scott."

Enraged, Preston charged Normandy, his muscles firing in quick succession. Osian's eyes went wide and round as Preston collided with the old man, knocking him to the ground. He straddled his chest, the frantic beat of Normandy's heart hammering a frenzied drumbeat against Preston's hamstrings. The doctor's thin arms slapped and tugged at Preston's button-down as the Council Leader flattened his palm against Normandy's face, forcing his wrinkled cheek against the floor.

"Why would I play with my doll . . ." Preston whispered against Normandy's ear, "when I can play with yours?"

Preston drew the syringe back and plunged the needle into Normandy's leaping jugular.

The doctor's hands ceased moving and his shoes quit squeaking against the tile in fruitless attempts to gain purchase. Preston's veins thrummed as Normandy's jaw slackened and his chest ceased its panicked rise and fall.

The world around Preston blurred as he slid off the doctor's torso and fell back onto the cool tile. His body hummed and sparks of light flashed across his vision. Blood surged through his middle, a peak rising in the lap of his pants.

The plan for his future was nearing completion. He only needed to read through Normandy's files and create a dose of his own. But he could spend a few moments and enjoy this heady bliss to completion. He slid his hand down his stomach, stopping to wrestle with the button of his trousers.

Boom!

Preston startled, his gaze flitting to the unconscious girl sprawled across the gurney.

Boom! Boom! Boom!

He stood, loosening his tie as he strode to the drawer and removed another syringe. The vial of potassium chloride was empty, but there was something far more delicious in the lab across the hall.

Boom! Boom!

He would do his duty as Council Leader and sort out the racket, and then he would come and have his fun with *her.*

He stuffed the syringe into his pocket, his fingertips once again going numb as he dragged them along the girl's thin arm.

"I'll see you soon, *pet,*" he murmured as he made his way to the exit.

The door slid open as another series of explosions sounded. "It seems there really is no rest for the wicked."

XXXVIII

Aiden was tired. The kind of tired that ached deep in his bones and turned his muscles to putty. But he was alive, sprawled out on the hard tile of his hopelessness-white room after what felt like years of VR torture. But alive. Although, he was quickly learning that this life wasn't truly worth living. He couldn't get to Blair, couldn't keep his sister safe. Council Leader Preston Darby had made sure of that.

"I could make her open to just about anything."

Aiden's swallow tugged on the boulder in his throat. He was now only of help to Eos, but he didn't think he could be for much longer.

Within his sore joints and weak limbs, fear gained a handhold. He wasn't sure if he was strong enough to keep his darkness at bay. It wanted to release his secrets, strike a deal, walk away from this place and never look back. The evil part of him didn't care about family or friends or love. It cared only for self-preservation.

The lock to his door clicked as someone gained entry. Aiden tensed. He might not be strong, but he was ready. He would give Darby and his own darkness a run for their money.

"Fancy meeting you here." Tavi's helmet of neon-pink hair was the most glorious thing Aiden had ever seen.

His mouth was dry, and his lips cracked around a silent *Tavi?*

She sighed and rested her hands on her narrow hips as she approached. "You look like shit."

His arms shook as he pushed himself up. "Nice to see you, too, Tavi."

"It's *Racer.*" She shook her head, tucking her small frame under his arm to steady him as he stood. "But I guess I'll allow it since I already know you are the worst at following directions."

Aiden could have melted into her, but instead, he froze. Was this real? Was she real?

How many times will I have to ask myself these questions?

How many rounds would Preston Darby and Dr. Tetch put him through?

Darby had tried to trick him into thinking he was close to rescue before. The first time, in Zone Seven and beyond, the Council Leader had been successful. The rest of the VR rounds had just been for show, an exercise of power, a breeding ground for fear. Could this be another attempt?

The Key might know about Tavi, but they didn't know her the way Aiden did.

"Octavia?" he croaked.

That's how the corporation knew her. That's how Holly had introduced her on his first day in the End-of-Life Unit, and it hadn't gone over well.

She stared up at him, a frown creasing her brows. "I can leave you here, you know."

A rush of gratitude flooded him, and he wrapped his arms around her and squeezed. "You're really here."

"Gross." She grunted and wiggled out of his grasp, patting her solid mound of pink hair. "Just because we can touch doesn't mean we should."

"Sorry, won't happen again." His cheeks heated. He'd only ever impulsively hugged one other person, and that had been Cath.

She gave him a once-over before she looked around the bare room. "Still no shoes, huh?"

He shook his head.

She let out a noise somewhere in between a sigh and a groan. "It's always something with you."

He could have hugged her again but didn't. Instead, he followed her to the open door and waited behind her as she peered out into the hall.

"We don't have much time." She grabbed his hand and yanked him into the hall. She was faster than he'd expected, or maybe he was more exhausted than he thought possible, either way, his lungs burned and legs ached as he rushed to keep up with her short, feverish strides.

The halls were empty. There should be soldiers. There was no way Tavi could have gotten him out of that room without triggering some kind of alarm. His stomach roiled and he couldn't help but think that it was happening again. That he was back in Dr. Tetch's lab, strapped to a chair, tentacles reaching into his brain and plunging him back into the corporation's made-up virtual world. Would he escape just to awaken in the bowels of the MediCenter?

His legs wobbled beneath him as he charged up the stairs after Tavi, who didn't pause before bursting through the door and into the hall that led to the MediCenter's lobby. His muscles burned as he slowed to catch his breath, his inhales and exhales rushing in and out in soupy, uncontrolled gasps.

There was one way he could check. One way he could know for sure that he was in the real.

He pressed his fingers against the spot behind his right ear. Pain bit through his skin and flashed down his neck. A cry caught in his throat as he prodded the crusty, scabbing wound.

There was no pain in Dr. Tetch's VR world—only the weight of the weapon that Aiden always came to hold and the fear that lived like ice in his bones as he sorted through what was real. The physical pain would come later, after the doctor had gathered more information from his test subject. It was strange being viewed as an experiment, another body only useful as long as it supplied information.

Tears burned Aiden's eyes, and he blinked them back. Tavi, the escape . . .

It's really happening.

They were running and no one was chasing them.

Boom!

Aiden's heart leaped and his eyes found Tavi, still as stone a few paces in front of him in the MediCenter lobby. The glow from the secondary after-hours lights muted her hair to a dull salmon.

She tilted her chin toward the front of the lobby. "It's brighter than I thought it'd be."

He followed her gaze out the MediCenter's grand glass entry doors. A flash of light exploded in the sky above the buildings of Zone One—a burnt-orange ball shaped like the sun with a golden *E* blazing in its center.

It was beautiful and bold, and he felt its meaning crack through him like lightning.

"What is it?" He held his breath, hoping he was right.

She bit her bottom lip as more fireworks shattered the sky, bathing them in flashes of white, then purple, green, blue . . .

"A proclamation." Her eyes glimmered with unshed tears. "There's no more hiding. Eos is out."

He stared up at the colorful bursts, tears gliding warm down his cheeks. Cath had told him this would happen—that one day there would be a revolution. She didn't think she'd live to see it. She had been right.

Tavi wrapped her hand around his.

His mouth moved, but he couldn't force any words past the tightness in his throat.

"Don't say anything," she whispered. "You'll ruin the moment."

Another burst of light the same brilliant tangerine as the rising sun.

"I'm glad we're friends," he said anyway.

With a groan, she released his hand and blinked back her tears. "We're definitely not friends." She sniffled and rubbed the round tip of her tiny nose.

With a grin, Aiden wiped his wet cheeks on the sleeve of his shirt. "Deny it all you want, but I know the truth."

Lips pursed, she glanced down at her cuff. "We have to get moving. Don't want to keep Echo waiting or get caught standing here gawking."

An electric-red flash filled the lobby as if Aiden's blood had drained from his body and into the space around them. "Echo?"

Tavi moved to the bank of elevators and passed her cuff beneath the scanner. One elevator opened immediately as three others chimed their arrival. Tavi darted into the metal box and yanked Aiden in behind her.

Grunted commands and thundering footsteps filled the lobby as a blur of soldiers clad in Key Corp red filed out of the elevators and into formation with their backs to the elevator doors—and Tavi and Aiden. A commanding officer stood in front, inches taller than the other soldiers, his white-blond hair alight with the exploding fireworks. His attention was on the front doors as he pointed, shouting orders that Aiden couldn't make out over his pulse roaring between his ears.

Tavi jerked, smashing her small frame against the elevator's metal wall. "Twelve." Her hushed shout was filled with panic, but the elevator didn't move. "Twelve, twelve, twelve!"

The doors began to close as Rhett's gaze swung over the squadron. His amber eyes met Aiden's. Neither man moved, frozen by the decision, the consequences, the freedom of choice.

It's over.

Aiden straightened. He wasn't a stranger to being caught. At least this time, when Rhett plunged him back into hopelessness, he would know what to expect and how to prepare Tavi. Or perhaps he would spare them both from the torture and give in to his darkness, spew his secrets, and hope Preston Darby would end his life before he had a chance to feel guilty, or worse, see his sister open to him.

Rhett's chin dipped slightly, almost imperceptibly, before he turned his attention to his company and his back to the elevator.

The doors closed, and Tavi's legs nearly collapsed beneath

her. "That was way too close. I thought I was going to pee." She righted herself, tugging on her blue scrub top. "That's what we get for having such a squishy moment."

Aiden rubbed his trembling hands together. Rhett Owens, a major in the Key Corp military, Elodie's fiancé, had let them go.

"And learn how to more quickly identify a whisper, you dim-witted box!" Tavi shouted and delivered a swift kick to the elevator.

The twelfth floor . . .

"You're taking me to Blair." Aiden felt lightheaded. He wasn't sure if it was Darby and Dr. Tetch or Rhett or the idea that he was about to see the only family he had left.

"I'm taking you to Echo."

"But—"

Tavi shook her head. "Spoilers."

If Blair had taken Cath's place as Echo, what did she know? And what would she do with her newfound power?

Aiden's stomach roiled as the elevator reached its destination and the doors noiselessly opened. He took a deep breath and stepped out into the empty space lined with glass-front offices. It didn't matter that it was after hours, he was sure his sister would have insisted the occupants of each cubicle were relocated as soon as she took up residence. Blair wasn't one for being watched, inspected.

Tavi held back the elevator door with her arm but didn't follow him out. "This is where I leave you."

The light from the fireworks poured in through large windows, illuminating the twelfth floor in birthday-party colors.

"She'd be proud of you, you know."

"Who?" Aiden glanced down at his bare feet before brushing his hand through his disheveled mohawk.

Tavi rolled her eyes. "Oh, Wonder Boy, you still have so much to learn."

The corner of his mouth quirked in a crooked smile. "Thankfully, I have you as a teacher."

She stepped back, returning his grin as the doors closed.

Aiden's palms were sweaty, his breaths uneven while he walked toward the narrow corridor outside his sister's office. When he was sure he would never see her again, he'd come up with a million things to say. A million ways to apologize. Now, with each step toward the inevitable, words evaporated, rising from him like steam.

He stopped short of the hallway that dead-ended at Blair's office and peered across the corridor into the only space that still had its lights on. There were no photos or decorations or personal touches in the glass-front office directly across from Blair's, but someone had been there. The steaming cup of coffee and the slowly rocking desk chair were proof of that.

Behind him, the door to Blair's office hissed open. His sister appeared, silhouetted by flashes of brilliant oranges and golds. Blair pressed her finger to her lips and peered around him to the illuminated office before motioning for him to come inside her own.

"Racer told me you made it to the floor," she said as soon as the door closed. "I was afraid you'd decided not to come."

Aiden padded over to the fluffy rug and dug his bare toes into the synthetic wool. It hadn't been that long since this white rug had been dappled with Cath's blood. "Racer told me you were Echo."

"I can explain." Blair tucked a curl behind her ear and worried her bottom lip with her teeth. "If you want me to."

The sister he knew would never have cared about what he wanted. She lived only for *her* goals and *her* needs. It seemed like, in the same way no one knew him, Aiden hadn't truly known her, either. "Go ahead."

Blair closed her eyes for a moment and inhaled, as if steadying herself against an oncoming storm. "Cath left me a note." She began pacing, her lips tight as she wrung her hands and walked back and forth. "She told me everything."

Everything.

He swallowed.

"She wrote about Cerberus and Eos . . . and you." She stopped pacing to stand in front of him. "I know the truth now. I wish I would have opened my eyes and seen it sooner."

She took a breath and leaned forward, wrapping her arms around him.

Aiden's stomach squeezed and his heartbeat sputtered.

"I'm sorry." Her voice cracked as she settled her chin on his shoulder. "I'm so sorry."

He hugged her back, his face buried in her curls. He inhaled her scents of lilac and vanilla. She smelled like their mother. She smelled like home.

Tears rolled down his cheeks as memories flooded. Laughter and sunshine. Wet grass beneath his feet. His mother and father, whole and alive and brimming with joy.

"I love you, Blair."

She quaked against him, and he held her tighter.

"I love you," he said again. "And I'm sorry, too."

XXXIX

Elodie's heart beat in her throat as she and Sparkman exited the Max and headed toward the MediCenter. With Blair's help, Thea had reprogrammed their cuffs with the same permissions the director herself had. But, other than her clothes, Elodie couldn't change her appearance that much, and she and Sparkman were wanted by the corporation.

In their brief Eos-encoded chat, Thea had assured her that Key Corp soldiers would be too preoccupied by the next part of the plan she'd developed, with the help of other Eos members, in the hours since she'd left the safe house to even notice a herd of elephants walking through the front doors of the MediCenter, much less Elodie and Sparkman. However, as the streetlamps switched on and they grew closer to the most important building in the city, Elodie wasn't so sure.

"We should go back." Her eyes darted to the red-brick walkway beneath her feet as two suit-clad men walked briskly by.

Sparkman adjusted her cap and peered down the block at

the MediCenter's smooth concrete facade framed by bronze sconces now lit by piercing white bulbs. "If Thea says we don't have anything to worry about, there's no point in wasting energy doing just that."

Elodie swallowed the sour taste in her mouth. "But what if she's wrong?"

"She's not," Sparkman said matter-of-factly, the violet orb around her painting her pale skin a soft purple. "And we would have received word if something happened and we needed to abort."

Elodie couldn't help but think about Echo and the fact that she, the leader of this faction of Eos, had died, and Elodie had been the one to inform them.

As if Sparkman had read her mind, she added, "Thea isn't working alone. None of us are."

They paused in front of Jackrabbit, three buildings down from the MediCenter's grand glass double doors. Sparkman cracked her knuckles, one after the other, as she glanced at Elodie. "We have to trust them as much as we trust ourselves."

Elodie didn't have much practice trusting herself, but there was nothing like a baptism by fire.

She averted Sparkman's probing gaze to stare at her reflection in the restaurant's expansive windows. Her Violet Shield was a shimmering bubble, her hair hung in wavy sheets from under the hat Sparkman had given her to hide the still-numb wound behind her ear. Her shirt was too big, her pants inches too short. She looked completely unremarkable. They both did. And yet, they were on their way to change the world.

Elodie flexed her hands, her fingers tingling with nervous anticipation.

I don't know if I can do this.

The words rested on her tongue, and she bit them back before they had a chance to escape.

"You're right," she said instead. "I trust myself. I trust Eos. We can do this." And, this time, she believed.

A loud *boom* rattled the windows and sucked the air from Elodie's lungs. Light exploded in the air. A fiery orange sun burned across the sky. In its middle, a sunflower-yellow *E*.

Sparkman's lips lifted into a smile for the first time since Elodie had met the lieutenant colonel. "After the storm . . ."

"Comes the dawn." Elodie murmured.

The sun crackled and popped, leaving a shadow of smoke as the colorful embers fizzled down to earth.

Sparkman brushed her braid from her shoulder and locked eyes with Elodie. "It's started."

Adrenaline buzzed through Elodie's limbs. "And so will we."

Another explosion sounded, and a sinewy trail of light whined across the dark sky as the door to the MediCenter opened and a sea of red emerged.

Sparkman and Elodie scooted closer to Jackrabbit's windows, nearly disappearing in the shadows of the overhang. The restaurant's patrons had risen from their seats to rush to the glass. Fireworks were only reserved for one time of year, and the Rose Festival had ended abruptly without the traditional final night's celebrations.

Elodie turned her back to the guests, their hands pressed against the windows as wide-eyed as children outside a toy store, and forced herself to keep her attention on the bursts of color as a line of Key Corp soldiers marched past. She was just like everyone else, unremarkable and caught up in Eos's distraction. Between the loud booms and crackles of the fire-works, she listened to their hammering footsteps take them farther and farther away.

Sure the soldiers weren't returning, Elodie leaned forward and peered around Sparkman to the entrance of the Medi-Center. "It's clear."

She stepped from the shadows, shedding her doubts and fears and leaving them in front of Jackrabbit and its patrons. She'd been working up to being decisive and determined, and she would no longer let her insecurities stand in her way.

She and Sparkman did as Thea had instructed and approached the MediCenter as if this was another ordinary evening of another ordinary day. Before she passed her newly outfitted cuff under the scanner, Elodie peered through the front doors of the MediCenter, the loud explosions of light reflecting off the glass.

"Once we're in, we should take the stairs." Sparkman's whisper was more of a hushed growl as she passed her cuff beneath the access panel. "At some point, Eos will cut the power. We don't want to be in an elevator when they do."

She followed the lieutenant colonel into the lobby, glancing over her shoulder for one last look at the distraction, declaration, call to arms that burst in vivid colors against the darkening sky.

"Oof." The air wheezed from Elodie's lungs as she slammed against a firm blockade. She rubbed her cheek and glanced up. Rhett's lips twisted into an embarrassed grin as he brushed his knuckles against his chest. The chest she'd just run into. She sighed. When it came to entering the MediCenter, it seemed she was destined to smack into something.

"Sorry about that," Rhett said, adjusting his fully equipped duty belt, his gaze never quite landing on her. "I guess I'm not very good at the lurking-in-the-shadows brand of espionage."

A grin ticked against Elodie's mouth. It was the most relaxed, least Rhett-like thing he'd ever said, but she still felt awkward in front of him—the same way she'd felt the first night they'd met in VR. She needed space from him. From men.

"We should head down." Again, he didn't make eye contact as he nodded toward the stairwell.

Sparkman eyed Rhett, her gaze lingering on the jutting end of the stock prod he'd casually rested his hand on. "Lead the way," she grunted with a tick of her jaw.

Elodie appreciated that Sparkman followed her own rules. She didn't fully trust Rhett, but she did trust Elodie. Now, Elodie trusted herself to know when she was making the right decision, and that was all that mattered.

They headed down the stairs to the basement, their footsteps in time with the quickened beat of her heart. It was ironic that this level housed the End-of-Life Unit when it was, and continued to be, where each different stage of Elodie's life began.

Rhett opened the door at the bottom of the stairwell and paused, his head swiveling back and forth as he surveyed the white halls of the basement before they entered. "I sent everyone topside, but it's important to make certain they followed orders."

Sparkman let out another grunt as she passed Rhett and entered into the lower level of the MediCenter. Elodie trailed after her, her footsteps as light and noiseless as the lieutenant colonel's.

Sparkman halted, jutting her finger at a door labeled MAIN-TENANCE, her long braid brushing her back as she cocked her head. "What's in there?"

Before Elodie could open her mouth to state the obvious, Rhett cleared his throat. "Mistakes." The word was barely a whisper.

Elodie's eyes roamed his face, but there was nothing to be found in the placid stiffness of his soldierly exterior.

Sparkman and Rhett continued forward, and Elodie had to jog to keep up with their long, hurried strides as he led them around another corner, pointing at the entrance two doors down from the end of the wide hall. Elodie didn't wait for an explanation. Her pulse thundered through her ears and her stomach pressed against her spine as she ran to the door and passed her cuff beneath the scanner.

The row of Xs loomed heavy against the wall over her mother's gurney.

"Mom!" She tore across the room, tears burning her throat.

Gwen lay motionless, stretched across the metal table, covered only by a paper-thin hospital gown.

Rhett's footsteps thundered after her. "Is she—"

His unspoken question was a knife in Elodie's back, and she sucked in a breath to quell the stab of pain as she pressed her fingers against her mother's cold wrist and waited.

Elodie's knees shook and a cry of relief passed her lips as a strong pulse beat under her fingertips. "She's alive." She breathed, her eyes searching the room, trailing up the long IV tubes to the same pump station she'd been hooked up to.

"Will this help?" Rhett thrust his holopad into her hands.

Elodie's eyes searched the six squares on the screen. Three were filled with patient information, the others with different alphanumeric codes. Elodie's finger hovered over the square labeled 92 before clicking on the citizen ID number she knew to be her mother's. She would get Aubrey out, but she had to save her mother first.

Elodie reviewed her file, thankful that the Key had done one thing right in funneling her into the nursing program. Without that knowledge, she would have had no way of knowing her mother was only on a simple dose of tranquilizers meant to keep her under until the morning when—

Her stomach dropped to her toes. "What's Update Ninety-Two?" She angled the screen toward Rhett.

"Normandy," he spat, the tendons in his neck straining with the cherry-red anger that ate up his skin. "He's been running tests on Aubrey. Extracting things from her—*doses.*" He stormed over to the pump station. With one smooth motion, he ripped it from the wall. Liquid spewed, and Elodie was certain that somewhere within the MediCenter, alarm bells sounded.

"That's one way," Sparkman said from her place on watch just outside the room's open door.

Elodie set down the holopad and gently removed the IV from the crook of her mother's elbow.

A few moments later, Gwen stirred, making confused huffs and gentle moans as if waking from a bad dream.

"It's okay, Mom. I'm here." Elodie ran her fingers over her mother's bleach-blond hair and grown-out roots. It was as soft and light as it looked. It was a shame that the Key had lied to and tricked Gwen into keeping simple moments like this away from her daughter. How different their lives would be if they'd only been allowed to touch.

"Elodie?" Her mother's voice was small and thin as she struggled to keep her eyelids open. "I thought—" Tears welled and slipped past her temples, disappearing into her hair. "I thought I'd never see you again."

Elodie swiped the back of her hand against her own wet cheek. "I'm getting you out of here."

Gwen's hand hovered above Elodie's, but she pulled it back to her chest before making contact. "I've done so many things, so many dreadful things. I—"

"We don't have to do this now," Elodie said, blinking through another swirl of tears. "Let's get you somewhere safe first."

Rhett slid his arm around Gwen's shoulder and helped her up. She recoiled under his touch.

"It's okay, Mom. You won't get sick. The Key has—"

"*He* did this." She shrugged away from Rhett and slipped off the gurney, leaning against its metal lip to steady herself. "He told me that he would take me to you. That I could apologize. That you were safe." More tears slid down her cheeks, dotting the thin fabric of her gown as she glared up at him. "I trusted you, and you lied to me."

Rhett stepped back. His throat bobbed, but no sound escaped his lips.

Sparkman stepped into the room, her jaw set and hands fisted at her sides. "Someone's coming."

Elodie tucked her arm around her mother's waist and guided her to the open door.

"Let me," Sparkman said, taking Elodie's place by her mother's side before thrusting the Eos communique device into Elodie's grasp. "I'll be in touch as soon as we're settled."

She stared down at the gadget. She had no choice but to let her mother go with the lieutenant colonel. This part of Elodie's story wasn't over. She'd made Aubrey a promise, and she would keep it.

Sparkman cupped Elodie's hand in hers, forcing her fingers to close over the tech. "Your mom will be safe."

Footsteps echoed in the distance, moving closer, closer.

Elodie placed her fist over her heart and bowed. "I trust you." She turned to her mother whose wide-eyed gaze swung from Elodie to Sparkman and back again.

"You're leaving again?" Gwen asked, plumped lips trembling.

Elodie hadn't left the first time, but she supposed there was plenty of time to explain the truth after she'd found Aubrey and Aiden and gotten them to safety, too.

Elodie smiled, unsure of exactly how she felt now, faced with her mother whose worry hadn't turned into disdain. Maybe it was coming, or maybe kindness would take its place. Either way, their relationship would be forever changed. "I'll see you soon, Mom."

As Sparkman led Gwen out of the room, her mom's cold fingers caught Elodie's. "I love you. You know that, right?"

She'd saved her mother. She would every time, but she wasn't sure if she was still willing to accept Gwen's particular brand of love. "I know."

The footsteps grew closer as Sparkman whisked Gwen from the room and disappeared behind the closing door.

Elodie turned her attention to Rhett. His arms were extended, and his white-knuckled grip swallowed the edge of the gurney as he bent at the waist, his head between his outstretched arms. At any moment, she expected him to vomit.

"You ready?" A few weeks ago she would have asked if he

was okay, but she was different then, and so was he. Now, the way he felt didn't matter, and she wasn't quite certain that she even cared. He was no longer a priority. They had to be ready for action.

He regained his composure and nodded, stalking toward the door as the footsteps neared and hushed voices filled the hall.

Elodie clenched her hands into fists. She'd never been in a fight, but she'd learned the basics from Violet Royale. And, Elodie supposed, there was a first time for everything.

XL

Blair wiped her nose on the sleeve of her blouse as she led Aiden to her desk and the holopad that held the only file she'd found that hinted at what Darby and Normandy had in store for Westfall and its citizens. Blair clicked on the folder's icon and handed the holopad to her brother.

"Upgrade Ninety-Two . . ." He shook his head, pointing to the black lines that covered nearly every line of the document. "Everything's redacted."

"Turns out, being director doesn't get me many privileges." Blair crossed her arms over her chest. "The only things I know is that there's some sort of dose being prepared for each citizen and that the upgrade will follow." She glanced at the holopad. "The upgrade has something to do with a girl—Patient Ninety-Two."

"Aubrey, Elodie's patient. She's the one who went missing." He set the holopad back onto Blair's desk and scrolled though the pages that had more empty spaces than a slice of swiss cheese.

"Turns out, she's been here the whole time. In a basement

lab." Blair ground her teeth, frustrated that secret experiments and upgrades had been carried out right under her nose. How much more was there that she didn't know about?

"We have to get her out." Aiden's temples pulsed with the rhythmic tensing of his jaw. "Go door to door down there until we find her."

Blair's gaze slid to the wound behind his ear. She reached out, hand hovering next to his cheek. Gingerly, she brushed her fingers over the lines of crusted blood along his neck. It felt so strange to touch. "What did they do to you?"

He looked at her and grinned the same mischievous expression he'd been giving her since he was a little boy. "I did that myself."

She nearly chuckled, but the haunted, unreadable look that passed over his face made her pause. "Are you sure you're okay?"

Another flash of straight teeth stained blue by a brilliant flash of fireworks. "Right as rain."

She didn't believe him, but she didn't want to push him away by being too insistent. She'd already lost him too many times.

A loud shriek snapped Blair's attention to the wall of windows and the world outside the MediCenter. An amplified voice, muffled by the panes of glass, shouted clipped instructions to whoever hadn't already fled downtown.

"Key soldiers." Aiden's eyes met hers. "I'm pretty sure you started a war."

Blair swallowed. "It was better than the alternative." She tucked her holopad back into her desk drawer as the messaging thread she shared with Maxine appeared across her vision.

I'm glad you found your brother. There's something else you need to see. I can't talk about it here. They might be screening our messages. Meet me in the basement. Sending you the coordinates.

Blair entered a reply and made a futile attempt at smoothing the wrinkles from her shirt. "Looks like we won't have to go door to door after all. I just got word about something in the basement that needs my attention." A flashing light appeared in her field of vision, marking the rendezvous location.

Aiden ran his hand through his curly mohawk. "Was it from Rhett?"

Blair nearly tripped over her rug on her way to the door.

"He saw us, Racer and me, getting into the elevator. He could have stopped us, but he didn't."

Aiden stared at her expectantly as she unlocked her office door and hurried into the hall. Her cheeks burned, and she was thankful it was after hours and the corridor that led to the stairwell was only lit by the fiery balls of light that exploded outside. "Major Owens has also come to certain realizations about the Key and has changed his behavior accordingly."

Aiden rolled his eyes and padded after her. "You sound like a textbook."

Blair's blush deepened. At least it had kept him from asking any questions she didn't yet know how to answer.

"There is one more thing," Aiden said as the door to the stairway closed behind them. "You haven't seen Darby, have you?"

Blair gripped the railing and focused on her quick steps and putting one foot in front of the other. "Unfortunately, I've seen him quite a few times." A lump sat in the back of her throat and her eyes burned with tears that she wouldn't allow to fall. "Another perk of my new position." She hoped he heard the sarcasm and disgust in her voice and not the anguish. "He told me about his plan to dose and upgrade each citizen."

She continued forward. Maybe if she put enough time,

enough words, enough space between her and what had happened with him in her office, it would fade away like any other nightmare.

"Although, I'm not sure exactly how it's all related to Patient Ninety-Two, but if we can get her away from Darby and Normandy, I know it will prevent them from completing their plan," she said as they charged toward the large B that denoted they had reached the basement level. "Maxine found something. It has to be related to what's going on. She can help us find Aubrey."

Aiden nodded, stepping in front of her as the door to the basement opened. He was so grown-up, and she had missed the whole thing.

The hallway was clear, and Blair rushed forward, following the directions Maxine had sent while silently cursing the tight pencil skirt that made each clipped step short and loud.

"Once we find Aubrey," Aiden began, whirling around to check behind them, "where should we take her?"

Blair frowned. She'd started a coup, started a war, and was trying to do right by her adoptive mother, but hadn't had the time to think everything through like she would have before. Turns out, the truth required a bit more thought than her usual automatic lies.

"Eos has safe houses," he continued. "But I don't know if any have been made since I—"

Up ahead, a door hissed open. Blair skidded to a stop next to Aiden, who stood tense and ready.

Elodie emerged from the room, flanked by Rhett, his fist wrapped around the handle of his stock prod. He deflated when he saw her but stiffened again as Aiden charged forward and scooped Elodie into his arms. Her stomach warmed and familiar butterflies returned. In the future, if they wanted to, she and Rhett would be able to do the same.

"I was worried about you," Elodie and Aiden said in unison.

Elodie smiled and brushed a clump of lint from Aiden's shirt. "They had my mom. We got her out. Sparkman's taking her to a safe house. We were going to get you, too," she said, motioning over her shoulder to the major.

"Rhett." Aiden nodded stiffly.

"Aiden," Rhett returned with a tight nod of his own.

Blair remained silent. If she locked the three of them in a room and left them there for a week, they'd still have more to sort through. And if she locked herself in a room with Rhett . . .

She pressed her hand to her flaming cheek and focused her attention on the restless, awkward trio in front of her.

While she did owe Elodie an apology—she had clearly misjudged her and been unnecessarily cruel—she preferred to do so after a thorough interrogation of the young woman and finding out her intentions with Aiden.

Her brother scrubbed a hand through his hair and cleared his throat. "Thanks for earlier, Rhett."

Rhett scratched his chin and muttered something unintelligible.

Cupping his hand to his ear, Aiden leaned forward. "What was that?"

Rhett shrugged, his gaze landing everywhere except on Aiden or Elodie. "I didn't say anything."

"Right," Aiden scoffed.

Elodie held up her hands and stepped between the men. "A lot has happened, but we can sort through all of it later."

Aiden crossed his arms over his chest. "We can sort through it once your *fiancé* stops being a dick."

"Ex-fiancé." It was Elodie and Rhett's turn to speak as one.

Blair took a breath and opened her mouth to put an end to the bickering when Maxine rounded the corner. The trio halted their argument and stared, unblinking, at Blair's assistant.

"Oh." Maxine's eyebrows rose as she adjusted the strap of the large purse slung over her shoulder. "I didn't realize you'd have an entourage."

Her gaze settled on Elodie who seemed to coil, ready to strike. A stark change from the young woman who'd blended into the walls of Blair's office during their last interaction.

"Well," Maxine continued, brushing back a stray hair as she turned her attention to Blair. "I found a room full of paper files about the patient you mentioned. Of course, we can visit them another time if you're busy."

Blair smoothed her skirt and hung a practiced smile on her lips. "They have quite a bit to sort through, so we will leave them to it." Aiden opened his mouth to object, but Blair spoke before he had the chance. "Find me after you three manage to get on the same page. We don't have time to get weighed down by these arguments." She hoped her wide-eyed glare was enough to convey the message that, when the time came, they needed to be a unified front against the Key.

As she turned and followed Maxine to the nearby door labeled MAINTENANCE, she was almost certain she heard Elodie scoff.

Maxine passed her cuff beneath the scanner and gained entry into the cold, purple hallway beyond. "You can imagine my surprise"—she paused to wait for the door to close behind them—"when I realized that this maintenance room is not a maintenance room at all." Her lips tightened into an O as she pointed to the door to their right. "But it does hold all the answers."

Blair passed her cuff beneath the access scanner. It flashed red, denying her entry.

"Oops, I'll get that." Maxine stepped in front of Blair and scanned her cuff. The panel flashed green, and the door opened.

"How did you—"

Preston Darby leaned against the control panel in the center of the room, hair mussed, clothes wrinkled, his tie dangling loosely around his neck. Around him, holographic pages shimmered and the control panel's lights blinked. Blair's gaze slipped to the black spot on the floor next to shiny boots as if he'd spilled a bottle of ink.

Blair cleared her throat, forcing the tremor from her voice. "Why are you here?" She knew she'd have to see him again. Darby wasn't one to go down without a fight. But for some reason, she thought she'd feel ready. Instead, being in the same room with him transported her back into her office, legs forced against her desk, him forced against her.

She fisted her hands and took a deep breath in through her nose and out through her mouth as her gaze fell back to the small black pool on the floor. She squinted. No, it wasn't a pool. It was a hole, its edges as soft and mushy as a wet cracker.

He shrugged. "Same as you, I suspect."

"I doubt that very much." Blair's laugh was hollow as she turned to face her assistant. "Maxine, why don't you gather the files you spoke of and meet me out in the hall?"

Darby leaned against the control panel and crossed his arms

over his chest. "Come now, Blair. Don't you want to finish our game?"

The hairs on the nape of her neck rose in warning, and she gave him a wide berth, choosing a point in front of the wall of filing cabinets as far from him as she could get. "You're sick, Preston. I never started a game with you. It's all in your head."

She bit back the rest of her thoughts about his entitlement, fragile ego, mental health, and how he would soon be ousted. There was no reasoning with him. She knew that, and he had to see that with her new understanding of him, and Maxine in the room, he would lose.

"Maxine, I'll wait for you out—"

"Blair," he interjected, a petulant child ignored by the adults in the room. "It's no fun if you don't engage."

"You know what? No," she snapped, well aware of the fact that he'd most likely never had the word directed at him. "You don't get to talk to me. You haven't earned the right."

He arched a brow and the corner of his mouth slid into a smile. "Why earn something when you can just take it?"

"Excuse me. If I may . . ." Maxine stepped between them, her slight frame not enough to block out Darby's prying gaze. "Blair, in all of her wisdom, said something when we were in the hall that I think rings true for this situation as well."

Blair released a measured exhale, relaxing a bit as Darby's attention shifted, and Maxine claimed the brunt of his focus.

"We really don't have time to get weighed down by these arguments." She adjusted the strap of her bag and clasped her hands in front of her. "Especially since we're all after the same thing."

Blair let out a dry laugh and rested her hands on her hips.

"I appreciate what you're trying to do, Maxine, but you have no idea what's going on or what that man actually is."

"Unfortunately for you," Maxine said as she reached into her bag, "I know exactly who he is." Her lips tightening into her signature O, she removed a yellow plastic gun from her purse and pointed it at Blair.

The red dot of the laser glowed against her blouse, and Blair's stomach dropped to her toes.

"So, Director Scott." Maxine cocked her head and tucked her short hair behind her ear. "How's that for predictable?"

XLI

They were so close to the end, and Elodie hated to admit it, but Blair had a point. This squabbling had to stop before they went any further. And it had to stop now. If they could get Aubrey before Eos came, the added chaos would ensure an easy escape. Clearly the boys weren't going to be able to move forward until the ridiculous drama was sorted, so Elodie would sort it.

"Yes, Rhett and I were Matched," she explained, crossing her arms over her chest. "But I think we can both agree that that's definitely not a thing anymore."

"El?"

She held up her hand, quieting Rhett. Regardless of whether or not he thought they could work things out and end up together, she didn't. When it came to their relationship, what he wanted didn't matter. She was no longer going to live her life ruled by a man's desires. "And it's not just him. I don't want to be with anyone right now."

"Oh." Aiden winced. "I mean, I didn't think that we were

going to be, like, *together* together, but . . ." He bit his lower lip. "What about Zone Seven?"

Elodie's cheeks flamed.

"El—"

She skewered Rhett with a glance. She would definitely rather not have this conversation right now, and the whole thing was made worse by the fact that her *ex*-fiancé loomed next to her.

"I feel like we can do that kind of thing without being completely together," she offered.

"Elodie!"

Rhett's tone made her flinch. "If it makes you uncomfortable, you don't have to stand here and listen to our private conversation."

"*That*," he motioned to the room Blair and her assistant had entered, "is not a maintenance room."

Cold sweat beaded on Elodie's brow as she and Aiden turned to stare at the door. "What is it?" she asked.

"Labs. Two of them."

Aiden took a tentative step forward. "So, there are no paper files?"

"There are, but—" His hesitation was the only answer Elodie needed.

She charged toward the door, smacking against the metal when the scanner denied her access.

"Only four people have the correct permissions," Rhett said, reaching around her to scan his cuff.

The door opened, and Elodie blinked under the brilliant violet light of the antechamber.

"What did you have to do to become one of the chosen ones?" Aiden asked, passing Rhett to stand next to Elodie.

Rhett brushed his hands through his hair, his gaze moving back and forth between the doors on opposite sides of the small enclosure. "I'm starting to think I'm always in the wrong place at the wrong time."

He made a quick decision and scanned his cuff beneath the access panel for the door on the left.

Elodie picked at her nails, anxiety gnawing at her gut as she waited for the door to open.

Inside, the walls of the lab were covered with cabinets, drawers, and unused pump stations. In the middle of the room, Patient Ninety-Two lay stretched across a gurney as small and frail as she'd always been.

"Aubrey!" A rush of satisfaction made her lightheaded.

It's almost over.

Elodie rushed in, her gaze searching the room. "Blair's not in here," she called over her shoulder, gripping the edge of Aubrey's gurney as another wave of dizziness crested.

Aiden's footsteps ate up the ground behind her, but Rhett stayed in the open doorway, half of his face painted purple like he'd been dipped in paint.

"Dude," Aiden said, pausing next to Elodie. "Just go after her."

Rhett's teeth grazed his bottom lip before he nodded to himself and marched in after them. "Take this." He removed his gun from its holster and thrust it toward Elodie.

She recoiled, clasping her hands behind her back. "I won't need that." She took a step away from him as if distance could make the offer disappear. "Even if I did, I wouldn't use it. And that's the whole point of having a gun."

"No one needs it," Aiden grumbled, taking the firearm and stuffing it into his pants pocket. "But we don't have time to argue."

Elodie snorted. *Now* they didn't want to argue.

"I'll leave my cuff outside the other door so you can get in when you're done." He left the room, submerging himself into violet.

Slowly, Elodie rounded the gurney, checking each of Aubrey's IVs as Aiden made his way to the pump station pressed into the wall. As she neared Aubrey's feet, Elodie let out a squeal of horror and clapped her hand over her mouth. On the other side of the gurney, Dr. Normandy lay on the floor, the needle of an empty syringe plunged into his neck, his eyes open, cloudy, staring at nothing.

In an instant, Aiden was by her side. He nudged the doctor's shoe with his bare foot. No response. Elodie didn't expect one. It was clear that the doctor was dead.

"What happened here?" she whispered.

Aiden shook his head. "I don't think we want to know."

Elodie's legs trembled as she stepped over the doctor and forced away the image of his hazy white eyes to resume studying Aubrey's tubes. They didn't come here for Normandy, and after what she learned about him from Sparkman and Thea, she wasn't sure his death was the worst thing.

"I told the doctor you were coming, but I guess it doesn't matter now."

Aubrey's words streamed between Elodie's ears and she glanced down at the little girl. Aubrey's eyelids fluttered open, revealing her brilliant purple irises.

Elodie didn't let herself look back at Normandy's stiff corpse. "The doctor's dead."

Aiden glanced over his shoulder, his brow creasing. "Right. That's what you said before."

She nodded. "Just letting Aubrey know."

He glanced down at the girl whose mouth hadn't opened since they'd entered the room.

Elodie cocked her head. "You can't hear her?"

"*No.*" The word was long and drawn out, as Aiden eyed them both suspiciously.

"*Only you,*" Aubrey said, loud and clear. "*His destiny is different. Yours has just begun.*"

Elodie ignored the tight squeeze of her stomach and busied herself with the various tubes, IVs, and ports that sprouted from Aubrey's body like roots. There were too many to know for certain that removing them would do more good than harm.

Elodie cleared the apprehension from her throat. "Eos has doctors."

It wasn't a question, but she was thankful Aiden answered her anyway. "Yeah, reach out through the network," he grunted from the pump station, his back to her, his biceps flexing as he wrestled with it. "You can find a safe house equipped with the right medical gear for whatever you need. Ask for a doctor, and one will meet you there."

A final loud grunt and a metallic screech, and he turned around, the metal box in his arms. "One of the good things about hopping career fields," he explained, wheeling over a silver pole with a shepherd's hook on the top, "is that you learn a little about a lot." He hung the pump station on the hook and rolled it over to Elodie.

I'm . . . so . . . tired. Aubrey's voice was breathy and tired.

"Rest," Elodie said, running her hand along Aubrey's sweat-streaked forehead. "When you wake up, you'll be safe and away from here."

Aubrey's heavy eyelids closed as the drugs reclaimed her, and Elodie helped Aiden steer the gurney and the pump station out the door.

In the purple light of the antechamber, Elodie glanced down at the cuff Rhett left outside the other lab. "I can't come with you. I have to get Aubrey out and make sure my mom's okay."

Aiden's lips quirked in a half smile. "You've done what you came here to do. Don't worry about the rest of us. Like you said, Eos is coming." He unleashed a full smile as he rocked onto his toes. "And it's not like I haven't gotten myself out of difficult situations before."

She reached up and traced his sculpted jaw the way she had in her mind, in her fantasy, in Zone Seven. "Aiden, I do want you, but I have to put myself first."

He cupped her hand in his and brushed his lips against her palm. "I understand," he murmured, his breath featherlight against her skin.

She guided his mouth to hers and kissed him. A kiss that promised more but didn't promise forever.

"Thanks for the adventure." She smiled, her heart fluttering as she rolled the gurney and the pump station into the white hall.

He smoothed his fingertips against his lips. "Thanks for the kiss."

XLII

Preston licked his lips, a slow, languid movement that made Blair shudder. This time, he wouldn't be foolish. It wasn't desire that made her quake, but soon . . .

Another pass of his tongue along his mouth.

Soon, it would be.

The door hissed open, and Preston's eyes narrowed at the intrusion. Only four people had access to these secret labs. Preston had taken care of the old coot, and he and Maxine were already in the room.

"Rhett," he growled.

Maxine turned to face the man who wore his own narrow-eyed look of determination. "Your timing is impeccable, Major."

He reached for the stock prod poking out of his duty belt.

Maxine tsked, switching the aim of her Taser from Blair to the major's chest.

A laugh bubbled in Preston's throat as he took in the yellow

Taser and the petite woman holding it. She looked like a child, the Taser a toy.

Another chuckle spilled from his lips as he ran his fingers over the warm barrel of the specially made syringe behind him. He'd filled it with the doctor's unique blend—a black, tar-like substance that ate through whatever it touched. He'd prepared it for Normandy, to get rid of his body, but Maxine had distracted him with news of Blair and her brother. If he didn't empty the barrel soon, its contents would corrode the treated plastic and end up creating another hole in the floor.

A final chuckle made Rhett's gaze collide with Preston's.

Now is not the time for jokes, a small voice inside him chided.

Preston shrugged. "You have to admit, this whole scene *is* a little funny."

Rhett seemed to swell, a storm cloud, churning, darkening with each passing moment, as he surged forward.

Maxine pulled the trigger. The probes shot out and hit their mark. The major went rigid, a rough bark tearing from his mouth while his muscles and joints locked and the electronic weapon cycled, emitting small ticks that sounded to Preston like rounds of applause.

Rhett fell backward. His head smacked into the metal door with a loud *thwack*.

Blair's choked sob was a stab in Preston's gut. He wrapped his hand around the syringe. He should make her watch the major's body be eaten from the inside out. They could both learn something from the experience.

Maxine's sigh interrupted Preston's frustration. "Can't help but feel bad for the giant lug. Always getting taken out right before the finale." Her frown could have won an award as she

THE KEY TO FURY

discarded the spent weapon onto the soldier and jabbed his ribs with the pointed toe of her shoe. "So like a man to talk all big and bad but not perform when it really matters. Wouldn't you agree, Blair?"

Clearing his throat, Preston released his hold on the syringe and pushed himself away from the control panel before Blair could answer. "Not *all* men."

Maxine turned to him and smiled. "I did good?" she asked, biting her lower lip.

He held his hand out to her and her heels clicked against the tile as she strode over to him and took it. "Yes, my dutiful little monster."

Blair pressed her hand against her mouth and stepped back, colliding with the wall of filing cabinets behind her.

"Don't look so shocked," Darby said, reeling Maxine into him until her back pressed firmly against his front. "I had to have someone keep an eye on you when I couldn't." He wrapped his arm around her chest and hooked his hand over her shoulder. "I thought you deserved a certain level of respect that having cameras in your office and home would overstep. I was wrong. But a scientist is never correct one hundred percent of the time."

Maxine's gaze turned heavy lidded as she dropped her head back against his shoulder. "I only want what's best for you, Council Leader," she purred against his neck.

He frowned and shrugged her away from his bare skin. Bad accompanied good, and Maxine Wyndham was always pawing at him like a bitch in heat. "You could take a lesson from your assistant, Blair."

The almost unnoticeable tremble of Blair's chin made his heart squeeze. He'd won.

Her gaze glossed over Rhett a final time before it settled on Preston. "What do you want?" Her voice was calmer than he'd expected. Perhaps the ball was still in play.

Maxine gasped as he pushed her to the side and stalked toward Blair. "You . . ." He dug his fingertips into the blade of his rumpled tie. "The world . . ." His cold limbs turned hot as he stared into her hazel eyes. "Nothing less than what I deserve."

"The world is a very big place," she said, her chin high, her posture stiff. "Even if you fool some, you will *never* fool me."

"It's not about *fooling* you." He brushed the curls from her forehead and smoothed his palm down her jawline. "It's about taking."

Her wild, pleading gaze fell over his shoulder and landed on Maxine.

"She won't help you." He smiled, closing the distance between them to press his forehead to hers. "She's already mine, and I didn't even have to dose her."

The toe of Blair's stiletto connected with his groin. He sagged against her, his stomach seizing as pain shot through his core. He fell to his knees, and she squirmed out from under him and bolted toward the door. He bared his teeth and let out a savage growl as he struck out and grabbed her. He dug his fingers into her shin and jerked. Her legs flew out from under her and she smacked into the tile. Spittle flew from his lips as he grunted and seethed while he slid his hand down to her ankle and caught her other one as she kicked.

"Don't make me hurt you, Blair," he roared as he pulled her farther from the door, her palms squeaking against the tile with each worthless attempt to escape.

He dragged her back to the cabinets and grabbed her wrists with a bone-crushing grip, yanking her to her feet.

Spit sprayed his face. "Fuck you!"

He pushed her into the cabinets, and she cringed when her back struck the metal. He dug his fingers into her curls and brought a fistful to his face, wiping away the saliva.

"No matter what games we play, I will always win." He wrapped his hand around her neck and squeezed.

Spittle bubbled in the corners of her mouth, and he had to secure her hands between them, pressing his body to hers to keep her claws from marring his face.

"Update Ninety-Two will give me everything. First, a simple mRNA dose to teach your cells that the implant, *my* implant, is a part of you. That it should be welcomed as its tendrils spread and take hold of all your mushy bits. I suppose the process is a bit complicated. I won't bore you with its intricacies." He released his grasp on her throat and his heart skipped when her chest heaved against his as she gulped in wheezing breaths. "After I hook you to the pump station next door and dose you, you'll be pure and ready for my update. Won't it feel good to let it all go and let me take control?"

This time, when he clamped down on her neck, she didn't fight back.

"Good girl," he whispered, brushing his lips along the line of saliva that slid down her chin.

XLIII

Aiden stared at the closed door between Elodie and him for a full minute before bending to pick up the cuff Rhett had left behind. He'd needed the time to bring himself back down to earth. As much as it stung, it was a good thing that she wasn't ready to be with him. He needed space to vanquish his darkness before he was deserving of her.

He passed Rhett's cuff beneath the scanner. The door whirred and clicked, struggling to open. Aiden's brows knit and his heartbeat quickened as a low whimper met his ears. He forced his hands between the narrow space between the door and the jamb and pushed. Rhett spilled into the hallway, his partially open lids revealing the whites of his eyes.

Sirens wailed, drowning out Aiden's thundering pulse, and emergency lights flashed overhead. His gaze swung around the room as the overhead sprinklers rained water onto the scene—Maxine scooping wet papers off the control panel and into her huge purse while Darby choked his sister.

Without a second thought, Aiden reached into his pocket and pulled out the gun he'd taken from Rhett. "Get away from her!" he shouted, aiming the pistol at Darby.

"Little brother." Darby had to yell to be heard over the sirens and the rushing showers. "Are you going to shoot me?"

Aiden swiped away the water streaming into his eyes and pulled back the weapon's slide.

Darby didn't release his grip on Blair as he arched a brow. "Aiden, let's think about this—"

His words were swallowed by the loud *pop* of the gun.

Aiden's arm vibrated with the discharge. He hadn't only pulled the trigger for Blair. He'd fired for his birth mother, for his adoptive mother, for Elodie, for all the love that he lost and the people he would die to protect.

Darby and Blair fell to the ground in a tangled heap, their wet *slap* punctuated by Maxine's high-pitched scream. Blood seeped from their joined bodies, swept up in the current of water that pooled along the floor, lapping against Aiden's bare feet.

"Blair—" The gun clattered against the floor as he rushed to his sister.

Pain racked his side as a wailing body struck his and they crashed onto the tile. Water flooded his nose and mouth and he sputtered and coughed as he fought to flip onto his back.

Maxine dropped against him, her knees like anchors on top of his chest.

"After everything I've worked for!" she screeched, her pupils white rimmed as she drew back her fist and plunged a needle into his shoulder.

He howled as fire poured from the syringe and seared his insides.

Another cry mixed with his as Blair fisted Maxine's hair and yanked her backward, throwing her into the filing cabinets. Maxine yelped and slid down the metal, her unconscious body resting against Darby.

With shaking fingers, Aiden sat up and pulled the needle from his shoulder. He eyed the half-empty syringe of black liquid before tossing it into the deepening water.

Blair knelt next to him. Rivulets rushed down her face, and he knew by her puffy eyes and quivering chin, some of them had to be tears. "Are you okay?"

He winced as he rolled his shoulder, but he could deal with the pain. He'd done it. He'd rescued his sister.

"Is Darby . . . ?"

He followed Blair's gaze to the Council Leader. Ribbons of red swirled in the water around him, broken up by floating bits of flesh and muscle, all of it surging in and out of the oozing, gaping hole where the side of his neck had been.

He finally got what was coming to him.

Urgent shouts snapped Aiden's attention to the open door. Elodie seemed to fly into the room, followed by a line of Eos soldiers, their wet helmets the same golden orange as the rising sun.

XLIV

Elodie's heart was a caged bird flapping wildly inside her chest as she ran through the open door. Water splashed onto Aiden's already soaked shirt when she dropped to her knees next to him. "Eos intercepted Aubrey and me on our way out. We heard the shot." She intertwined her fingers with his and squeezed a little too tightly. "Are either of you hurt?"

"I'm fine." He sat up a bit straighter as she regarded him suspiciously. "Seriously."

Elodie's gaze lifted to Blair, her bloodshot eyes, and the dark bruises blooming around her neck. "And you?"

Blair lifted her chin. "I will be."

Aiden returned Elodie's tight grip with a gentle squeeze of his own. "Let's get out of here and to someplace that's not loud, flashy, and wet," he said with a grunt as he attempted to stand.

With Elodie on one side and Blair on the other, they helped hoist him to his feet.

Blair pursed her lips. "You can see why neither of us believe you when you say you're fine."

Elodie nodded her agreement, her arms and legs trembling with adrenaline.

"Just a few war wounds." He cringed and massaged his shoulder. "At least I'm not working on my second concussion," he said with a nod toward Rhett, whom Eos soldiers had managed to revive.

Rhett shrugged out of the stiff Key Corp–red officer's blazer the water had stained a deep crimson as he blinked and looked around the room. He leveled his gaze on Elodie, Aiden, and Blair and frowned. "I fucking missed it again." He used the Eos soldiers at his sides as crutches before standing tall and waving them away. "How does this keep happening?"

Elodie shifted, holding on to Aiden's waist a little tighter as he tried to support his own weight but couldn't.

"You clearly need some Eos training." His exhale was a hiss as he grimaced and landed a friendly blow to Rhett's arm.

Fear took hold of Elodie's lungs, constricting her breathing as she studied Aiden. He had no visible wounds, at least none she could see through his wet clothes, but his obvious pain put her on edge.

Blair reached up and gingerly touched the back of Rhett's head, a smile plumping her cheeks. "We'll be sure to get him whatever he needs."

Elodie swallowed her unease and watched Blair and Rhett and the way their lips curved and eyes rested on each other and made a mental note to play matchmaker later.

Some of the color had drained from Aiden's skin as he looked around the room. "Where's Maxine?" A wail exploded with his next breath, and he clapped his hand over his shoulder and collapsed against Elodie.

"Aiden!" she shouted as he slid down her body and crumpled onto the floor. Elodie followed him down, unsure if she was hearing her cries or Blair's.

The shoulder of Aiden's shirt was marred with black liquid. She tore the fabric away and sucked in a shuddering breath. Black slime oozed from exposed muscle, sinew, and bone. The obsidian maw grew, a ghost chomping and devouring, bit by bit.

"Denny!" Blair clutched Rhett's wet coat in her hands, and she pressed it against the spreading wound.

Inky black liquid stained Aiden's teeth and seeped from the corners of his mouth as he worked to choke out a response.

"Stay with me, Aiden." Elodie's voice caught on a sob. "We haven't had a chance. You can't—"

But he was gone.

Blair's scream rattled Elodie's insides as his chest collapsed and the poison ate through what was left of his middle, up his neck, across his face, down his legs. Ravaged flecks of skin and fiber swirled with the steadily rising waters as Elodie whispered her final goodbye and closed her hand around what was left of his.

Then it was gone, too.

She opened her fingers and released his ashes to the pulsing waters, just as she had to the winds beyond Zone Seven.

EPILOGUE

There were no Violet Shields at Aiden's funeral. Not as a farce or a show of togetherness, as it had been at the former Director Holbrook's, but because each person who had come to pay their respects knew the truth.

As it turned out, the truth did what Cerberus had done: split society into warring factions, each with the belief that they were right and knew the best way to shape the new world. Elodie questioned whether or not either side, the freethinking, bohemian followers of Eos or the traditional, fear-mongering, steadfast Key supporters, was correct, and it was clear that neither had all the answers.

Elodie stood next to the pine box that held nothing but the memory of the man she could have loved. There was no body to bury. Whatever Maxine had injected into him had nearly erased him from existence.

Elodie set her hand on the coffin. As long as she was alive, he would be, too.

Blair wrapped her arm around Elodie's shoulders and pulled her close. The women didn't need to speak. Their combined sorrow was another person in the room, a silent spectator.

Elodie blinked back tears and watched as the funeral-goers filed past the coffin before filtering out of the warehouse that had once been Wonderland, then a battleground, and now a final resting place. Most wore a blazing orange sash around their bicep, signaling their loyalty and adding to the ever-increasing divide, but some wore Key red.

Why could death bring them together but the pursuit of life could not?

A flash of neon pink caught Elodie's attention and pulled her from her thoughts. The petite young woman's cheeks were nearly as pink as her hair, her eyes puffy, but she didn't cry as she set a single sheet of paper on the pine box. Her lips moved, her words silent, as she placed her hand over her heart and bowed to Aiden's memory before following the line of mourners to the door.

Through a swirl of tears, Elodie glanced at the page. "O Captain! My Captain!" was handwritten in bold, scrawling script across the top of the poem. She wasn't sure of its significance, but she was sure of one thing: the gesture swelled with love.

Elodie caught a glimpse of Sparkman's long braid and Thea's shining black hair as they made their way through the processional. The secure communique device in Elodie's pocket buzzed.

TFUJIMOTO: 🖤

A smile sputtered against Elodie's lips. They'd come a long way since their meeting in the tunnels beneath Westfall. It had only been a couple weeks, but Elodie had learned enough about herself and the world to span a couple lifetimes. Unfortunately, the same could not be said for her mother. Sparkman and Thea had successfully freed Gwen from the Key, had informed her of the truth, had made sure she was healthy, mind and body, and then left her to make her own decision. She'd returned to the corporation as soon as she was able, and she hadn't spoken to Elodie since.

Even though Elodie wanted it to, not everything ended in happiness and understanding.

Rhett brought up the tail end of the line and made his way to Blair's side as soon as the last person paid their respects. In a pair of jeans and a button-down, he looked more relaxed now than Elodie had ever seen him before.

When he reached her, he bent over and whispered something to Blair, who nodded.

"It's time," she said, giving Elodie a final squeeze before heading to one of the rooms deeper within the warehouse.

Rhett remained there, silent and contemplative. She appreciated the quiet and that he no longer felt the need to fill it with his own self-importance. No matter how slow his evolution, he was moving in the right direction.

"How is she?" Elodie asked, her hand still resting on the coarse wood.

"She's started talking aloud, which is a huge step forward, not to mention less startling." He clasped his hands behind his back and stiffened. "Her file says that she's eight, but she doesn't talk or act like a kid. She's . . . different, older somehow."

Elodie nodded. Aubrey had always seemed stuck between two times, the little girl who wanted her mommy and a soul equipped with the knowledge of an ancient.

"Her patient number is also interesting. For the past eight years, the MediCenter has been assigning citizens patient numbers in the tens of thousands. I know Normandy had his own way of categorizing the people he experimented on, but—"

As his pregnant pause swelled around them, Elodie glanced up. Rhett chewed the inside of his cheek while he stared at the coffin, his gaze searching for something in the swirls and grooves of the wood.

"What is it?"

His shrug was barely noticeable. "I'll let you know when I figure it out." He cleared his throat and blinked back his faraway look. "I should check in with Blair."

She offered a small twitch of a smile and watched him disappear behind the same door Blair had ventured through.

Alone, Elodie bent and pressed her lips to the pine. She lingered for a few beats of her heart before walking away. She didn't need to tell Aiden goodbye. She already had.

Elodie stepped carefully over the freshly tilled dirt that would feed and protect a new field of crops and flowers. She would delight in information about Wonderland's rebirth, but she would never return to this place. This had been a part of the life she'd once thought of as a storybook, an adventure novel, a fairy tale.

But life wasn't a series of scenes from a book. Life was figuring out desires and hopes. It was warring with inner thoughts and those who meant harm. It was a constant reevaluation of ideas and morals as more was learned and understood.

Life was change, and Elodie was different now.

INCOMING PRIORITY ONE ALERT FROM THE KEY CORPORATION

**YOUR HEALTH. YOUR LIFE. YOUR FUTURE.
YOU ARE THE KEY.**

Blair Scott stared into the camera, her funeral-black attire an ink stain pressed into the brilliant white backdrop behind her.

"This is the last time I, or anyone, will reach out to you in this manner. At the end of this broadcast, the implant program will go offline and implant removal appointments will be scheduled, free of charge, for every citizen who wishes to have theirs removed."

She glanced down at her hands clasped in front of her hips and took a breath before continuing. "The coming days will bring with them a lot of change and even more questions. I hope I can answer them. I hope you can trust me when I do."

"I ask you to remember that we are in this existence together. Be kind to yourself and to others, and we will make it through. Perhaps, on the other side, there will truly be liberty and justice for all."

Blair's image faded, and a blazing orange sun took her place.

ACKNOWLEDGMENTS

Traditionally, this is where an author lists all the people who helped bring this book from a thought or a few scribbled notes to the thing you're listening to or holding in your hands. Instead, I'm going to list some resources to help you if you're struggling.

Before I do, I want to talk about Blair. What Preston did to her in her office was sexual assault. Survivors often blame themselves or think that they caused the attack or encouraged the perpetrator, which we witness with Blair's feelings afterward. It's important to understand that she is not to blame. The victim is never to blame.

If you're a survivor of sexual assault, you are not alone, and it was not your fault.

If you or someone you know is in need of help, please contact

- RAINN—National Sexual Assault Hotline providing 24-7 confidential support. Learn more at RAINN.org and (800) 656-4673.

- National Suicide Prevention Lifeline—The Lifeline provides free and confidential support 24-7 for people in distress, prevention and crisis resources for you or your loved ones, and best practices for professionals. Contact them at SuicidePreventionLifeline.org and (800) 273-8255.

- Crisis Text Line—You get 24-7 text access to crisis intervention with a live, trained crisis counselor. The volunteer crisis counselor will help you move from a hot moment to a cool moment. US and Canada text 741741.